"Why?" Mac finally asked in a soft voice. "I've missed you. What would be the harm in reconnecting?"

This question so dumbfounded her that Hailey stared, speechless. And then, while she was still trying to formulate a response, he leaned over and kissed her.

It wasn't a demanding kiss, or a punishing one. The brush of his lips on hers felt soft, welcoming and familiar. And because of that, sensual as hell. When he finally lifted his mouth away, she couldn't stop shaking.

Of course he noticed. "Are you cold?" he asked, even though she suspected he knew the truth.

"No." Right then, right now, she knew she should stand up, move away and demand in a forceful voice that he never do such a thing again. But it had been far too long since she'd been touched, and the cold, empty shell of a person she'd become felt like a flower opening to the sun. She wanted more.

* * *

If you're on Twitter, tell us what you think of Harlequin Romantic Suspense! #harlequinromsuspense

D0957781

Dear Reader,

Some books are more difficult for me to write than others. This book was one of those. I started working on it while still raw from losing my father just two years after losing my mother. Several times while writing it, I had to force myself to face my pain and dig deep. The story, while alternately painful and uplifting, hit close to my heart, and now that the book is finished, I feel it is among my best work. The love shines through.

Previous loves and second chances are my very favorite to write. Throw in a massive need for forgiveness, for understanding and the fact that a very giving woman needs to finally learn it's all right to reach for her own happiness, and you have part of the reason why this book was so important to me. Raw and emotional, some of it culled from my own recent experiences, I viewed this story as redemption and the true power of love. There's beauty in sacrifice and joy in love. This particular couple is special to me. I hope you feel the same. I'd love to hear from you and see what you think.

Karen Whiddon

THE TEXAN'S RETURN

Karen Whiddon

HHARLEQUIN® ROMANTIC SUSPENSE

Recycling programs
for this product may
not exist in your area.

ISBN-13: 978-0-373-40206-9

The Texan's Return

Printed in U.S.A.

www.Harlequin.com

Karen Whiddon started weaving fanciful tales for her younger brothers at the age of eleven. Amid the gorgeous Catskill Mountains, then the majestic Rocky Mountains, she fueled her imagination with the natural beauty surrounding her. Karen now lives in north Texas, writes full-time and volunteers for a boxer dog rescue. She shares her life with her hero of a husband and four to five dogs, depending on if she is fostering. You can email Karen at kwhiddon1@aol.com. Fans can also check out her website, karenwhiddon.com.

Harlequin Romantic Suspense

The Texan's Return

The Coltons of Texas

Runaway Colton

The Coltons of Oklahoma

The Temptation of Dr. Colton

The Coltons: Return to Wyoming

A Secret Colton Baby
The CEO's Secret Baby
The Cop's Missing Child
The Millionaire Cowboy's Secret
Texas Secrets, Lovers' Lies
The Rancher's Return

Silhouette Romantic Suspense

The Princess's Secret Scandal
Bulletproof Marriage

The Cordiasic Legacy

Black Sheep P.I.
The Perfect Soldier
Profile for Seduction

Visit the Author Profile page at Harlequin.com for more titles.

To those who take care of others. The caregivers—of the elderly or of children, of spouses or friends. Know that while an often thankless job might seem unappreciated, in the end it truly is.

Chapter 1

The sharp sound of someone knocking on her front door made Hailey Green narrow her eyes. She'd posted a No Soliciting sign years ago, but every once in a while, a very persistent salesperson would pretend not to see it. She supposed they felt somewhat entitled after walking all the way up her long, winding drive.

Still… She put down the whisk, wiped her hands on the front of her faded jeans, and marched to answer the knock. Prepared speech all ready, she flung the door open. And stared, the words dying on her lips. Her heart flip-flopped in her chest, like a caught catfish on the end of a trotline.

Him. Mac Morrison.

"What…" Stunned, she took a step back, in disbelief, in defense, or a combination of both. Once, her younger self had dreamt of this moment. That dream, like all the others, had faded. Every time his face drifted into her thoughts, she'd chased the image away, telling herself after so many years, she had no idea what kind of man Mac had become.

Now she knew. She let her gaze drink him in, too shocked even to attempt to hide her reaction. After a decade away, he was no longer a boy, but a man. And oh, what a man.

He'd filled out, his body finally catching up to his height. Time had hardened the craggy perfection of his face and given him a masculine virility that his younger self had only had a hint of. He'd gotten muscular, too, his bare arms powerful, his broad shoulders filling out his black T-shirt. He wore his thick, dark hair longer, shaggier, but this also just enhanced his appeal. Only the warmth in his gray eyes as he gazed at her hadn't changed.

"Hi," he said, his easy smile and husky voice making her catch her breath. "How've you been? It's been a long time, but you still look the same. Even down to the earrings. I'm glad to see you kept them."

Purely on reflex, she brought her hand up to her ears. The tiny diamond ear studs he'd given her for her sixteenth birthday were in place, just as they always were. She took them off every night and put them on every single morning. They were the only piece of jewelry she wore.

She could have slammed the door and locked it, turned and run down the hall to the bathroom so she could retch up the remains of breakfast. She could have, probably should have, but instead she couldn't make herself move. One devilish quirk of a smile and all the memories, wants and desires came rushing back as if they were yesterday rather than almost a decade ago.

Mouth dry, she struggled to find the words to make a response. Instead, to her absolute horror, her eyes filled with tears. She would not cry, not in front of him.

"What…" she tried again. "What are you doing here? After all this time." The harshness of her tone spoke more of her pain rather than anger.

"What, no friendly welcome?" Mockery and regret combined to darken his eyes to slate. "I thought at least that you'd want to catch up with an old friend."

Friends. They'd been that, once. And more. Much, much more. Not only best friends, but lovers and soul mates. She'd loved him, with all the fervor of a teenage girl. And he'd loved her back, or so she'd believed. Though when he and his family had moved away, under the cloud of shame caused by what Mac's father had done, he hadn't even said goodbye. Hailey had never heard from him again.

Not that she'd wanted to. That was what she'd told herself to mitigate the hurt. After all, there'd only been so many things she could grieve at seventeen. Her sister's murder had been difficult enough. Once upon a time, Hailey had believed in true love, happily-ever-after and fairy tales. That was Before, with a capital B. Before everything had changed and she'd learned monsters really did exist.

"Hailey?" He cocked his head, clearly waiting for her to respond.

The sound of her name on his lips sent a shiver up her spine. Words. She needed to answer him. So she said the first thing that came to mind. "I thought you moved far away. Another state? Up north somewhere."

"No. Mother and I settled in Huntsville, to be near my dad."

She couldn't suppress a shudder.

He continued on as if he hadn't noticed. "My mother passed away three years ago."

"I'm sorry," she said, meaning it. Then, because she had to ask, she did. "And your father?" Holding herself stiffly, she waited for him to say the words that, even now, might set her free.

Swallowing, Mac looked away for the first time since he'd arrived. "He's been ill. Pancreatic cancer. It's terminal."

Heaven help her, she wouldn't allow herself to feel pity. His father deserved none, that was for sure. Crossing her arms, she settled for a nod. "What are you doing here, Mac?" This time, she softened her tone. "Nothing good can come of dredging up old memories."

Finally, he appeared uncomfortable. Shifting his weight from foot to foot—sturdy black motorcycle boots, she noticed—he sighed. "I'm home, Hailey. My father and I both. We've moved back into the old place on Front Street."

"They let him out?" Shocked, she didn't have time to think of the impact her words might have on him. He winced, and she scaled back her outrage, just a little bit. "I've been notified every time he's come up for parole," she informed him, her voice firm but softer. "I'd know if they were going to release that man."

"That man is my father." He rolled one shoulder in that shrug she remembered. "He's sick, Hailey. Very ill," he told her, his tone matter-of-fact since he definitely knew he couldn't ask for her sympathy. "He's dying, actually. His one wish was to come home and spend his final days in the house he built with his own hands. He needed someone to take care of him when hospice isn't there, so I came with him."

Hailey stared. She'd never been cruel, not to him. Even when the accusations had been flying like mud under a galloping horse's hooves, she hadn't blamed him for what his father had done. She wouldn't be cruel now either.

Lips tight, she nodded. "Good luck."

Before he had time to muster up a reply, she closed the door in his face and, for good measure, clicked the dead bolt into place.

Breathing as hard as if she'd just completed several runs up and down the stairs, she stared at the back of the closed door and tried to adjust to the sudden shift in her reality. As she trembled, she pressed her hand to her midsection, trying to regain her equilibrium.

She had a sneaking suspicion nothing would ever be the same again. Mac had returned. Despite knowing better, her heart had given a spontaneous leap of joy at the sight of him, proving old habits died hard.

Mac Morrison. The only boy she'd ever loved. He was a man now, devastatingly handsome, and even more ruggedly virile. The sight of him still captivated her. Despite everything. He'd come back. Who would have ever believed such a thing could be possible? Stunned, dismayed and confused, she wasn't sure of herself anymore. The flare of sudden attraction at the sight of him made her feel as if she'd been catapulted into the past, before her entire life—both of their entire lives—had been irrevocably changed. She'd not only lost her sister, but her mother had descended into the depths of alcoholism, her stepfather had left and Hailey had become caregiver to her three younger siblings. For them, she'd had to be strong. For them, she'd buried her grief and sorrow deep inside and worked hard to make sure they'd have the most stable lives she could give them.

Since then, she'd clawed her way back to a semblance of normalcy. She refused to let that be jeopardized because of his return.

Why had he come to see her? Just to let her know he was back in town? Along with the monster he called his father. She supposed she should be glad for the warning. That way, she could make sure she avoided them.

Giving herself a mental shake, she straightened her shoulders, exhaled and turned to make her way back to the kitchen. She'd never liked change, but it sure looked like things were changing. She'd do her damnedest to keep any repercussions from touching her or her brothers and sister.

Mac Morrison had known his stomach shouldn't have been twisted in knots because he meant to say hello to his old high school flame. Yet it was. The fact that he'd never forgotten her factored in heavily as one reason, but it could also be due to the possibility that she still hated him.

Did she, after ten long years? Wanting to know the answer was part of the reason he made this unannounced visit.

The other part? He simply wanted to see her. To find out if the years had been kind to her. To hear her speak in that slow, sensual Southern drawl he'd never forgotten. Even if she looked at him with her bright blue eyes full of hate, he thought he could take that. Maybe.

Maybe now enough years had passed that he'd no longer feel that sharp stab of betrayal.

Foolish, he knew. But in the aftermath of Hailey's sister's murder, he and his family had been part of the fallout. The entire town had been in upheaval. He could have taken that; he could have taken anything. But when Hailey turned against him, that had been the final straw of many.

Now looking back, he could see a bit more clearly. They'd all been in agony. The unspeakable had happened right in the middle of their idyllic little town, and the consequences had been enormous. There'd been so much pain on both sides. So much loss. Surely not the worst, but definitely not the least of all had been their breakup.

If he'd wanted a fresh start, he wasn't sure this town would be the best place to get it. But he owned the house and farm free and clear. This was what his father wanted, so Mac had come home. Because despite everything, no matter where he'd lived since then, he always considered Legacy, Texas, home.

Once he'd arrived back in the place that had haunted him since leaving, the first thing he'd done after getting settled was ask around in town about Hailey. He figured she might have gotten married by now, have a couple kids of her own. He'd been stunned to learn she hadn't, even more surprised to find out she'd remained living in her childhood home with her mother and three younger siblings.

Of course he knew he had to head out to Hailey's place. He'd driven there slowly, the winding, tree-lined roads as familiar as if he'd never left. The thick foliage, glowing in various shades of vibrant green, reminded him how beautiful spring could be in this part of Texas. With the backdrop of a cloudless sky in that particular shade of cornflower blue, the natural beauty lightened his heart. He thought it might be the prettiest thing he'd ever seen, except for the sight of Hailey's gaze softening as she looked at him.

Once, he'd been certain he and Hailey would end up together. Ever since they'd split, he'd felt a yawning ache in his heart, right where she used be.

As he walked up her sidewalk, still edged in what he swore were the same type of colorful flowers from the previous decade, his heart hammered in his chest. He tried to remember the words he'd rehearsed. They'd all flown out the window at his first glimpse of her tidy little white house, unchanged by time.

Unaccountably nervous, he swallowed hard. Then, before he had time to change his mind, he lifted his fist and rapped on her door. Again, he rehearsed his speech, hoping to sound casual, friendly even.

When she opened the door, annoyance in her sky blue eyes, he swallowed back whatever he'd been about to say. Their gazes met, locked and every single word he'd prepared fled again.

Damn it. He could do nothing but drink her in with his gaze. Hailey looked even better than he remembered—gorgeous, stunning and sexy. If anything, the decade since he'd seen her had ripened her lush beauty, maturing a younger prettiness into a sensual sort of beauty. She still wore her blond hair straight and uncut. Now it came nearly to her slender hips. Even in an old T-shirt and well-worn jeans, she outshone any other woman he'd ever known.

A roiling mix of emotions stampeded through him.

Longing, joy and lust, of course. And more. All the memories of the time they shared, all the regret at missing the future he'd planned with her.

One thing he knew with absolute certainty. He'd been gone too long. Way too long. Still standing like a tongue-tied fool on her front porch, he realized another utter truth. He should have come back years ago and tried to right things between them. Even if she had believed the son should suffer for the sins of his father, he could have at least tried.

Perceived sins. Despite what she and everyone else believed, his father, Gus, hadn't killed Hailey's sister Brenda. Mac knew his dad. The elder Morrison was a kindhearted man, always helping others. He'd been a good father, a great father, and Mac had looked up to him, even after he'd been tried on trumped-up charges and sent off to prison for a crime he hadn't committed.

When the prison had called with the news of his dad's impending release—they'd called it Compassionate Release—due to severe and terminal health issues, Mac had been shocked. He'd immediately hightailed it up to the prison to see for himself. The sight of Gus Morrison, a once stout man, with his bones riding too close to the surface of his loose and paper-thin skin, had hurt.

"Pancreatic cancer," Gus had rasped. "Stage four and inoperable. I don't want your pity, son. I just want to go home to die."

By home, he meant the family home in the town that had castigated him. Since they still owned the house free and clear and were current on the property taxes, Mac saw no reason not to give his father his wish.

So for the first time in a decade, Mac had driven

back to east Texas, to the little town of Legacy, north of Mineola.

He'd finally gotten his dad settled in the wreck of a building that had once been the family home. Years of abandonment had taken its toll on the place. Mac had gone in and chased out the rodents, patched up the holes and made sure the electrical and plumbing still worked. By some miracle, they did.

Hospice had brought out the hospital bed and a bedpan, though they only checked in a few times a week. If he wanted round-the-clock care for his father, he'd have to hire a private nurse. For right now, Mac figured he'd do the best he could.

Then, with Gus settled and the hospice nurse visiting, Mac had driven out to attempt to make peace with Hailey. Her decisive reaction had put a quick end to that idea.

What had he expected after all?

Had he honestly thought the passage of time would have magically mended the huge rift between them? Closure, that oft-bandied-about term, clearly wasn't going to be easy in this situation. In fact, he almost felt like he'd never left.

The thought made him feel uneasy. Determined to do the right thing for his father, he hadn't thought about what going back would actually mean. After all, Gus hadn't been around town after his arrest. He hadn't seen the way the townspeople had reacted to the news of Gus Morrison's indictment. Or how his wife and son were made scapegoats. Shopkeepers had refused to wait on them, waitresses wouldn't serve them. Things had gotten so bad they'd had to drive to the next town over to buy groceries and gas.

Small towns could be brutal sometimes. But now that a decade had gone by, Mac hoped things would be different. They sure as hell better be. He wasn't an uncertain teenager anymore.

Taking a deep breath, he shook his head at his own foolishness. Ten years had passed. People had moved on with their lives. He doubted anyone would even remember him, never mind consider holding him accountable for what they believed his father had done.

While the real killer, the monster who'd attacked Brenda Green and strangled her, had gotten away scotfree.

Though beautiful flowers adorned Hailey's neat home, his place looked old, beat and barren. With all the major repairs he had to make to get the place livable, he knew he wouldn't get around to doing anything cosmetic for a good while.

Letting himself into the small house, he followed the scent of bleach mixed with medicine. His father sat up in the bed, valiantly trying to eat while Dolores, the hospice nurse, looked on and quietly encouraged him.

Mac had read volumes on pancreatic cancer. He knew the progression of the disease would make it increasingly difficult for his father to eat.

"Son." Spying Mac, Gus motioned him over.

Mac pulled up a chair next to the bed. "How're you feeling, Dad?"

"Like hell." A ghost of a smile flitted over the older man's face. Since he'd lost weight, his skin hung loose on too-sharp bones.

Mac's chest squeezed. "I'm sorry."

Shaking his head, Gus waved away his words. He glanced at Dolores—a curly-haired older woman with thick eyeglasses—and winked. "Dolores, do you mind taking a break? I want a private word with my son."

"Of course." Dolores stood. "I need to stretch my legs anyway. I'll be outside if you need me."

Gus waited until the front door had closed behind her. "I need one more favor from you, Mac. I'm sorry, because I swore I wouldn't ask for more than you've already given me. But I can't die with this stain on our good name." He took a deep breath, then erupted in a short bout of coughing.

Waiting, Mac had a feeling he knew exactly what his father was about to say. He couldn't say he blamed him; he'd want the same thing if their positions were reversed.

"Find out who really killed that girl," Gus finally rasped. "You know I didn't do it. Clear my name before I pass away. Could you do that for me, son?"

How could he not? Slowly, Mac nodded. He'd actually been expecting this request. Of course, his father had no idea that Mac had been trying to find the real killer without success for ten long years. "Sure," he said, his chest aching. "I'll get started immediately."

It was the first time he'd lied to his father since he'd been a teenager.

Mac's return was all Hailey could think about. Though he probably didn't remember, the anniversary of Brenda's murder was one day away. At first, they'd marked this date with somber visits to the grave, bearing flowers. They'd done a few interviews, skirting the deep emotions, vocalizing how glad they were that the killing hadn't continued.

After a few years, they'd begun pretending the day

didn't exist. Hailey had tried to keep up the tradition by taking the kids to visit a sister they didn't even remember, but June had finally told her tiredly to stop.

Now, Hailey would mark the anniversary with a quiet prayer. June would do her best to stay drunk, beginning the moment she opened her eyes until she passed out, oblivious to both pain and memories. This year, her mother had started early.

Hailey did her usual chores while her mother slept off her drinking binge. At least she'd come home this time. Someone had dropped her off, and she'd staggered into the house right before Hailey got up to begin the day. This was infinitely preferable over getting a call in the middle of the night asking Hailey to pick up June at the Legacy police station. As long as she didn't drive, the officers remained sympathetic toward her. The woman's daughter had been murdered after all. No one could blame her for turning to alcohol to drown her sorrows.

Except Hailey did. She understood grieving—heck, she'd grieved over her baby sister's loss, too. But June had other children. Eli had just turned one when Brenda died and the twins were four. June had let her seventeen-year-old daughter shoulder the responsibility for her entire family. Hailey had needed her to be strong, especially after her stepdad-slash-adoptive father, Aaron—the younger kids' birth father—had taken off. He'd given both Brenda and Hailey his name, but little else. As far as Hailey knew, he and June had never actually divorced, but he certainly didn't pay child support or make any effort to see his kids.

Or—and she winced at the thought—if he did sporadically, June drank the money away.

Hailey blinked, realizing she'd been standing near

the sink staring blindly, the task at hand forgotten. Seeing Mac again had made her lose track of the present and revisit the past. Since the past couldn't be changed, Hailey believed in moving forward. She tried not to dwell on things that would make her sad. After all, she had her life to live and enough responsibility for two twenty-seven-year-olds.

Speaking of responsibility, right at this moment it meant boiling noodles to mix with tuna and peas for their dinner tonight. She shook her head at her own foolishness and got back to peeling carrots, cutting them before adding them to the broth.

In a few hours, she'd leave to go pick up Eli from elementary school and then Tom and Tara from middle school. Their mother might or might not wake up to eat supper, but Hailey would take her a plate anyway.

After dinner, Hailey would help her younger siblings with their homework, and later they'd all watch some television. She'd monitor their internet usage, a fact of life that totally irked the fourteen-year-old twins, though not nearly as much as the fact that they still had dial-up since they couldn't afford broadband, and later tuck them into bed with a kiss.

Despite being their older sister, she did everything her mother should have done but wasn't capable of.

Again she thought of Mac and his father. Mac had never believed in Gus's guilt, even when a jury had convicted him. Too bad Mac couldn't have seen what Brenda's murder had done to her family. Luckily, Hailey had been strong enough to pick up the pieces. She'd been determined to give her brothers and sister the best, most normal life possible, even if doing so meant sacrificing her own.

Now that the kids had gotten older, Hailey had begun taking an occasional class at the junior college the next town over. She paid for this—and for the kids' essentials—by operating her own resume business, walking the neighbors' dogs, cleaning houses during school hours, taking in laundry and ironing, running errands for elderly shut-ins, basically picking up any work she could. She also tried to make sure to get her mother's disability check before the woman could drink it all away. They weren't rich by any means, but Hailey made sure the children were fed and clean and, most important, loved.

If she sometimes longed for a life of her own outside of tiny Legacy, Texas, she didn't allow herself to wallow in self-pity for long. She simply had too much to do.

She didn't date, unwilling and unable to divide her time any further. Plus, she didn't need the complications having a boyfriend would bring. Her busy life had settled into a sort of static routine that felt normal and safe.

Except today… Seeing Mac on her doorstep made her feel alive in a way she hadn't for years. Ten, to be exact. She found this both terrifying and exhilarating.

Of course, she wouldn't be seeing him again. Just because he'd moved back to Legacy didn't mean they'd be running into each other all the time. Nothing was going to change.

Maybe if she told herself that often enough, she'd come to actually believe it.

Chapter 2

After a restless night, Mac abandoned any attempt at sleeping and got up with the sun. He showered and dressed, then quietly padded into the kitchen to make coffee and a pan of oatmeal. He fixed his breakfast and ate, leaving the rest of the oatmeal for Gus to have when he woke.

The sound of the television coming on alerted Mac that Gus was up. Gus loved to watch the morning news, a habit he'd no doubt developed while in prison as he'd always been an evening news kind of guy before.

"Are you ready for breakfast?" Mac called. He'd nuke the oatmeal, add raisins, a spoonful of protein powder and milk, and carry it in to his father.

"Mac!" Gus tried to shout, but only succeeded in a loud croak. "Come in here. You've got to see this."

Mac hurried in, just in time to hear the news reporter

comment on a teenage girl's murder that had happened a few hours ago in the tiny east Texas town of Legacy. The reporter informed them excitedly that this was the first murder in ten years, the first since Brenda Green's body was found in this exact same spot.

Stunned, Mac reeled. Glancing at his father, who wore a grim expression of pain mingled with satisfaction on his wasted face, he looked back at the television.

Ten years to the day. And right after Mac and Gus had come back to town. Then, a combination of relief and horror flooded through him. Relief, because anyone looking at his father could tell instantly he wouldn't have been able to do it—the man could barely even walk, for pity's sake—and horror because of the killer's choice of date and place. Ten long years had passed since the first murder. What would make someone do such a thing to celebrate such a gruesome anniversary? It had to be the original killer. Had to be.

"See?" Gus said quietly, switching off the television once the segment had ended. "You know as well as I do that this has to be the same person who killed Brenda Green. Why else would they kill again at the same location, on the same date? More proof I didn't do it."

While Mac agreed, he had to wonder about the timing. Ten long years had passed since a killing. If it had been the same person, what had been the reason for the huge gap? Now Gus had returned to Legacy and immediately another girl got murdered? It sure sounded like someone was trying to set Gus up.

But why? For what reason? It might have worked, too, except whoever it was had no idea how fast the illness had marched through Gus's body.

"Now you have even more incentive to find out who

the real killer is," Gus continued. "Not just to clear my name, but to make sure no other young girl suffers a horrible fate." The older man's eyes glistened.

"I'm sure the police will be working hard to solve the case," Mac said.

"Right. Like they did ten years ago? No. They didn't find the right man then, and I doubt they will now."

Gus swiped his hand across his face and shook his head. "The hell I've been through. While I know it's nothing like what the Greens suffered, knowing everyone believes you're a monster is its own kind of torture. Not to mention rotting in prison for something I didn't do."

Not sure what to say, Mac squeezed his father's shoulder. "Now how about that breakfast? Or do you need to use the restroom first?"

"Already been." He sounded like a little kid who'd pulled a fast one. Since he wasn't supposed to try to walk unassisted, in a way he had.

Mac had already lectured him on this the day before, so he decided to let it pass this time. "Then I guess I need to bring you some food."

"Okay," Gus said, grimacing. "To be honest with you, I'm not sure how much I can eat."

"I made oatmeal. Your favorite. At least you can try."

"That I can do. I sure wish I could have coffee, though."

"I'll make you some decaf."

After putting everything on a tray, Mac carried it in and placed it in front of his dad. He pulled up a chair next to the bed, figuring he could make conversation while getting a look at how much his dad managed to eat.

To his surprise, Gus ate most of the oatmeal. He

drank all the juice and took a few sips of the decaf coffee before proclaiming himself done.

"You did great," Mac said, pleased.

"Thanks. Now, how about you help me make it to the bathroom? I want to take a shower."

Mac had installed handrails in the master bedroom shower. Luckily, it was a walk-in, so Gus had no problem getting in or out.

After Gus had showered and dried off, Mac helped him dress and took his arm to lead him back to bed. Gus tired easily these days, and they'd discovered early on it was better to let him stay in the bed rather than a chair. One incident of him sliding down the floor and being unable to get up had proved that.

Settled back against his pillow, Gus proclaimed himself comfortable. Mac asked him if he needed anything. He'd planned to do more repair work on the exterior of the house. Checking on Gus every thirty minutes, of course.

"Sit and talk awhile." Gus jerked his chin to indicate the chair next to the bed. "I won't take much of your time." He grinned as he glanced at the clock. "My game show comes on in ten minutes."

Smiling back, Mac took a seat. He treasured this time with his father and was grateful to have it. It almost made up for the ten years lost—almost, but not really.

"So tell me, have you seen her yet?" Gus asked.

Even though they both knew who he meant, Mac considered feigning ignorance just to tease. But in the end, he simply nodded. "I have."

"How is she? Still as pretty?"

Mac sighed. "Even more so. She didn't really want

to talk, to put it mildly. I let her know we were back in town, and that was about it."

"I'm sorry, son." Gus reached up and squeezed Mac's arm. "I know how much you loved her."

Loved. Past tense. Sometimes Mac wished that's where his feelings could stay. But to hope such a thing was foolish. One glance at Hailey and he'd known that.

"Still do," he confessed. "I'm hoping to get a second chance with her."

"Glad to hear it." Gus studied him, his gaze sharp as ever. "But don't just hope. Act. Good things only come to those who work hard to get them."

Hearing his father repeat the old adage Mac had heard growing up made him grin. "Yes, sir," he said. "Now I'd better get to work. And you've got your game show to watch."

Nodding, Gus clicked on the TV. Even as the opening music came on, his eyes were already drifting closed.

Getting up and moving quietly away, Mac left him alone to rest. He removed and replaced three back window screens before heading inside to check on his father. He found Gus sound asleep, the television still on.

Next up, Mac wanted to fix a leaky pipe under the sink in the guest bathroom. He spent the next several hours repairing small things, checking them off a long list he'd made.

Come lunchtime, Mac made a couple of sandwiches. He fixed both him and his dad identical plates, chips and a large dill pickle for both of them. After pouring two glasses of iced tea, he carried everything into the living room and loudly cleared his throat.

Startled, Gus opened his eyes and sat up. "What's going on?"

"Nothing much. Just brought us a little lunch."

Side by side, they ate. Once again, Gus pleasantly surprised Mac with his appetite. "You're really eating well today," Mac told him. He'd noticed some days were better than others.

Gus shrugged. "I'm hungry for some reason." He covered his mouth with his hand and yawned. "But all this food makes me sleepy."

"You go ahead and rest." Gathering up the plates, Mac carried them to the kitchen. "I'll check on you later."

Yawning again, Gus nodded. When Mac glanced back on his way to the kitchen, his father was already asleep.

The rest of the day passed quickly. Mac kept busy, tackling all the smaller jobs first before he attempted the bigger ones. He'd gone inside to check on Gus and to fix himself a drink when Trudy Blevins, the lone reporter for the local radio station, showed up at the front door. She rang the bell, which only made a dry buzzing sound. Of course, this was one of the many things Mac needed to repair but hadn't gotten around to yet.

When he answered, he stepped out on the porch, unwilling to let her inside. She identified herself, and he nodded, deciding not to tell her he remembered her from the time she'd given a talk on career day during his senior year in high school. She hadn't aged that much since then.

"I guess you heard," she began, clearly not wanting to waste any time on small talk. "Since the murder sort of coincides with you and your father's return, I wanted to see if you had any comments you wanted to make. I work for the newspaper, too, and I've been receiving calls from some of the larger TV stations in both Dallas and Houston."

"Are you kidding?" he asked, more out of shock than any real curiosity.

Trudy didn't even crack a smile. Chewing gum so violently her dangly earrings swayed, she stared at him hard. "Nope."

Now he was really glad he hadn't invited her in. "My father is sick. Actually, he's dying. While he's not yet completely bedridden, he's getting to where he can barely walk. It's a major effort for him to make it to the bathroom. So if you're out here fishing for some clue that would make you think he did it, you're barking up the wrong tree."

"Oh, it wasn't him I was curious about," Trudy said. Something in the caustic tone of her voice should have warned him. "It was you. Like father, like son and all that. Continuing the tradition, are ya?"

If she'd been a man, he would have decked her. Instead, hands clenched into fists, he settled for turning around, stepping inside and closing the door in her smug, supercilious face.

"Who was that, son?" His father's querulous voice trembled with the effort required to speak.

"Somebody selling magazines," he lied one more time, since there wasn't a chance in hell he'd have his dad worrying about this while struggling with the process of dying.

As usual, Hailey had the early evening news on while cooking dinner. The twins were up in their room, supposedly doing homework but probably using their shared cell phone to text friends. Eli had finished his schoolwork and had gone outside to ride his bike. And her mother had not yet roused herself enough to venture out of her bedroom.

Which meant when the news story came on, Hailey heard it alone.

Shock had her frozen as she listened, unable to move. The reporter's words echoed inside her head, as if everything had slowed down to a crawl. Another. Murdered. Girl. Anniversary of Brenda's death.

It had happened that morning. Suddenly, Hailey was fiercely glad she hadn't watched TV or listened to the radio all day.

They showed the dead girl's picture, culled from Facebook. Slender, her pert nose covered in freckles. Blond hair, blue eyes. She could have been Brenda's twin.

Pain slammed into her, followed by disbelief. Not again, not again. How was it possible that such an atrocity had been allowed to reoccur after an entire decade had passed?

Finally she sucked in a gasp of air, then another. And then she remembered. Gus Morrison. Mac had brought him back to town. The killer had been freed, and he'd killed again.

Her surroundings spun as she battled to maintain her bearings. Though Mac had claimed his father was sick, the timing was just too awful to be a coincidence. *Gus goes to prison and no more killings. Gus is released and bam. Another young girl loses her life. Another family is torn apart.*

Feeling physically ill, she reached for the phone. She needed to alert the police, to let them know a monster had returned to their midst. Though they probably already knew, she'd feel better checking, just in case.

As her fingers connected with the receiver, the phone rang. Though she didn't recognize the number, she answered anyway. "Hello?"

"Hailey? Have you seen the news?"

She would have recognized the voice anywhere. Ice and heat simultaneously coursed through her veins. "Mac." Her throat closed, making it impossible to say anything else.

"I take it you've heard another girl has been murdered."

This time, she managed to croak a response. "Yes."

"It's horrible. I considered calling you this morning, but I figured you needed time to process it. I wanted to let you know, I'm going to talk to the police. I'm hoping they'll consider reopening the investigation into your sister's murder."

Whatever she might have expected him to say, it hadn't been this. "I don't understand. Why would they do that? The case was solved. They got a conviction."

"Don't you see? If anything, this proves my father didn't kill Brenda."

Stunned, she wasn't sure how to respond. She'd always known Mac believed his father to be innocent. But this…

She replied the only way she could, letting her own emotions show. "Does it? Does it really? Because from where I sit, it's the opposite. No one was killed while your dad was in prison. He gets out, and immediately there's another murder. It doesn't take a police detective to figure that out."

Silence. Then, he sighed. "He's not capable of hurt-

ing anyone, Hailey. He's really ill. I promised him I'd
try to clear his name. Now that someone else has been
killed, the police might be more inclined to look at
Brenda's murder again."

She felt like she was living a nightmare. "If you get
them to reopen the case, then that will stir everything
up again. My brothers and sister don't remember any of
this, and June…" She swallowed hard. "June drinks."

"I'm sorry," he said.

"No." Deep breath. And again. "You aren't. You
couldn't be, since all of this is your fault. I don't understand why you brought him back here. How can you
be so blind?"

"You need to come over and see him. Come see for
yourself."

Clearly, he hadn't carefully considered his words
or how they'd affect her. Or maybe he'd lost his mind.
"No, I don't. I don't feel the need to ever lay eyes on
that man again."

"He's dying, Hailey," Mac repeated, his voice breaking.

She steeled her heart, quashing the rush of pity she
felt at his words. "So you say. But as long as he's still
alive, I can't feel safe. Nor should any other female in
this town." The harshness of her words made her in-
wardly wince, but she didn't call them back or apologize. She only spoke the truth, whether or not Mac
wanted to hear it.

"That's why you need to come. See for yourself.
You'll know he's not well enough to have done this."
He inhaled sharply, making her remember the old way
he'd given her warning that she wasn't going to like

what he was about to say. "I'd never have pegged you for a coward, Hailey. Clearly I was wrong."

He ended the call before she could respond.

Staring at the phone, she didn't know whether to laugh or cry and throw the damn thing against the wall. Coward.

She fumed all through dinner, his words echoing over and over in his head. He knew, of course, that she'd taken real pride in her courage, her ability to face the greatest challenges head-on. This belief in her own ability had been necessary to help her get through the dark days after Brenda's death. She'd had no choice but to pull herself together and step into the shoes her mother had vacated. She'd been the glue that held their small family together, with no real adult guidance.

She'd done the best she could. She still did. Every single day. A coward, she was not.

But for Mac—someone she hadn't seen or talked to since she'd been seventeen—to blatantly try to use this word to compel her to do what he wanted—struck her as pretty low. Lower than low, actually.

Yet she still hadn't broached the subject of the most recent murder with the kids. So maybe part of her was a coward. She knew she had to tell them, eventually. But they needed to get to enjoy their meal first.

"Are you all right?" Tara, usually completely absorbed with her phone, eyed her. "You seem... Are you mad about something?"

Her twin, Tom, snorted and kept shoveling macaroni and cheese into his mouth. Ever since the previous year when he'd turned thirteen, he could eat as much as all of them put together. Growing boy.

Eli, the youngest at eleven, continued eating, too,

though he paused long enough to frown up at her. "Are you getting sick?" He twisted his mouth at her. "At school Jody Peirce said his mom says your boyfriend was back in town." He cocked his head, eyeing her with open curiosity. Tara and Tom both swung their gaze to her, waiting for her answer.

"I don't have a boyfriend," she countered, even though hearing another child had said this to her brother made her fume. "Ya'll know that. When would I have time to date anyone?"

Eli shrugged. She thought that might be the end of it, but Eli wasn't done. "Jody said he was your *old* boyfriend. From back when you were in high school."

Tom and Tara exchanged looks at this. "Whoa," Tara said. "Is this that hot guy who was in all your old photo albums?"

"What were you doing snooping through my things?" Best to counterattack rather than give a direct answer. "Those photo albums were locked up."

"In that beat-up old hope chest in your room." Scorn dripped from Tara's voice. "The lock is so old and rusty, a paper clip opened it."

"Tara Jean…"

"What? I wanted to see what you looked like back when you were young."

Ouch. That stung.

"And I saw your old boyfriend. So what? I didn't hurt anything. I put everything back exactly where you left it."

"That isn't the point," Hailey began. Before she could finish, their mother shuffled into the kitchen and headed for the refrigerator. Opening it, she perused the contents. Finally, she grabbed the orange juice and began drinking it, straight from the carton.

Both Hailey and Tara winced.

"Do you want any dinner, Mom?" Hailey asked. "I made tuna casserole with macaroni and cheese and peas." She made this often because it was one of the best ways she knew to stretch dollars to feed them for a couple of days. Except with the way Tom ate these days, they'd be lucky to have enough to have again tomorrow.

"Not that." June viewed the casserole dish with scorn. "I'll just have some cereal."

Except if she did, there wouldn't be enough milk for the kids to have breakfast tomorrow. With the ease of habit, Hailey moved to intercept and redirect her. "You need protein, Mom. Tuna has lots of protein."

Steering June to the empty chair across from Eli, Hailey helped her get settled. Eli shifted in his seat, clearly uncomfortable. Tom continued devouring his meal, while Tara pretended a sudden interest in her fingernails.

June didn't appear to notice the silence. She took a second swig of her orange juice. "This would go great with some champagne," she muttered.

Hailey hurriedly fixed a plate, careful not to put too much food on it. June rarely ate while nursing a hangover. For whatever reason, food seemed to appeal to her only when she'd started drinking. When she had a buzz, as she called it. The kids were used to it; over the years this had become their normal.

Able to remember a time—Before—when her mother hadn't been like this, Hailey had never grown accustomed to her mother slurping down wine or bourbon or beer—whatever she could get—her eyes growing shiny, her words slurring as she took staggering steps toward the fridge or television, holding on to the wall.

She used to say she drank to dull her agony. These days, she drank because she was addicted, an alcoholic. Hailey wanted to get her help, but she didn't know how. She also knew her mother had to want help before she could begin the process of changing. June wasn't there yet. Hailey didn't know if she'd ever be.

"What's this about a boyfriend?" June's gaze sharpened, as she picked the peas out of her casserole. "Hallelujah, if you finally got one. It's got to have been forever since you got la—"

"Mother." Firmly, Hailey interrupted. She knew what June had been about to say, but there was no way she wanted any of the kids to hear it. "I don't have a boyfriend. Not at all."

Frowning in confusion, June looked from Hailey to Tara and back again. "But I thought I heard…"

"He's from the past," Eli put in, no doubt trying to be helpful and completely unaware he was making things worse. "An old high school boyfriend."

Hearing this, June dropped her fork with a clatter. "What?" Eyes narrowed to slits, she glared at Eli before transferring her focus to Hailey. "You only had one boyfriend in high school that I know of. What are you doing talking to Mac Morrison after what he did to our family?"

Great. Now Hailey felt obligated to defend him. "First up, Mac didn't do anything to anyone. And second…" Then she closed her mouth, not sure exactly what she could say that wouldn't cause her mom to vent an explosion of rage or descend into a black hole of self-pity. Either one would be considered a good enough reason to get drunk, as if June needed a reason.

"You were saying?" Arms crossed, chin up and dinner forgotten, June appeared spoiling for a fight. Hailey's heart ached as she remembered the woman her mother used to be. Though it had been a long time, Hailey had never lost hope of someday getting that woman back.

"Nothing." Ducking her head, Hailey resorted to a ploy from childhood. "Aren't you going to eat? You need to get something in your stomach if you want to feel better."

June glared. Then she shoved her plate away so hard she jostled Eli's glass, spilling milk all over the table. Eli jumped up and grabbed a paper towel to try to mop it up. "I ain't eating this slop," she declared. "And don't try to change the subject."

Tom scraped the last bit of macaroni off his plate and mumbled an excuse before fleeing the room. Eli shot Hailey a panicked look. Shifting side to side, he appeared torn between following his brother or staying to support his oldest sister. Meanwhile, Tara made it plain she wasn't going anywhere. She kicked back in her chair and watched the verbal exchange with interest.

Hailey knew this was her mother's disease, not hers. At least not the mother she used to be. "I really think you should—"

"No." June's tone had the petulance of a small child. Eli finally decided he'd had enough and rushed out of the kitchen without a word.

Watching him go, Hailey sighed. Her mother's lips tightened, which meant she'd noticed.

"Mother, please." Trying again, Hailey gingerly

moved June's plate closer to her. "At least try to eat a little."

"Not until you promise me you won't go see that Mac Morrison."

Though Hailey had already decided she wouldn't, for whatever reason her mother's dictate made her want to jump in the car and drive over there. He'd called her a coward. She wasn't. There was no way she could manage all she did and let fear rule her life.

Yet the possibility of seeing Mac's father terrified her. Because she wasn't sure what she might do. What if she lost control and let out the primal, long-buried part of her that thirsted for vengeance? She didn't think she would, but the sad truth was that the possibility would always be there, lurking underneath the polite veneer of manners.

Gus Morrison had not only taken her sister's life, he'd destroyed Hailey's, too.

"That man ruined my life," June continued. "There's no way I want any daughter of mine hanging around someone like that. Consider our family's reputation."

Since this statement so boggled the mind, Hailey wasn't sure how to respond. Did June not think staggering around town, slurring her words and passing out in bars had any bearing on what people thought of their family?

Once again, Hailey knew better than to comment. She had no plans to escalate anything. Her first consideration always had to be of her brothers and sister.

Her lack of response seemed to have caused June to lose interest—or her train of thought. She dropped back into her chair with a thud, slid her plate over in front of her and took a couple of rapid bites. "You really believed you loved that boy," she commented, not raising her eyes from her food. "Head over heels. Aaron and I were sure the two of you would be married someday."

Surprising how that truth could still hurt. Rather than talk about Mac, Hailey changed the subject to her stepfather, Aaron. He'd taken off in the middle of the fallout and chaos after Brenda's death.

"Do you ever hear from him, Mom?" Hailey asked in a conversational tone. "I know you two never finalized a divorce or anything."

"Why would we do that?" June's tone regained its former sharpness. "Someday we might get back together. Stranger things have happened."

And there you had it. June alternated between a dark sort of reality and some bizarre fantasyland. If Aaron hadn't reappeared after ten years, Hailey sort of doubted he would.

Of course, Mac had returned. Who knew, maybe her mother was on to something. Now Hailey just had to figure out whether or not to tell her about the most recent murder.

In the end, she decided to stay quiet. The way June carried on, Hailey figured it'd be better if she didn't know, at least for now. She'd gather the kids upstairs and fill them all in. After they were aware, then and only then would Hailey discuss it with her mother. That way, everyone would be prepared to deal with June's reaction, whatever that may be.

Chapter 3

Mac hadn't gotten much sleep the first few nights after bringing his father home. Though his bedroom was down the hall from the living room where they'd placed the hospital bed, every little sound had him getting up to check and make sure his dad was okay. Paranoid, true. But he couldn't seem to help himself.

While he knew intellectually his father had come home to die, part of him felt as if by being vigilant, he could somehow prevent it. Indefinitely, even.

But after the first week, Mac had relaxed somewhat. Gus seemed stronger, he was eating well and despite his marked lack of energy, he appeared happy. Things seemed to be looking up.

Then another young girl had been murdered. Mac wondered if he'd ever sleep again. In all his life, Gus had only asked two things of him. One, that they come back to Legacy and, two, to find out who'd really killed Brenda Green and by doing so, clear his name. Not only his, but the reputation of their entire family.

Now that another killing had occurred with obvious ties to the first one a decade earlier, Mac imagined the police were in an uproar. They needed to find the killer before anyone else got hurt. In fact, he'd only just had the thought when a police cruiser pulled up in front of the house and stopped. Mac felt his entire body tense.

One day. One day since the murder. He actually was surprised it had taken them this long. Since he'd been expecting this once he'd learned the news, he simply waited on the front porch. Two uniformed cops exited the car and came up the walk toward him.

"Afternoon," the officer who'd been driving, wearing a dark blue uniform and mirrored sunglasses, greeted him. "Are you Mr. Mac Morrison?"

"I am." Mac kept his tone cordial. "What can I do for you?"

"We'd like a word with your father, Gus. We understand he received early parole. Is he home?"

"He is. I believe he's asleep. He's basically confined to a hospital bed, you know." Imparting this information as casually as if chatting about the weather, Mac forced a smile. "Come on in. We'll wake him if we have to."

Both officers' boots clomped heavily on the creaky wooden porch as they followed him inside.

In the living room, Mac stepped aside so they could see. The room smelled of medicine and disease. His father slept, a shrunken version of his former hearty self, with his mouth open, and slight gurgling sounds escaped him.

The two policemen exchanged glances. "This is Gus Morrison?"

"Yes. His illness is the reason he was released from prison early." A rare exception had been made. Timed with the fact that he'd be up for parole, and someone in the prison hierarchy had given Gus his first—and only—break in ten long years.

Officer Number One nodded. "Mr. Morrison?" he said, looking at Gus. "Sir, we'd like to ask you a few questions."

When Gus continued sleeping, the second officer stepped forward. Loudly clearing his throat, he leaned in. *"Sir?"*

Startled, Gus jumped and opened his eyes. "Who, what?" When he caught sight of the uniformed policemen, distrust flashed across his face. Mac couldn't actually blame him. He hadn't been treated fairly since the day he'd been arrested and charged with a murder he didn't commit.

Still, a second later Gus regained his composure. "How can I help you fellas?" he asked, his tone cordial.

"We'd like to ask you a few questions. Starting with, can you tell us your whereabouts the night before last?"

Shaking his head, Gus exchanged a glance with Mac before giving the officer a wry smile. "Here. I was right here in this bed. It may have somehow escaped your notice, but I'm terminally ill."

The two cops looked to Mac for confirmation. "He's not very mobile at all," Mac said.

"No disrespect intended, sir, but do you have proof of that?"

Mac crossed to the side table and picked up the thick manila folder containing all of Gus's medical diagnosis records. Another folder, marked in red, came from the hospice provider. Silently, he passed these over to the first policeman and waited while the other man skimmed the paperwork.

When that man had finished, instead of giving them to his partner, he handed them back to Mac. "My mother died of pancreatic cancer," he said, his mouth turning down at the corners. "I'm sorry. We didn't know."

This despite the fact that any good investigator would have checked the prison records. Everything, from what time Gus got up in the morning, to when he used the bathroom, was detailed there.

"I understand," Mac lied. "There's a lot to deal with. May I ask, since you have a new murder to investigate, if anyone is considering reopening the old Brenda Green case?"

At the question, Gus's tired eyes brightened. Again he tried to sit up as he waited to hear the answer.

"I…um… I'm not sure," the officer stammered.

"Who's in charge of this investigation?" Mac pressed. "I want to give him a call and set up a meeting."

From the perplexed expression on the two men's faces, clearly they hadn't been expecting this. "We're not sure, actually," the first guy said. "I think the FBI might be helping us out with this one."

"Good, but someone in your office is running point. I need to know who."

"Detective Logan," Officer Number Two finally answered. "And he reports to Lieutenant Gage. Either one of them would be able to help you, though it'd be easier to get an appointment with Logan."

"Thank you." Mac looked from one to the other. "Do either of you happen to have a card?"

"No," Officer Number One muttered. "We don't. Sorry."

Mac decided to let it go. "All right then. Is there anything else we can do for you?"

A quick glance at his father showed the elder Morrison struggled to stay awake.

After the two policemen had left, Mac headed off to take a shower. He'd give Detective Logan a call first thing in the morning and check on the possibility of reopening his father's old case.

The next morning, after showering and preparing breakfast, Mac watched the clock, wondering when would be the best time to call. He and Gus had settled into a comfortable routine.

At nine sharp, Mac made the call while Gus listened. When he asked for Detective Logan, he got voice mail. After leaving his name and number, he pocketed his phone. "Don't worry, Dad. I'll keep after them. If I have to go down there, I will."

The rest of the day, Mac kept himself busy. The old house needed constant repairs, springing a leak here or there, and it seemed he'd no sooner fixed one thing when another needed his attention. Since the work required his hands rather than his mind, he couldn't help but think of Hailey. He'd let her get away once. Not this time. Somehow, someway, he had to persuade her to give him a second chance. To give them a second chance.

He just didn't know how. After a lunch break during which he also fixed his father some soup, since the elusive Detective Logan still hadn't called, Mac phoned again. Once more he got voice mail. He resigned himself to having to make a trip to the police station in the morning. For now, he needed to complete his rewiring of the doorbell. Once he'd finished that, he made a glass of iced tea and planned to sit on the front porch and drink it. He carried it there and grasped the handle to go outside.

The little kid standing on his front porch stepped back in surprise when Mac opened the front door. Towheaded, with freckles and bright blue eyes, he couldn't have been much older than ten or eleven. A battered blue bicycle leaned against the porch railing.

"Can I help you?" Mac asked, keeping his tone kind.

Nodding, the boy swallowed hard, before meeting Mac's gaze. "I'm Eli," he said, holding out his hand. "Eli Green."

Stunned, Mac shook Eli's hand. "Hailey's brother? You were barely walking when I saw you last."

With more dignity than his age warranted, Eli nodded. "So you are the right guy."

"The right guy? For what?"

The little guy lifted his chin. "My sister Hailey's old boyfriend from high school."

For whatever reason, Eli's choice of words made Mac smile. "I'm not all that old," he teased. "But, yes, I was Hailey's boyfriend back in school."

Eli nodded solemnly. He eyed Mac, looking him over as if inspecting him. "I need to know what's wrong with you."

"Wrong with me?"

"Yes. Our mother doesn't want Hailey to go anywhere near you."

That didn't surprise him. Mac hadn't been in town long enough to find out the Green family dynamic, but the family had been heavily fractured by Brenda's murder. The loss of her daughter had damn near destroyed Hailey's mother, June. She'd turned to solace in the bottle. Mac wondered if she'd managed to make her way out of the depths of despair.

He thought not, since Hailey still lived at her childhood home.

Shaking his head to clear the cobwebs off his thoughts, Mac squatted down in front to Eli. "What'd you come here for, little man?"

"I wanted to check you out for myself." Again, the kid's quiet dignity made him seem older than his what— ten? eleven?—years. "Hailey deserves to be happy. She does everything for us and hardly anything for herself."

Still not sure where Eli was going with this, Mac nodded. "She's a good person."

"My other sister Tara showed me and Tom the photo albums. The ones from when Hailey and you were boyfriend and girlfriend. She looked like a different person."

"Well, it's been ten years," Mac pointed out. "We're all older now." His legs had started to ache from crouching down, so he stood and walked over to the porch steps and took a seat. Patting a spot next to him, he motioned for Eli to join him.

After the boy had gotten settled, he sighed heavily, sounding more like a middle-aged man than a young kid. "I'm not talking about being older. She looked different because she was happy." His solemn expression matched his tone. "Poor Hailey. I can't even think of the last time I saw her laugh like that."

Concerned, Mac couldn't help but ask. "She's not happy now?"

"No." Sadness colored his young/old voice. "She tries, but she's not happy. Not like that."

"What do you mean?" He felt kind of bad, pumping a kid for information about Hailey, but Eli had come to him, not the other way around.

Eli shrugged. "She's tired a lot. Whenever she's not taking care of us—and Mom—she works. We're really poor. She thinks I don't know, but it's hard not to, you know? Our mom is an alcoholic."

Stunned that a kid this young knew such a word so intimately, Mac realized he might not really know Hailey anymore. Not now.

"How old are you?" Mac had to ask, since he couldn't remember exactly how old Eli had been ten years ago.

The kid's chin came up, the gesture so like Hailey's, Mac caught his breath. "I'm eleven. But I see things, too, you know. I might only be eleven, but even I can tell that Hailey needs more."

"More what?"

When Eli met his gaze, Mac saw wisdom far beyond the boy's years. "More smiles. More happy times. Tara—that's my other sister—says after high school, and our other sister's death, Hailey never got to be young again."

Mac felt a sharp stab of pain. This kid wasn't old enough to remember. He didn't understand the chain of events that had pulled the rug out from under them all. So much pain. The town had become a cesspool. People had taken sides, drawn lines, made enemies. Even time hadn't been able to heal the old wounds. Coming here made them all fresh and new again. He could only imagine how Hailey felt, still living here, reminded constantly.

"Do you like baseball?" Eli asked, apparently ready to change the subject.

"Sure. What about you?"

"It's my favorite sport. I'm hoping to get to play Little League someday."

This seemed slightly odd. From what Mac could remember, T-ball started really young, like four or five years old. From there, the kids played in leagues, all the way up to Little League baseball.

"Where do you play if you're not in a league?" he asked.

Eli looked down. "Sometimes my brother and I play catch. And in school, we have games. But no one will pick me for their team because I haven't played Little League." He shuffled his feet. "I'm not really very good."

"That stinks," Mac said, meaning it. "But I bet all you need is some practice. How about you and I hit the ball around? I've got time."

The kid's head snapped up so fast it's a wonder he didn't pop his neck. "When?"

"How about now?"

As he turned to go rummage around for his old baseball equipment, he heard a screech of tires as a car came around the corner. It barreled down his street, a little too fast. He recognized the car. Hailey's, the same jalopy she'd been driving back in high school.

Eyeing it, he was surprised it still ran. Various creases and dents marred the shape of the body. In the not crumpled areas, the red paint had faded and chipped, and the tires didn't match. It slowed as it pulled up in front of Mac's house and slammed on the brakes.

Eli groaned. "Great. I won't get to play catch." He swallowed hard. "And I'm also in big trouble."

Mac didn't have time to ask him what he meant. The door creaked open, and Hailey burst from the driver's seat. She hurried up the path, her expression grim and furious. Of course the second Mac saw her, he felt that same instant zing of attraction.

"Eli Green." Her crossed arms and stern tone left no room for argument. "What on earth are you doing here?"

"Talking to your friend." The boy stayed put, his expression defiant. "We were just about to practice baseball."

"You know better," she said, directing her comment at both of them.

Biting back a smile, Mac nodded. "I promise you, he's safe. I could have run him home."

"I have my bike," Eli pointed out.

"You're in so much trouble, young man." Hailey shot Mac a fierce glare. "You still haven't explained what you're doing over here, clear across town."

"I told you, I—"

"Mac?" His father's voice, both unsteady and querulous. "Who's here? What's happening?"

Hailey froze. She looked torn between jumping in her car and driving off at breakneck speed, and standing in between Eli and the house, as if to protect him.

"Just a second, Dad," Mac called back. "I'll be there in a minute. Everything is okay."

Eli looked at his sister, frozen in place, her eyes wide with shock. Then he glanced at Mac, who tried like hell not to relay tension. "Is your father sick?"

"Yes. Yes, he is. Very sick."

"Let me go say hi to him." Before Hailey could protest, Eli bounded up the steps and disappeared into the house.

Hailey cursed. "Now look what you've done," she cried out. Casting him a withering look, she sailed up the steps after her brother, hell-bent on protecting him from the perceived menace lurking inside.

Hailey stopped short at the sight of the hospital bed. The withered man in it wasn't recognizable as the larger-than-life Gus Morrison she remembered. Eli stood close to him, chattering away. Too close, she thought, her stomach clenching as she wondered if her baby brother was in danger.

"Eli?" She kept her voice calm, not wanting to alarm her brother or Mac's dad. Mac had come up behind her, standing between her and the doorway. She wanted to ask him to move since she'd need a clear path if she had to flee. Well, she'd just barrel into him if she had to.

"Just a minute, Hailey," Eli answered. "Me and Mr. Morrison are talking about baseball."

She remembered Mac's father had been a baseball fanatic, just like her baby brother.

"Hailey?" Struggling to rise up on his elbows, Gus failed. He settled back into his spot with a grunt. "Come here, baby girl, and let me have a look at you."

A shudder skittered up her spine. She couldn't make herself move, not a step toward him or away.

"Please, don't hurt him," Mac murmured in her ear. "Just go over and say hello, then I promise I'll figure out a way for you and your brother to beat a hasty retreat."

Retreat. Like a coward. Except he was right. Retreating was all she wanted, with every fiber of her body. She wanted to snatch Eli up and run.

Instead, she found herself taking one step, then two. She stopped when a good three feet separated her from the man in the bed.

Gus's faded gray eyes, so like Mac's, searched her face. "You came to see my son?" he asked, hope lightening the raspy exhaustion in his voice.

Heaven help her, she didn't have the heart to disappoint him. Why? Why was that? This man had all but destroyed everything important to her.

Instead of outright denial, she settled on the truth. "I came to get my little brother Eli. His other brother told me where he'd gone."

"Tom?" Eli squeaked, shocked and hurt all at once. "He promised he wouldn't tell."

"Well, maybe he realized he needed to," she retorted back. She held out her hand for him to take, aware the second their fingers connected, they'd beat a fast track to the door.

Meeting her gaze, Eli slowly shook his head. He cut his eyes toward the man in the bed. "I'm not finished yet."

"It's okay." Gus sighed, clearly exhausted from even this brief interaction. "You go ahead and go. I'm sure I'll see you again."

Not if she could help it.

Opening his eyes again, Gus pinned her with his gaze. "But first, I'd like a word with you in private."

While she searched for a way to decline without alerting Eli to the fact that something was wrong, Mac grabbed Eli's hand and tugged him toward the door. "We'll be just outside on the front porch," he said. "Take all the time you need." When he caught Hailey's eye, she saw the entreaty there, the plea to remember this was his father and he was dying.

She knew that. What she couldn't forget was that this man had murdered her sister and destroyed everything she held dear.

Swallowing hard, she steeled herself to get through the next minute.

"Thank you for coming to see me," Gus said, once everyone else had gone. "It means a lot to me, considering how you once believed the unthinkable. I hate that this happened again to another girl, but at least that forces people to see the truth. I can at least die happy knowing that you know I didn't kill your sister."

Throat tight, she stared. She could picture June's reaction here, something incoherently vindictive or violent or both. She felt a bit like she was letting her mother down, but for whatever reason she couldn't bring herself to do anything more than listen.

Apparently taking her silence for acquiescence, Gus continued. "Mac has promised to get the case reopened. Now that the police know someone else killed this latest girl, they should be willing to take a look at Brenda's murder, too. It's about time the real murderer is brought to justice. I'm hoping he can clear my name before I die."

Two things struck her. One, Gus's father truly believed what he said. And two, was it possible he had a point? All along, he'd maintained his innocence, claiming the police were railroading him into a conviction, with trumped-up evidence and no real proof.

If this was true—and she wasn't certain it was—Gus Morrison had spent ten years in prison for a crime he hadn't committed. What a bitter pill to swallow if that was the case. To have been robbed of ten years of your now-too-short life for nothing.

"He missed you, you know," Gus continued on, the raspy thread of his voice wearing thin.

This comment startled her, making her blink. "Who?" she asked, even though she knew.

"Mac. He never forgot you. I think he might still carry a torch for you." Gus's eyes drifted closed again. "If everything works out, please take care of my son after I'm gone. He won't have anyone else."

Since she couldn't in a million years agree to a promise like that, she stood silently, staring down at the man who for the past decade she'd regarded as a monster. What if he was telling the truth? What if—and this might be a huge stretch—he wasn't actually the one who'd killed Brenda and torn two families and an entire town apart?

Even as she had this thought, she clenched her jaw and shook her head. Enough of this foolishness. Mac and Gus returning to Legacy had done nothing but dredge up the past. Their presence had brought pain and uncertainty right back to the surface.

Gus's eyes drifted closed. Even though she hadn't responded, she took this as her cue to exit. Moving noiselessly, she went to the door. Outside, Mac and Eli sat on the top step of the porch. They both looked up as she approached.

"Ready to go?" she asked her brother, keeping her tone light and avoiding Mac's gaze.

"Can't I stay a little longer?" Eli pleaded. "Mac's promised to teach me how to hit a baseball. You know

I've always wanted to play in Little League. If he helps me practice, I might get better at it."

She swallowed, trying not to let herself feel guilty. Every single year since Eli had been old enough, he'd begged to join Little League. Unfortunately, they barely had enough money to buy food to feed the family. They simply couldn't afford it, so every year she'd had to tell him no. Undeterred, he'd ask the next year. As if things had changed. She guessed since he was so young, he didn't understand.

"I can drive him home after," Mac added quietly. The afternoon sun lit up his dark hair with gold, shadowing his craggy face and reminding her how she'd used to find his raw masculinity beautiful. Despite the tingle in her veins every time she got near him, she needed to make sure all that stayed in the past.

Tears stinging the back of her eyes, she shook her head, steeling herself at Eli's disappointed look. "Not today. Come on, Eli, let's get going. I'm sure you have homework you need to do."

Right about now, June would be staggering into the kitchen, rummaging around for something to eat. Their mother would go on a major binge if she found out about today. Of course, as her addiction to alcohol got steadily worse, June seized the slightest excuse to lose herself in drink.

Eli hesitated, disappointment and resignation plain on his young, freckled face. But he finally got up and went to get his bike.

"Let me help put that in your backseat," Mac said.

Refusing to look at him, she nodded. Once the bike

had been secured and Eli buckled in, she started the car and drove off without even saying goodbye to the man standing on the porch, watching them go.

Chapter 4

What had he expected, a miracle? Mac knew better, but when his father had asked to talk to Hailey, hope had risen in him so fast he nearly drowned in it.

But Hailey had emerged unchanged, at least as far as he could tell. She'd always been stubborn; in the old days he'd found it charming and amusing and often teased her about it.

Bless Eli for giving them this opportunity. Mac had been wracking his brain trying to figure out a way to get Hailey over here to talk to his dad. Now, thanks to one headstrong eleven-year-old, the chance had fallen into his lap. And while he wasn't sure what his father had said to Hailey, at least he'd gotten the opportunity to say it.

He glanced at his watch. He might as well shower and call it a day. Too late to do much more. This morning he'd gotten started on repairing the roof. Luckily, in the ten years since graduating high school, he'd become a jack-of-all-trades. He'd gone to work for a local custom home builder in Huntsville and had learned a myriad of skills. Everything from carpentry to tile to roofing. In a pinch, he could also do basic electrical and plumbing, too, though he wasn't licensed or certified. The skills would serve him well while he worked to fix up the old family house.

Since right now, with the need to look after his father, he wasn't able to work, he knew he'd have to be thrifty. Luckily, he'd been socking away most of his money in the hopes of starting his own construction company. While he still wanted to do this someday, for now it was good to have a backup in a pinch. Most important, he would be there for his father. No amount of money could ever make him regret that. He'd missed out on ten years while his dad was in prison. Damned if he'd miss out on this.

While he took his second shower of the day, he replayed Eli's words over and over in his mind. Hailey wasn't happy. The family needed money.

And Mac needed help with his father.

It would be a win-win. He'd get to spend more time with Hailey, she'd get some financial assistance, and maybe she'd even come to accept the truth of his father's innocence. Especially if he could help the police find the real killer.

And if he was hoping for the moon and the sun and the stars, maybe Hailey could find her way back to loving Mac again.

Feeling more positive than he had in days, he grabbed his phone and made the call. He couldn't ask her on the phone—this was something he wanted to do in person. But he didn't want to show up at her house unannounced either.

"I liked Mac. He was really nice," Eli enthused on the way home from Mac's. Either he didn't understand he shouldn't have done what he had, or his gushing was meant to hide it.

She shot him a quelling look, but since he bounced up and down in his seat, she doubted he saw it. "Eli, you know you aren't supposed to go anywhere after school without discussing it with me first."

His restless movements stilled. "I know," he said quietly. Then he lifted his chin and met her gaze. "I had to, though. We talked about it, all three of us. I wanted to meet him."

"Why?"

He looked down, then out the window, anywhere but directly at her. When he spoke again, he spoke in a voice so small she could barely hear him. "I wanted to see if he'd be your boyfriend again. We—Tom, Tara and me—decided that would be a good thing."

Dumbfounded, she couldn't figure out their logic. "And why would that be?" she asked.

His sigh sounded much too old for his eleven years. "Because we want you to be happy again. You know, like you were in those pictures from when you were young."

Any other time, his choice of phrase would have made her smile. She guessed at his age, twenty-seven must seem old. "I *am* happy," she told him. "I don't understand why you'd think I'm not."

He shrugged. "I dunno." Which meant he was done

trying to explain himself. Either way, she knew just how to fix this mess. She couldn't have Eli going off to the other side of town and visiting with strangers.

When they pulled into her long drive and parked in front of the garage, she took a deep breath. "Don't go far," she ordered, the instant they stopped. With his hand already on the door handle, Eli froze.

"In fact, I want you to go and find your brother and sister. I need to see all three of you in the kitchen. It's family meeting time."

Waiting in the kitchen, Hailey saw no sign of her mother. If June had already made her normal afternoon raid for snacks, she saw no sign of it. Usually June would leave open cookie or chip bags scattered around on the counter and table. Despite Hailey's attempts to get her to eat healthy, they could barely afford junk food. Healthy food was, unfortunately, often way too expensive for their meager budget.

As the kids shuffled in, she noticed them all looking around for signs of June. The relief she saw in their faces mirrored her own, which made her feel sad.

"Sit," she ordered, pointing at the kitchen table. "We need to talk."

Eli sat. A moment later the twins did the same.

"Now tell me who thought it would be a good idea to send an eleven-year-old over to a stranger's house. Especially with everything that's been going on."

"I didn't think he'd really do it," Tara protested. "It was a dumb idea, and I thought we were all just talking."

"Uh-huh. But you, Tom." She speared him with a glance. "You knew, right?"

"No. Not really," he protested. Then, as she continued to eye him, he swallowed and finally nodded. "As soon as he rode off on his bike, I knew it was the wrong thing to do. That's why I told you."

Eli crossed his eyes and stuck his tongue out at his brother. "Tattletale."

"Enough of that." Hailey kept her voice sharp, though she wanted to smile. Including Tara in a look, she pulled out a chair. "Now I want to know where you got the idea that I'm not happy."

Still silent, Tara began studying her hands, ignoring the way both her brothers looked in her direction.

"Tara?" Softening her voice, Hailey reached out and cupped her younger sister's chin. "Honey? Why do you think I'm unhappy?"

Tara bit her lip as she raised her gaze. "Not unhappy, not really. It's just…"

"You looked different then," Eli put in.

"Yeah." Even Tom had a comment.

"Different how?" Hailey looked from one to the other.

"I don't know. Just…happier. Brighter, even. Like you glowed." Having said that, Tara returned her attention back to her fingernails.

Brighter. Happier. In love. Hailey blinked. "I'm fine," she said firmly. "And while I really appreciate everyone thinking of me, in the future, please, discuss with me any other schemes you might come up with, okay?"

All three of them nodded.

"Good. Now that you understand, wash up and get ready for dinner. After we eat, I want everyone to make sure their homework is done, okay?"

Again, the kids nodded in unison.

For the evening meal she made hamburger meat and pasta again. Not the healthiest choice, but an inexpensive one that all the kids liked. June didn't put in an appearance at all, so they ate without her. Hailey resisted the urge to go check on her, aware that right now she couldn't handle finding her mother passed out, drunk.

As a treat, she'd bought ice cream. Once they'd finished, she got each of them a single scoop and watched their young faces light up.

After, everyone brought their homework out to work on at the kitchen table, at Hailey's insistence. Truth be told, she enjoyed this feeling of togetherness, of family. She only hoped their mother didn't do something to ruin it.

Her cell phone rang. As she glanced at the number, her heart skipped a beat. *Mac.* She actually considered not answering, or sending the call to voice mail, but in the end she said hello.

"Would it be all right if I came over?" Mac asked. "I have something important I need to discuss with you."

Nonplussed, she swallowed. Suddenly, she realized she badly wanted to see him. Not good. "When?"

"Now."

She glanced over her shoulder at the three avid faces shamelessly attempting to eavesdrop. "Now isn't a good time."

"Then how about later? In an hour? I just need a few minutes of your time."

There were several ways she could answer that. If June saw him, that alone might be enough to set her off and on a two-day bender. And of course the kids, playing at matchmaking, would have reason to think they'd been successful.

Yet despite all this, she realized she craved him, with an intensity so powerful, it hurt.

She had to be strong. Too much was at stake. "I don't think today is good at all."

Silence. Then he sighed. "I just need five minutes, Hailey. Five quick minutes. I can meet you somewhere, or come there, or you can stop by here. Please. This is important."

It must be, for him to push so hard. "Fine," she said, relenting. "Five minutes. Now. I'll meet you at the end of my driveway." That way there was zero chance that June would see him. And the kids, despite their attempts to listen in, wouldn't be able to watch.

"Give me fifteen minutes to get there," he said. "And, Hailey?"

"Yes?"

"Thank you." He ended the call.

Dropping her phone into her back pocket, Hailey looked up to find all three of her siblings openly staring at her.

"Well?" Tara demanded, barely able to contain her excitement. "Was that Mac? Do you have a date?"

The quelling look Hailey shot her should have been intimidating. Instead, Tara grinned. "You do, don't you?"

"Not a date," she clarified. "A meeting. He says it will take five minutes. He wants to talk to me about something. Probably about Eli showing up over there uninvited and unannounced."

Eli shook his head. "No, I doubt it's about me. If he wanted to say something about my visit, he could have done it over the phone. It's got to be more personal than that if he needs to say it to your face."

What? Now Hailey stared. How had Eli gotten to be eleven going on thirty? Sometimes he acted older and wiser than both of the fourteen-year-old twins combined.

"You're right!" Tara jumped up. "He probably wants to ask you out on a date."

"I doubt that." Hailey was quick to respond. "And once again, that's also something he could do over the phone." She made a show out of checking her watch. "I'd better get going. He's on his way over here right now."

"Here?" Tara squeaked. "We get to actually see him, in person?"

Oh, geez. "No. Settle down. I'm meeting him at the end of the driveway. To talk. Alone." She met each of their gazes. "Got that?"

One by one, each kid slowly nodded. Satisfied, Hailey headed to the bathroom to check her reflection in the mirror. She excused this little bit of vanity, refusing to think about it. Then, with one last warning glare at Tom, Tara and Eli, she headed out to walk down the driveway and meet Mac.

Unaccountably nervous, Mac made it to her place in record time. He considered himself lucky he hadn't received a speeding ticket. She wasn't there yet, which was good. Parking at the end of her driveway, he got out and sat on the tailgate of his truck. Though it had been a different pickup, he and Hailey had spent a lot of time sitting on tailgates. Football parties at school, summer bonfires out near the lake. Then, she'd nestled close to him, fitting so perfectly under his arm. He wished he'd been able to capture those moments somewhere other than his memory.

They'd been perfect for each other. He couldn't

help but believe they were meant to be together. All he needed to do was help Hailey see that.

Waiting, his heartbeat slowed, resuming its normal steady rhythm. The pine trees lining the curving drive formed a picturesque canopy while the setting sun sent golden fingers of light through their branches, dappling the pavement with flecks of gilt.

A moment later, he saw her, strolling down her driveway toward him, and his pulse picked up again. Hailey. Everything else ceased to exist as he focused on her.

She still walked with the loose-limbed saunter, her quiet confidence sexy, though she didn't realize it. She wore her long blond hair in a ponytail, which swung jauntily with every step she took.

Longing had his entire body clenching. Breathing deeply, he forced himself to relax again, to appear expressionless. Because he knew if he gave away the depths of his need and longing, she'd be frightened.

"All right," she drawled, by way of greeting. "What was so important that it couldn't wait for another day?"

He cleared his throat, and then dove right in.

"I need to hire someone to help out with my dad." His tone matter-of-fact, he held her gaze. "I need to work, at least part-time, and I can't leave him alone. I was hoping you'd consider it."

At first she didn't respond, didn't say anything, only continued to watch him from those bright blue eyes of hers.

"It's a paying job," he offered, deciding not to bother trying to pretend he wanted someone else to do it. "I thought I'd ask you first, since I know you could use the income."

She looked down and heaved a sigh. "I do need the

money, but I don't think I'd be the right person for the job."

He hadn't expected her to decline. "Why not?" he pressed. "You used to want to become a nurse. You might still go to nursing school one day. This would be good practice."

Hurt and disbelief flashed across her face. "That's not likely to happen."

"You're not too old," he argued. "In four years you'll only be thirty-one. That's not too old."

"No, it's not. But you're forgetting a few things. Eli is only eleven. I can't leave him alone with Mom. It'll be a long while before I'd be able to go to school. Assuming I could even afford it, which I can't."

His heart hurt for her. All her dreams had been put on hold, her entire life shattered, because some murderous SOB had taken her sister's life a decade ago.

His dad had paid, too. Paid for something he hadn't done. So help him, the police had better catch the right person this time.

"I really need the help," he reiterated. "I can't be with him twenty-four hours a day." He was telling the truth. If Hailey wouldn't do it—and he prayed she would— he'd have to hire a stranger.

"What about hospice?" Hailey asked. "I thought they came out periodically and relieved you."

"Two or three times a week. That's not nearly enough."

She wanted to say no, he could tell. But he knew how badly she needed money. "I'm willing to pay fifteen dollars an hour." He threw that out there, hoping it would help her make up her mind.

Her sigh told him how much it cost her not to say

yes. She tilted her head, considering, which sent a quick flare of hope through him.

"What are the hours? Because I have to take the kids to school in the morning, and pick them up after."

"We can work around that." He thought for a second. "Nine to two? That's five hours a day. Would that be good for you?"

Still considering, she frowned. He could see her doing the math in her head. "That's seventy-five dollars a day." Shock rang in her voice. "And if I worked five days a week, that'd be three-hundred seventy-five a week. How could you afford that?"

"If it makes my father's life easier, it's worth it." He meant his words. "And I make much more than that doing my work. But I should warn you, if you're considering doing it, that it won't be easy. My father is already very sick. Right now, his pain level is manageable. I'm not sure how long that will be the case."

Clearly torn, she swallowed hard. "I can't do any heavy lifting. You'd have to help me with that."

"I would, of course."

Again she went silent. He knew that kind of money would go a long way toward putting food on her table. And possibly more.

"Maybe Eli could finally join Little League," he said. "That extra money might enable you to pay for that."

"No." Mouth set in a grim line, her chin came up. "Don't you bring him into this. I don't want him getting his hopes up. If I let him do Little League, Tara will want to be a cheerleader. And Tom's been wanting to join the band and play trumpet. It wouldn't be fair to give to one and not the others. So, no, the extra money will go to pay the bills and buy groceries."

Stunned, he nodded, well aware he couldn't let her see how badly he wanted to offer to pay for them all to do those things. "Sorry. I didn't think."

Her shrug was meant to make him feel better. "You've never had three kids. I think you learn this kind of stuff through experience."

It obviously escaped her that she didn't actually have three kids either. But he supposed in her mind, it was sort of the same thing. She also took care of her mother. Now he was asking her to add one more person.

Still, it was better than scrambling around town looking for odd jobs and part-time work, he thought.

"I'm going to have to refuse. I just don't think it would work."

Shocked, he swallowed hard, trying like hell not to let his disappointment show on his face. He hadn't expected an outright refusal. "Do you mind telling me why?"

Her sideways look told him she thought he shouldn't have to ask. "Because it's your father. Because of what he did."

Her words brought a wave of pain so intense he had to briefly close his eyes. "I could swear to you on a stack of bibles that he's innocent, and you still wouldn't believe him, would you?"

"I…I don't know." She hesitated. Once, she would have offered an instant confirmation. "But as long as I don't know for sure, I don't think I can be around him."

Damn. "He's dying, Hailey." His voice broke. "He's dying and I love him. That ought to be enough." He wanted it to be. Oh, how he wanted it to be.

"I don't know that I can care for the man who killed my sister." She swallowed. "I'm sorry."

"He didn't." Though he knew his defense would fall on deaf ears, he had to give it a shot. "There was no real evidence. He had an indifferent attorney, and the police just wanted to close the case."

"Maybe so, but unless reopening the case shows me otherwise, I have no proof he didn't do it." She came closer, her earnest expression breaking his heart. "I'm sorry, Mac. If I think of anyone who could do the job, I'll have them call you."

He shouldn't have been so shattered, but he was. And even so, as she turned and walked back the way she'd come, he struggled with the urge to call her back, to ask her to take the weekend and think it over.

Had the rift between them grown so deep that there would never be a way to bridge it?

Once she'd gone out of sight, he climbed into his truck and started the engine. He still needed help. He'd wanted it to be her, but if she wouldn't do it, he'd have to find somebody else.

And figure out another way to get Hailey to give him a chance.

All the way back up her long, winding drive, Hailey berated herself. She didn't have the luxury of turning down work, especially work that paid so much. And this was Mac, who'd once been her everything, asking for her help.

Yet Gus… She considered Mac's words. What if the truth she'd believed for ten years wasn't really factual? What if Mac was right, and Gus hadn't committed the awful murder? Was there any sliver of reality in what Mac said, or had this just been a desperate attempt of a man to reconcile his love for his father with the possibility that Gus might be a monster?

She didn't know. She wasn't sure she'd ever know.

As she rounded the last corner and the house came into sight, her heart sank. June sat in the driver's seat of their one car, vainly trying to start the engine. Instead of a motor coming to life, every time she turned the key there was a clicking sound.

"Hey." June looked up as Hailey approached. "It's Friday night and I'm ready to party. But the car won't start. We either need a new battery or the alternator is gone."

Hailey winced. She'd just bought groceries and paid the electric bill. She had maybe five dollars left to her name, at least until she found some other work. Maybe she could pick up a shift waitressing in the café. Sometimes Jed Rogers would take pity on her and let her fill in when one of his waitresses called in sick.

Except without a car, how would she get into town to work?

She eyed her mother. "I don't suppose you have money to get that fixed?"

June started shaking her head before Hailey had even finished speaking. "My check doesn't come until next week," she drawled, not sounding the least bit concerned. "I don't have a dime."

Except somehow, from somewhere, she managed to come up with enough cash to buy a bottle or two. Hailey had searched numerous times, trying to find out where her mom hid her stash of cash, but so far the location eluded her.

"I don't either." Throat tight, Hailey refused to cry. This was the last straw. "I guess we're going to have to do without a car until we can come up with some money." Except she knew they couldn't, not past the weekend. Not only did she take the kids to school, but she picked them up. Eli's elementary school was close enough that he could ride his bike, but the twins' middle school was several miles away. She dreaded informing them that they'd need to ride the bus. They'd steadfastly refused every time she'd tried to suggest it, hinting how much money they could save on gas. Apparently to a fourteen-year-old, riding the school bus was the height of dorkiness.

Ah, well. They wouldn't have a choice if she didn't have a vehicle.

For the first time, June appeared slightly concerned. After all, how could she hang out at her bar without a way to get there? Then, staring at Hailey, her expression smoothed out, and her frown disappeared. "You'll figure something out," she said. "You always do."

Hailey shook her head and turned to go inside. Even though she was the daughter, she and her mother's roles had become reversed. Hailey was the one who worried if they had enough food, if she'd be able to clothe the children and keep the electricity and water turned on.

Now this.

There was no way she could turn down Mac's job offer now. More evidence of a hard truth she'd come to learn at an early age. Sometimes one had to swallow their pride in order to survive.

Chapter 5

The kitchen was empty. Hailey wasn't surprised. After her talk with them and insistence that they finish their homework at the table together, the instant she'd gone to meet Mac, the kids had scattered like leaves in the wind. For now, this suited her purpose. She didn't want any witnesses to her calling up Mac and eating a huge slice of humble pie.

The surprise in his voice when he answered his phone nearly coaxed a smile from her. He listened to her rambling apology without commenting, which she appreciated.

"So what I'm saying is that I've thought about it, and I've changed my mind," she said, winding down. "I'd like to accept your kind offer of a job. I can start Monday. I'll need the weekend to do personal things around the house."

"Fine." His immediate acceptance lightened the tightness in her chest, just the teeniest bit.

Except she had to ask for more. "There's just one problem. My car has broken down, and I don't have the money to fix it. I hate to ask this, but is there any way I could get an advance on my first paycheck?"

Again, he didn't even hesitate. "Sure. I'm not home yet. I'll turn the truck around and come and take a look at it."

She almost refused, envisioning her mother's reaction to Mac showing up. But then she didn't. She was tired of worrying about what everyone else would think while she was desperately trying to hold this family together. If her mother didn't like it, then tough. Hailey had simply had enough.

Right now, her number one priority would be getting the car running again.

When she went back outside to wait for Mac, June had gone. She must have slipped inside using the front door and headed straight to her room. That was the only way she could have bypassed the kitchen, which meant she hadn't wanted her daughter to see her. Whatever.

Hailey climbed up to sit on the hood of the car to wait for Mac to return.

When his truck turned off the road onto her drive, she took several deep breaths to calm her racing heart. She actually felt a bit rebellious, because she was tired of being the only one to do everything around there. She resolved to start making the kids pitch in more, and to try a little harder to get June to stop drinking. In the past, every attempt had been met with scorn and derision, and then outright rage. Her mother would then use the argument as a springboard to an excuse to drink even more. Hailey had finally given up and backed off.

Perhaps the time had come to make some changes around here.

And maybe, just maybe, she could give Mac a second chance.

As soon as she had that thought, she shut it down. She'd survived a lot of pain in her life. She wasn't sure she could handle opening up to him again.

Luckily for her, it had only been a dead battery, not something more serious like an alternator. Mac had not only purchased a new battery, but put it in himself. She'd taken quiet enjoyment in watching him work. The car had started immediately.

She'd stammered out a thank-you, but he'd waved her off, promising he'd deduct the cost from her first paycheck. Then, with a promise to see her at nine on Monday, he'd driven off.

The weekend passed uneventfully. Hailey cleaned, precooked meals and froze them, and did laundry. The kids played, occasionally lending her a hand, and her mother partied and slept. When Sunday night rolled around, Hailey glanced at the clock and debated. Soon it would be time to make everyone's lunches for tomorrow's school day. She always did that the night before. This time, she decided against it. The time had come for the kids to make their own lunches.

The next morning, she got up and did her normal things. She'd supervised the kids packing their own lunches the night before, but she still fixed them breakfast and waited while they ate before she'd load them up in the once-again-running car to take them to school.

Though Hailey tried hard to act as if nothing had changed, nervousness simmered just below the surface. She wiped her sweaty palms down the front of her jeans, attempting to keep smiling as she watched her siblings eat the oatmeal she'd prepared.

She dropped Eli off first. He hopped out of the car with his usual enthusiasm, waving as he hurried up the sidewalk to his school. His backpack almost looked bigger than him.

"It's heavy, too," Tom said after she'd voiced this observation. "I don't know what the heck he has in it, bricks?"

"Books, dummy," Tara corrected, elbowing her twin. "Not something you'd know anything about."

"Hey." He elbowed her back, harder.

"Stop it, you two." Luckily, it only took a few minutes to drive to the middle school. Grumbling, they subsided, each looking out their respective windows and doing their best to pretend the other didn't exist.

"Here we are," Hailey sang as she pulled up in front of the two-story brick building. "Both of you have a great day."

"I doubt that. We're in school," Tom pointed out, reluctantly climbing out of the car. He strode up the sidewalk without a backward glance, clearly not waiting for his sister.

Tara didn't move. "Hailey, what's wrong?" she asked. "And don't say nothing, because you stink at hiding things."

Surprised, Hailey turned to look into the backseat. "Neither of your brothers noticed anything."

"That's because they're boys." Disdain dripped from

Tara's tone. "They don't notice anything. Come on, Hailey. Spill. I'm your sister."

Her much younger sister, who'd already thought matchmaking Hailey with Mac would be a great idea.

"I'm fine," Hailey said. "I start a new job today. Hoping to pick up a bit more cash."

Tara nodded. "I can't wait until I can work so I can help out."

Her words squeezed Hailey's heart.

"I can." Hailey jerked her head toward the building. "Now get on inside or you're going to be late."

With an exaggerated sigh, Tara grabbed her backpack and climbed out. Hailey sat and watched until she disappeared inside the building. Then, with her stomach in knots and her heart beating way too fast, she pulled out of the school parking lot and headed toward Mac's house. Once there, after she parked, she sat in her car for a moment, trying to get up her nerve.

She'd never been a coward. Why start now? Taking a deep breath, she straightened her spine, yanked the keys from the ignition, and got out. She kept her stride brisk, marching up his sidewalk and up the steps to his front porch. Straightening her shoulders, she rapped smartly on his door, quickly, before she changed her mind.

When Mac opened the door, tall and broad-shouldered and way too ruggedly handsome, his slow smile was just like she remembered. The answering tingle in the pit of her stomach made her remember she never could resist that smile.

"Hailey." Closing the door behind him, he stepped outside to join her. Until he knew what she had to say, he didn't want to take a chance of his father hearing anything. "I wasn't entirely positive you'd show up. I have to admit I'm glad to see you."

Again her insides fluttered. Damn, he was charming. That was what her mother used to call Mac, back in the day when they were all normal, and life seemed uncomplicated.

And happy. She remembered her siblings' words.

"I think we should talk before I start work." Driving over here, she had told herself she would be cool, calm and collected. All of that resolve vanished with one molten look from his silver-colored eyes.

"Ok." He gestured at the porch swing, still hanging on the other end of the front porch. Years of neglect had chipped the paint, and the chains had rusted, but it still looked solid.

They'd spent a lot of time swinging there when they'd been younger. They'd been friends in elementary school, an item in middle school and an official couple all through high school. She'd always assumed they'd spend the rest of their lives together.

Still the hurt, still the need to push it down, to try to negate it. "A lot of water under the bridge." She used the cliché lightly.

"True." He waited until she'd gotten comfortably seated before settling next to her. This time, he sat at one end and she at the other. Their thighs didn't touch, and he didn't put his arm around her shoulders and draw her close.

Which was good. Because this was now, not then.

"I know I'll be working for you, but I want to make sure you understand that's all it will be."

"Employer/employee, you mean?" He seemed to find

this statement amusing, judging from the way one corner of his sensual lips quirked.

Hurriedly, she looked away. "Yes."

"Just out of curiosity, what's the difference?"

His question had her swinging around to look at him. "The difference?"

"Between how we are now?" Arms crossed, he tilted his head while he waited for her answer.

"I think you should stay away from my family," she blurted, refusing to feel foolish. Absurdly, her throat closed up the minute she finished saying the words, and tears stung the back of her eyes. Hopefully, she could blink those away.

Not outwardly reacting to her edict, he continued to regard her steadily. "Why?" he finally asked in a soft voice. "I've missed you. What would be the harm in reconnecting?"

This question so dumbfounded her that she stared, speechless. And then, while she was still trying to formulate a response, he leaned over and kissed her.

It wasn't a demanding kiss, or a punishing one. The brush of his lips on hers felt soft, welcoming and familiar. And because of that, sensual as hell. When he finally lifted his mouth away, she couldn't stop shaking.

Of course he noticed. "Are you cold?" he asked, even though she suspected he knew the truth.

"No." Right then, right now, she knew she should stand up, move away and demand in a forcible voice that he never do such a thing again. But it had been far too long since she'd been touched, and the cold, empty shell of a person she'd become felt like a flower opening to the sun. She wanted more. This utterly terrified her but filled her with longing, too.

"Mac..." She spoke his name, a whisper of air. Not defeat, certainly. Not hope either. Just a weird sort of acceptance. What they'd had between them once hadn't gone away. She didn't think it ever would.

"You know we belong together." His words echoed her jumbled thoughts.

"Maybe we did once," she answered. "But it's been ten years, Mac. We can't just pick up where we left off."

"Why not?" His gaze warm, he scooted closer. Wise enough not to get too close, though, because he knew she wouldn't like feeling pressured.

Even after all this time, he still knew her. Terrifying.

Pushing herself off the swing, she moved away toward the steps. "I can't," she whispered, hand to her throat. "My mother... You don't understand what she's like now. I'm barely keeping everything together as it is. And the fact that another girl has been killed...it's too much, Mac."

He nodded, his expression kind. "How about friends, then? Can you handle that? We were friends before anything else."

Friends. She didn't actually have too many of those either. It had just been easier—and safer—to keep to herself.

"I don't know..."

"No problem." He stood, dusting his big hands on the front of his jeans. Just looking at those long fingers made her remember how they'd felt on her skin, and her body heated. Friends didn't think of things like that.

"We're not kids anymore," he reminded her, carefully keeping his distance. "Our lives were in so much upheaval, we never had time or the skills to sort things out. Now, I've got my father to take care of, and you have your brothers and sister. I'd think friends would be simpler. I'm not sure I can act professionally toward you, whatever that means. Not right now."

"Simpler?" Now, that made her smile. When had anything between the two of them been simple? They'd been combustible, especially when they touched. How could she keep something like that from happening now?

Of course, she couldn't voice these fears out loud to him. Doing so would only acknowledge the truth she didn't want to admit, at least not yet.

"One thing I forgot to mention," Hailey said, needing to get this out of the way before she forgot. "Every other Tuesday, I iron for the Widow Caribiner. I'm supposed to be there this Tuesday and I can't cancel on such short notice. I'll need to let her know and figure out a way to reschedule her ironing."

"I understand." He nodded. "And I appreciate you agreeing to help more than you understand."

She kept her face expressionless, not sure how to respond, not entirely certain she'd be able to look herself in the mirror until this was over. Because she felt like a Judas, betraying her dead sister's memory. In essence, she'd be helping to ease Brenda's killer's passage from this life to the next. For money.

Countless times she'd justified her actions, if only to herself. The money wasn't for her, it was to keep their family fed, the electricity on and their lone vehicle running. As long as she held on to this truth, she could live with herself.

Evidently, Mac took her extended silence for indecision. "Please, Hailey." He spread his palms, towering over her, so virile and rugged and handsome. "I meant it when I said I really need your help. My father is dying. I'm doing the best I can, but this is uncharted territory for me."

He swallowed and looked away. When he swung his gaze back to meet hers, she saw grief there. Her chest constricted in commiseration. "I'm sorry," she whispered.

"It's hard. He's all the family I have left. You're going to be here, just about every single day. As soon as I can find work, I might be gone some of the time, but for now, I'm still here. Honestly, I can't go this alone anymore. I could really use a friend right now."

A friend. They'd been that, and more, until ten years ago. As she considered their shared past, she had fond memories spanning years of friendship. That was all he was asking for now. His request wasn't about Gus or what he'd done a decade ago. It was only about Mac. He needed her, wanted her to be his friend. While she didn't think she could open up her heart again to him, she thought she might be able to do this, at least. Maybe. She could at least try.

"Better friends than enemies, right?" He said this without expression. This was nearly her undoing. Because she knew him. No matter how many years had passed, she still got him. She understood what it cost him to have to practically beg for her friendship.

"Fine," she said, going for offhand and breezy, inside hoping she wouldn't regret her decision. "Friends it is. But you've got to promise me one thing. No more kissing."

He could have come back with some tired old cliché. Something along the lines of how he wouldn't kiss her until she asked him to. In fact, she braced herself for that.

Instead, he merely looked at her for a heartbeat too long before slowly shaking his head. "All I can do is give you my word to try not to. That'll have to be enough."

Equally flattered and worried, she took a deep breath. "Let's play it by ear, okay?" Jumping to her feet, she wiped the palm of her hands down the front of her jeans. "Now," she said briskly. "Why don't you show me what it is you'd like me to do?"

Mac hadn't told Gus he'd hired Hailey to help out. Part of the reason was what he'd told Hailey—he hadn't been entirely certain she'd show up. The other part—he knew what his father would think. That Mac had wanted Hailey around in order to engineer a second chance at a failed romance.

If Mac were honest with himself, he knew Gus wouldn't be entirely wrong. If Mac could have a second chance to regain what he and Hailey had lost, he'd take it.

He brought Hailey inside, fighting the urge to place his hand in the small of her back as he ushered her around.

Gus had fallen asleep, his head lolling to the side. He didn't wake as they entered the room.

After letting her watch his sleeping father for a few seconds, he motioned for her to follow him into the kitchen.

"He's still relatively able to walk to the bathroom," he told her. "With assistance getting up and back into the bed, of course."

She looked askance at him. "You do know there's no way I can lift him, right?"

"I do." He flashed her a slight smile. "That's not what I need you for. If you take his arm, he can manage on his own, though it can take him a few minutes. He gets lonely, even though I check on him every couple of hours. You'll keep him company, prepare food for him and help him eat. I should warn you, because of his disease, he eats very little. I try to get him to drink protein shakes when I can. But never force him. He's unable to digest very much, so just let him have what he can."

Eyes huge, she nodded.

"Hospice sends a nurse out two or three times a week," he told her. "She checks on his pain level and his medication. Often she sits and visits with him for a few hours."

Hailey nodded, her expression equal parts miserable and frightened. "What do you want me to do during her visits?"

Keeping his voice casual, he shrugged. "You can sit and visit with them both, or, if you want, you can come help me with whatever project I'm working on. It might be good for you to take a break from all of that."

Again she nodded. The myriad emotions crossing her face spoke to her inner conflict. She'd always been unable to hide her feelings.

He waited, loving her more and more with each second she hesitated.

"I'm not sure I can do this," she finally blurted. "I have no nurse's training, and I have no idea what on earth I would talk to him about. Especially since…you know."

He did know. All too well. And it still hurt his heart that she—and the rest of Legacy—considered his father a killer. He could only hope the police got a lead on the real killer soon, and acted on it.

"It's up to you," he replied. Because it was. In the end, money or no money, only Hailey could determine whether or not she was able to perform the task at hand. He wanted her there, needed her there, but only of her own free will. He wouldn't beg or offer more money. This was a decision she needed to make on her own.

Especially since it would only get worse.

After a moment of consideration—and really, she thought long and hard about saying a firm no and getting back into her car, Hailey finally took a deep breath and told Mac she was ready to commit herself to the job. She looked him in the eye and promised she'd work until the end came, whenever that might be. No matter how difficult the tasks might be, she'd do her best to complete them.

Their gazes had locked. Neither looked away. Hailey caught herself leaning toward him, drawn in by the warmth in his gray eyes. Therein lay trouble. The first to break eye contact, she righted herself. She needed to be especially careful now that she'd be seeing him every day. Straightening her shoulders, she'd wiped her palms briskly on the front of her jeans.

"I'd better get to it then," she said, still not entirely sure exactly what *it* might be.

Mac nodded. "I'll be outside working. Don't worry about me at lunchtime. I made my own and have an ice chest. Just remember, I'm available if you need me, okay?"

"I understand. Thanks." Relieved, somehow she managed a confident smile before turning away. A bit of the hard knot in her stomach eased now that she wouldn't have to worry about being distracted by Mac while she learned her way around taking care of his father.

The most difficult part, at least as far as she was concerned, would be training herself to see him as someone other than her enemy.

The first day wasn't at all what she'd expected. For one thing, Gus slept most of the time. She'd had to wake him at noon, attempting to tempt him to eat some chicken noodle soup she'd made. Grimacing apologetically, he'd managed only a few bites before shaking his head.

"My body won't let me take in too much," he told her, his eyes already drifting closed. He muttered something about his body not needing nourishment while in the process of shutting down before he fell back asleep.

As she gathered up his uneaten lunch to take back to the kitchen, the rush of pity that welled up in her surprised her. She'd sort of thought she might be able to remain objective and uncaring while doing her job. After all, this man had killed her sister. Supposedly.

For the first time in a decade, Hailey had actually taken a second look at the case. The night before, she'd spent hours reading transcripts and online accounts of the case and had come to realize Mac might actually be right. The evidence on Gus Morrison had been circumstantial at best. Photos of her baby sister had been found in Gus's glove box. A pair of her panties had been found under the driver's seat of his car. There was no DNA tying him to the body except for his prints on a bottle of beer found at the scene. They'd had no murder weapon, nothing but the single eyewitness who'd claimed to see Gus with Brenda the afternoon she'd been murdered.

She'd never in a million years believed she'd even think this, but Hailey had begun to consider the possibility that the wrong person had been charged and convicted of Brenda's murder.

Of course, that meant someone else had killed Hailey's sister. As usual, the familiar pang of sorrow went through her. If this was true, how awful false imprisonment must have been for Gus, knowing all along the killer had been someone else. But who? Could this actually be the same person who'd recently murdered another teenage girl? She hoped and prayed the police would figure this out soon, before anyone else got hurt.

She thought of the girl's family. The Lundgrens. Hailey knew how they must be feeling, all too aware of what the aftermath of such a horrific event was like. Several times, she thought about going over there, but she didn't know them, and she thought they might find a visit from a total stranger a little intrusive.

Still, when the hospice nurse, a nurturing, older woman with curly gray hair and thick glasses, came to tend to Gus, Hailey decided she had to at least try. Mac had told her she could run errands while Gus was with hospice.

"Dolores!" Gus smiled and tried to sit up. "Meet Hailey. She's the caregiver my son hired to help me. She also used to be my son's girlfriend." He winked.

A broad grin split Dolores's face. "My, you're in fine spirits today, aren't you?"

Hailey left the two of them chatting happily. She located Mac before she left, feeling obligated to let him know she was leaving. She found him on the back side of the house, standing on a stepladder, hammering.

"What are you doing?" she asked, shading her eyes with her hand and looking up at him.

"I'm making repairs to the wooden siding so I can repaint it." His boyish grin nearly took her out at the knees.

She inhaled deeply, holding on to the side of the house to steady herself. "Dolores from hospice is here. I'm going to run an errand for a little bit. I should be back within an hour."

Instead of sending her off with a wave, he climbed down. He wore a Texas Rangers baseball cap, which brought back so many memories she had to swallow hard to get past the lump in her throat.

"Where are you going?" he asked. "You look scared and worried as hell."

"I thought I'd go see the Lundgrens," she said quietly. He frowned. "Who?"

"The family of the girl who was murdered. I know what they're going through, so I thought I might be able to offer some comfort." Feeling suddenly self-conscious, she scuffed her feet. "I don't know, they might think I'm presumptuous, but I've got to at least try."

"Hailey…" A wealth of emotion in his voice as he spoke her name. Almost afraid to look at him, she forced herself to raise her head.

"Come here." He held out his arms. Maybe from habit, maybe because she simply wanted to, she crossed the space between them and let him pull her close and hold her. It felt good. So damn good. And right.

Tears stung the back of her eyes as she let herself hold on to him. So solid, so strong, so reassuring.

Wait. She tried to pull back, but he held her tight.

And when she looked up to find out why, the words died on her lips. His gray eyes had darkened, and for one breathless moment she thought he might kiss her, despite their earlier conversation.

Chapter 6

"No." Hailey gave him a little push, which made him instantly release her. "What's up, Mac?"

"The Lundgrens." Now he was the one who appeared uncomfortable. "I'm guessing you didn't hear."

Gaze searching his face, she shook her head. "No. Hear what?"

"They left town. As soon as they got Lora's body back, they all headed up north to Chicago. That's where they're from. I'm not sure if they plan on coming back or not. They have two other daughters, you know."

"How do you know all this?" Taking a step back, she eyed him. Even though, like her, he'd been born and raised here in Legacy, after ten years away, the folks in town would consider him a newcomer. Especially considering that Gus was his father.

"Dolores told me. She's Lora's aunt." He spread his

hands. "I'm sure if you have a message you want them to have, she'll pass it on."

Suddenly she wished he'd kissed her. Long enough to make her forget their past had been cut short. Instead, she made a show of turning to look down the long, gravel road. "Maybe I'll take a walk instead." One step away, and then another. It took every ounce of willpower she possessed to keep from flinging herself at him and holding on.

Instead, she did her best to pretend his touch hadn't affected her. "Okay, I'll think about it. I really don't know what I intended to say, just that I would be there if anyone needed to talk. I guess that's not necessary now." Stunned to realize she hovered on the verge of tears, she cleared her throat, praying he didn't notice. "Anyway, thanks for letting me know."

She strode off before he could comment or, worse, she could say or do something she'd regret later. Since she had no actual destination in mind, she took off down the road. She might as well get some exercise. Maybe the simple act of moving would make her feel better.

Two o'clock snuck up on her, arriving much more quickly than she'd thought it would. Stunned to realize that five hours had already passed, Hailey went outside to look for Mac and remind him that she had to leave.

She found him on the back side of the barn, shirtless and sweaty and now repairing fence. She watched him silently for a minute, unable to resist marveling at the play of his muscles, aching to reach out and feel them bunch under her hand.

This man, with his steel-gray eyes and his lean and muscular body... No wonder she hadn't been able to fall for anyone else. No other man could match him for masculine virility and sex appeal.

Sex. Her insides hummed at the thought. It had been way too long since she'd even thought of getting physical with a man. Now, with Mac back in town, it seemed that was all she could think about.

Blinking, she looked away and cleared her throat before glancing back at him. He turned and stared at her, the sun and the shadows changing his dark hair to gold and creating hollows in his handsome face.

"I've got to go." Suddenly aware she still stared, she looked back at the house. "Your dad's asleep. He wouldn't eat much—just a couple of spoonfuls of soup."

Mac grimaced. "Yeah. He's been eating less and less lately. The doctors warned me about this."

She knew she should say something, offer a word or two of comfort, but the words wouldn't come. Instead, she simply nodded and turned to leave. Then, remembering, she reminded him she wouldn't be back until Wednesday, since she'd already committed to ironing for the Widow Caribiner.

"All right." He'd already returned his attention to the fence. "See you Wednesday."

"Right."

"Oh, and, Hailey?"

"Yes?" She waited, willing him to turn around and meet her gaze again.

Instead, he kept on working. "Make sure you tell her you've got a regular job now, okay?"

Disappointed, she agreed. "Of course."

After picking up the kids from school, Hailey willed her life to feel normal, but she kept thinking about Gus, slowly dying, and Mac, doing his best to cope.

The twins bickered and Eli tried to sneak in a game on their old Xbox, but Hailey redirected him to his homework. "Tara," she said, motioning at the two boys. "I've got to run to the grocery store. Keep an eye on things until I get back, okay?"

Tara nodded. When she thought Hailey's back was turned, she stuck out her tongue at her brothers.

Hailey had never enjoyed grocery shopping, even when she had enough money to buy everything she needed. She especially detested it now with limited funds, yet still tried to plan inexpensive and nutritious meals that the kids would actually eat.

Impossible. But she had to try. Still, her stomach knotted up on the short drive to the store. She had exactly twelve dollars to feed everyone until she got paid—either from Ms. Caribiner or Mac. She'd managed on less. She had this.

Pasta featured heavily in her family's diet. A box of macaroni shells could be stretched to go a long way. Throw in tomato sauce, seasonings and ground beef, and she had a rudimentary Texan spaghetti. Add tuna, a can of peas and mayo, and she'd prepared tuna casserole. The possibilities were endless. Yet Hailey thought if she ate another plate of any kind of pasta, she'd be ill.

"Hey, there." Mac's voice, the husky timbre sending a jolt up her spine.

Deliberately casual, she turned slowly. "Hey, yourself. I thought you couldn't leave your dad alone."

"I really can't. But I realized we were out of a few things, so I ran up here. He's asleep, so I doubt he'll even notice I'm gone."

"Oh." From down the aisle, she registered Mrs. Darter frowning at her. Ignoring that, she eyed Mac's cart, trying to hide her envy. "You sure have a lot of vegetables and fruit."

He glanced at hers, noting the single head of lettuce and two tiny tomatoes. "I take it you have something against fresh produce?"

This made her smile. "No. I just can't afford to buy much of it." The second she spoke, she wished she could call the words back. Her face heated. "Ignore that," she said. "I'm not trying to complain." Or beg. She thought a silent prayer that he wouldn't offer to buy her anything.

Thankfully, he didn't. "The reason I have all this produce is that I'm attempting to get my father to eat as healthy as possible. He's not real thrilled with the idea. He has very little appetite now, and I've been trying juicing. So far, he seems to like what I've made."

Juicing. The idea of Mac using a juicer made her smile. Tamping down on the thought, she glanced at her watch. "I've got to go. I still have to make dinner for the kids."

"Your mother doesn't cook?"

Slowly, she shook her head.

"Hailey, how long has it been since you've taken a day to yourself?" he asked. "No kids, no mom, just you enjoying yourself?"

She stared blankly. "I have days to myself all the time. I iron for Ms. Carabiner. Sometimes she's there, but there's a lot of times she's not. I walk people's dogs, mow lawns, get mail and water plants when they're on vacation. I have a lot more alone time than you'd think."

"That's working." He chucked her lightly under the chin, the way he'd used to do when they were younger. It took every ounce of willpower to keep from leaning in to his touch.

"I'm talking about fun," he continued. "Jumping from the rope swing into the creek, going to a vineyard and sampling wine. Maybe an arts festival or antiques shop. When was the last time you did something like that?"

When I was with you a decade ago. Aware how pathetic they'd sound, she didn't say the words out loud. "Look, grocery shopping is bad enough. I don't need to sit around feeling sorry for myself, too."

His brows rose. "That long, eh? How about the two of us pick a day and spend part of it together?"

Mrs. Darter had moved closer, shooting them disapproving looks. As Hailey hesitated, the other woman loudly cleared her throat.

"Can I help you?" Mac said, looking directly at the woman.

"I can't believe you two." She spat the words. "You—" glaring at Hailey "—and you…" Her gaze swung around to Mac. "Trolling for slightly older victims, are you?"

The vileness of her remark made Hailey gasp. "How dare you?" she began, clenching her hands into fists. "I think—no, I *know*—you owe Mac an apology."

Instead, the woman shook her head and pushed her cart away, stomping her sensible shoes with every step she took.

Mac stood frozen, his expression impassive. Heart sore, Hailey could only imagine what he was thinking. This witch hunt was just like before, when his entire family had been vilified because of his father. Except worse. Because now a few people apparently thought it was him. How many? she wondered. How could people be so quick to jump to crazy conclusions?

Mac shook his head, then dragged his hands through

his hair, like shaking off bad vibes. "Whew," he commented.

"I didn't know it had gotten this bad," she quietly said, placing her hand on his arm. "I'm sorry."

"It's not your fault." His silver eyes had gone the color of slate. "People are what they are. I have no say over what they think or do. All I can control is my reaction to it."

Wise words. Suddenly, she very much wanted to spend a day with him, not working, just having fun. Or part of a day, at least. The part when the kids were in school.

Eyeing his shopping cart again, she transferred her gaze to him. "What do you do for a living these days? Or what did you do before you started taking care of your father?"

"Construction. Easy to pick up anywhere." He shrugged. "I worked hard and saved my money. That enabled me to take the time off to be with him."

Relieved that some of the tension had gone out of his shoulders, she continued asking questions. "Are you planning to go back to work anytime soon?"

"Maybe. It depends on how things go."

"Then how will you be able to leave?"

He tilted his head. "Hospice comes out three times a week, and you're there every day. If I coordinate things right, I can arrange for several hours. Plus, I can always do some cabinet-building or such at home. I've got tools in the barn."

"Good for you. I wish I'd learned some sort of trade, something I could do from home when the kids are in school." Smiling up at him, she marveled at how she felt. *Light.* Carefree. Young. Even though she'd just turned twenty-seven, she hadn't felt young in a long time.

For the first time, she understood what Eli had meant when he said he'd wanted her to look happy.

Over by the meat counter, two other women were staring. Hailey glanced over with a big smile plastered on her face and waved. They both instantly looked away.

"Well played," Mac murmured, his eyes flashing silver heat. "I see there are some things that haven't changed in this town."

"I'd better go." Hailey sighed.

After she got home and put the groceries up, she made spaghetti with small salads. June wandered in just in time to scarf down a plateful of spaghetti, washing it down with a huge glass of red wine. She kept the open bottle next to her. At least this time, she used a glass.

All four of her children eyed the wine, but no one commented. Hailey hated herself for remaining silent, but past experience had taught her all that would happen was a scene, which would make June drink more.

No one asked Hailey about her new job, and she didn't volunteer any info. Truth be told, she didn't know how June would react to learning who Hailey was taking care of. It'd be a lot simpler if June never found out.

The next morning after her usual ferrying the kids to school, Hailey drove to the middle of town to do the ironing for the Widow Carabiner. The elderly woman lived alone in a huge, perfectly restored Victorian house. She'd taught third grade at Holbrook Elementary for years until she'd finally retired, shortly after the death of her attorney husband. Now, she liked to stay active. She served on the city council and the boards of various charitable organizations, ranging from animal rescue to food pantries.

She'd been Hailey's teacher years ago. Mac's, too. And Brenda's. Hailey had always liked her. In fact, she suspected Ms. Carabiner came up with the ironing work just to help Hailey earn extra money. That was okay. Hailey needed all she could get. Now that she had a regular, if short-term, job, she hoped Ms. Carabiner wouldn't mind.

Ms. Carabiner often liked to chat while Hailey ironed. Ensconced in a dainty Victorian chair, she'd talk about everything from local gossip to what good works the church mission society had organized. Hailey enjoyed these discussions immensely. Despite being in her late seventies, the former teacher had her finger on the pulse of Legacy, and Hailey always learned something new from her.

When Hailey arrived, she didn't just get right to the ironing. There were certain rituals involved. First, there would be tea. And some sort of cookies, usually from the bakery in town, though sometimes Ms. Carabiner made them herself.

Sitting, Hailey waited until the other woman had taken her seat, too. Inhaling, she took a quick sip of her tea and explained about her new job, sticking to basic facts and not elaborating. Ms. Carabiner listened intently, taking small drinks and watching Hailey with a sharp-eyed gaze.

Finally, Hailey wound down, bracing herself for whatever Ms. Carabiner would say.

"You've found it in your heart to forgive him?"

"I didn't say that." The words escaped her before she

had time to consider. "I mean…" Hailey stopped, actually not sure what she meant.

"I see." Setting down her teacup, Ms. Carabiner stood. "There's quite a bit to iron this time."

Confused, Hailey got to her feet and followed the former schoolteacher into the sunroom. There, as usual, Ms. C had set up the ironing board, the stack of clothing neatly folded in a large laundry basket. Hailey always appreciated the scenic surroundings, which made such a routine task almost enjoyable.

Usually, Hailey ironed alone. This time, the elderly woman took a seat in a wicker chair to the side. She sat silently while Hailey plugged in the iron and waited for it to warm up.

She'd already ironed two blouses and started on a flowing black dress before the elderly woman spoke. "Life is too short to be unhappy."

Stomach in knots, Hailey nodded and continued ironing.

"It's okay to comment, child," Ms. Carabiner said, her tone dry.

Hailey barely looked up. "I'm not sure what it is that you want me to say."

Ms. C snorted. "Come on now. There's no need to pretend with me. You're taking care of the man who was convicted of killing your sister. That's got to be difficult."

"It wasn't as bad as I thought it would be," Hailey confessed, setting the iron aside. She'd learned at the expense of a skirt what happened it she didn't focus 100 percent on the task at hand. "Gus is so sick, it's almost like he's another person. He's not at all the way I remember him."

"What about Mac?"

Despite her heart skipping a beat, Hailey shrugged. "What about him?"

"I remember how you were with that boy. And he with you. Everyone with eyes in their head could see. You can't tell me that's changed."

While Hailey liked and respected Ms. Carabiner, she had no desire to get into an in-depth discussion of her feelings—or lack of feelings—for Mac Morrison. Especially since everyone knew that gossiping was a vocation for the elderly woman and had been for as long as Hailey could remember.

"It's been ten years, Ms. Carabiner," she said, picking up the iron and getting back to work.

"That's not an answer at all."

"Maybe not," Hailey responded. "But it's all the answer I'm able to give."

After she'd finished ironing all the clothing in the basket, Ms. C paid her, refusing change. When Hailey asked when she should come again, the older woman waved her away. "Not anytime soon, honey. You just focus on taking care of Mac's daddy. When it's over, you give me a call, okay?"

Touched despite herself, Hailey slowly nodded. She gave Ms. C a hug and let herself out. She figured this proved that the former teacher had invented an ironing job to help Hailey out. She wasn't entirely sure how she felt about that. Whether she realized it or not, Ms. Caribiner's kindness and generosity had enabled Hailey to put food on the table a time or two.

Now, Hailey would be reliant on her old high school sweetheart.

The next morning, as Hailey was leaving for work,

Trudy Blevins showed up on her doorstep. As usual, the reporter chomped gum so fast and hard that her dangly earrings swung in time to the motion.

Surprised, Hailey stopped short, car keys in hand. Trudy had been a fledgling reporter ten years ago; one of her first assignments had been covering Brenda's death.

A shiver of foreboding made her stomach clench. "Trudy, what are you doing here? Please, don't tell me there's been another murder."

"Oh, no, nothing like that." Trudy chuckled. "I'm actually doing a human interest story this time. I wondered if you'd mind if I asked you a few questions."

"Me?" Glancing at her watch, Hailey had a sinking feeling she knew what this was about. Ms. C had been talking.

A second later, Trudy confirmed it. "Yes. I wanted a few words from you about what it's like taking care of the man who murdered your sister."

Furious, Hailey opened her mouth, but no words would come. She shook her head and climbed into her car. "No comment," she managed to say, before closing and locking the door and starting the engine.

All the way to the Morrison farm, Hailey tried to plan damage control. While she'd known Ms. Caribiner loved to gossip, she somehow hadn't thought this would go beyond maybe a few of the elderly widow's close friends. She certainly hadn't thought the local news would want to do a story.

Which meant soon, the kids would hear about this at school. And June, either at the bar or one of her cronies would call her. Hailey tried to come up with some sort of damage control. She took care never to let Tom, Tara and Eli realize how close they stayed to poverty. Sure, her siblings understood that money wasn't plentiful. But Hailey had hoped to spare them from the depths she might have to go to keep the electricity and water on and food on the table.

All of which should have been June's job. Instead, Hailey had to make sure her mother never found any of the money Hailey earned. June already drank away every penny of her disability check each month. While Hailey understood June's alcoholism was an illness, it was hard not to feel resentful from time to time.

However, Hailey tried not to let the hard facts of life get her down. If she'd had enough money, she would have worked hard to get June into rehab. As things stood right now, June continued to deny she had a problem or that she needed help. Not a good situation for anyone.

Hailey hoped her siblings considered her an example rather than their mutual mother. She'd hate to think any of them could grow up and develop June's problems. In fact, she'd vowed to do whatever it took to ensure none of them did.

No matter what she had to sacrifice, Tom, Tara and Eli would always be her first priority. She couldn't let the resurrection of her feelings for Mac get in the way of that.

Hailey resolved to talk to June and the kids about everything that night, including the most recent murder, so they wouldn't hear about it from someone else.

One day led into another. A week passed, and she spent an uneventful weekend at home with her family. She thought of Mac way more than she should, yet she couldn't seem to stop feeling as though they were once again connected. But despite her feeling the need to shore herself up against him, nothing happened. Monday, as soon as she arrived at his place, Mac made himself scarce. He said he'd found work, and he spent a lot of time alone in the barn hammering and sawing.

When the hospice nurse arrived, Hailey sought him out, standing in the doorway and watching him work. The less time he spent with her, the more she craved being around him. Friends, she reminded herself constantly, well aware she didn't feel the slightest bit immune to his charm.

The next week, the days fell into a steady sort of rhythm. Every morning, Hailey got up as usual and helped the kids get ready for school while June slept in, just as she always did. Once, Hailey had used to wish her mother would actually get out of bed and help. These days, she was glad June didn't put in an appearance.

She lived in dread of Trudy Blevins actually publishing her article. Legacy was a small town and news traveled fast. Since she didn't get the paper and doubted something like this would make the television news, the only way Hailey would learn about the publication would be when someone mentioned it to her.

When Mac handed Hailey her first paycheck, the amount nearly made her cry. Somehow, she held it together long enough to smile and tell him thank you, but she'd already begun thinking of all the food she could buy. They'd been running dangerously low on provisions. Grilled cheese sandwiches and stale potato chips could only carry them so far.

"Wait," she told him. "You forgot to deduct for the car battery."

"No, I didn't." The warmth of his smile made her

toes curl in her shoes. "Consider it a starting bonus. Seriously, don't worry about it."

Pride had her wanting to protest, but she held her tongue. While money worries were a constant in her life, without this job she knew she might have had to hit up the charitable food pantry. She hated taking charity and June refused to apply for food stamps, but Hailey would do whatever she had to so the kids could be fed.

She stopped at the bank on her way to pick up the kids, using the drive-through so she wouldn't have to make small talk with one of the tellers. Only when the money had been safely deposited in her account did she breathe a sigh of relief. Now, her mother couldn't touch it. Even if June managed to find her debit card, she didn't know the PIN.

And, since Mac and she used the same bank, she figured the funds would be available immediately.

After dropping all three of the kids off at home with orders to get started on their homework, Hailey headed to the grocery store. Though she hadn't made a list, she knew she needed to stock up on the staples, as well as preplan some simple, inexpensive meals that would feed everyone for more than one meal. She had a Crock-Pot, which she used for soups, stews and chili. Chicken was cheap, especially the drumsticks, which the kids loved.

For the first time since she could remember, she grocery shopped without a knotted stomach, almost enjoying herself.

"Hey, do you have a minute?" Expression serious, Rod Bowers stepped in front of her in the cereal aisle. Hailey hadn't seen him in years. He and her stepfather, Aaron, had been best buddies. Rod had claimed to be as confounded as everyone else when Aaron took off, abandoning his wife and family. He'd come around a few times in the aftermath of the murder, but eventually he'd moved on with his life.

Slightly uneasy, but not sure why, Hailey nodded. "Sure. What's up?"

"I saw you from across the store and realized it's been years since I saw you or your brothers and sister. How's everyone doing?"

"Pretty good, actually." She managed a smile. "How about you?"

"I'm good." He scratched his head and then cleared his throat. "Listen, I heard something today, and I thought I'd ask you if it's true."

Crud. Though she'd been anticipating this, she still braced herself. Chest tight, Hailey took a deep breath. "What do you mean?"

"It's about Gus Morrison. Rumor has it that you've been over there taking care of him. Taking care of the man who killed your sister. I can't hardly wrap my mind around it, but I heard it from a reliable source. Hailey, tell me. Is it true?"

Thanks, Ms. Caribiner. First Trudy, now Rod. Hailey lifted her chin and met his gaze. The best offense was a strong defense. "I fail to see how that is any of your business."

If anything, her defiance made him appear even more determined. Jaw set tightly, he fixed his gaze on her. "Well, see, it is my business. Ever since Aaron disappeared, I've made it my purpose to take care of your family. The only reason you're able to buy groceries today is because of the monthly payments I give your mother."

Stunned, Hailey stared. "What are you talking about?"

"Don't pretend not to know. Every single month, on the first, I hand over three hundred dollars cash to June. I have for nearly ten years. June assures me that my money is put to good use."

Chapter 7

As horror sank in, Hailey had the strangest urge to laugh. She suppressed it and tried for a concerned look instead. "I'm sorry, but I didn't know about this. I've never seen a penny of this money and neither have my brothers or sister." She took a deep breath, aware she'd need strength and bravery to say what had to be said. "You are aware my mother is an alcoholic?"

Rod stared. "Yes, but…" His voice faded away as the full impact of what she'd told him sank in.

"Three hundred dollars will buy a lot of booze," Hailey said gently. "I'm only able to get groceries thanks to my new job." She looked down, then raised her gaze to meet his. "So if you really want to continue to help my family, don't give June any more money."

"You know I'm going to have to talk to her about that," he said, his tone indicating he wasn't sure she was telling the truth.

"Good. I suggest you do it as soon as possible. And if she has any money left over from your last payment, ask her if she'd mind giving it to me. The kids need new shoes." She managed a friendly smile and waved, before wheeling her cart away to finish her shopping.

Muttering under his breath, Rod stomped off. Once he'd gone, Hailey let out a shuddering breath. June had sunk to a new kind of low. And while she knew intellectually that her mother had a disease, the idea of June blowing through three hundred dollars a month—plus her disability check—made Hailey feel ill.

This had to stop. Determined, Hailey grimly filled her cart. She and June were going to have a long overdue chat before dinner that night.

But when Hailey got home, Tara ran out into the garage, her skin pale and blotchy, eyes red as if she'd been crying.

Alarmed, Hailey grabbed her and pulled her in for a hug. "What is it? What's wrong?"

"Emily McNair is missing."

Hearing this, Hailey's heart sank. Blond-haired, blue-eyed Emily had been over to the house numerous times. "What? When?"

"She didn't go to school today, but her parents didn't know she skipped. When her mom showed up to pick her up, everyone went crazy. No one can find her. Even Betsy—that's her best friend—says she has no idea where Emily is."

"Did her mom drop her off at school?"

Tara nodded. "Yes. But Em just went to first period. After that, she left."

"Just left? How is that possible?"

"It's not hard." Tara shrugged. "Lots of kids do it.

She just walked out the door and went wherever." Lower lip trembling, she sniffed. "What if the killer got her?"

"Why don't we think positive for now," Hailey said firmly. "Maybe she's just gone somewhere and she'll come home when she's done doing whatever it is she skipped school to do. Now help me unload these groceries. Keeping busy will help."

Silently, Tara grabbed a couple of grocery sacks and carried them into the house. Once the trunk had been emptied, Hailey asked Tara to help put the food away.

Sniffing, Tara complied. As she began to unpack each bag, her interest piqued. "You sure bought a lot of food."

"I got paid today," Hailey answered. Once everything had been put in its proper place, Hailey took her sister's hand. "It's five o'clock. Let's go see if there's anything mentioned in the news."

Of course the media had been unable to resist. A missing teenager, not long after one had been murdered? Add to that the fact that both girls resembled each other, and they were in a frenzy.

Hailey listened for a few minutes, then used the remote and turned the TV off. Tara had begun hyperventilating, turning wide eyes to stare at her older sister.

"They're speculating," Hailey assured her. She got up and pulled her sister in and held her.

"She's dead," Tara whispered. "I can't believe she's gone."

"No." Hand under her sister's chin, Hailey raised Tara's face. "Look at me. They haven't found her. They don't know if she's dead or alive. She could be alive, you know. I'd much rather focus on that then think something awful."

"What's going on?" Yawning, June wandered into the room. She wore a stained T-shirt and dirty yoga pants and looked like she hadn't showered in days. In one hand she held a coffee cup, but judging from the overpowering smell of alcohol, it didn't hold coffee.

The flash of anger Hailey felt was no surprise. All this time, while Hailey had struggled to keep food on the table and the lights on, this woman had been receiving three hundred dollars a month and said nothing. For ten years. A quick estimate brought that total amount to thirty-six thousand dollars!

"Tara, please go to your room," Hailey said, her voice cold. "I need to talk to Mom in private." She hated how she almost gagged over saying the word *Mom*.

Still teary-eyed, Tara nodded and got up.

"It's going to be all right, honey," Hailey told her, softening her tone. "Emily will be found." She hoped and prayed she was correct.

June narrowed her eyes. "Did another girl disappear?"

"Yes." Hailey indicated a chair. "Have a seat, Mother."

Though June tightened her jaw, she took a swig out of her cup and then sat, sinking down into the couch. "What's up, buttercup?"

The flippancy wasn't lost on Hailey. "I ran into Rod Bowers today at the grocery store. I haven't seen him in years."

A shadow of uneasiness crossed June's face. She gulped down more of her liquid courage before meeting Hailey's gaze. "How's he doing?"

"Why don't you tell me? I know you just saw him on the first. Did you know, he was mighty surprised to find out that I never saw a dime of that money he gave you."

"Why would you?" Defiant now, June lifted her chin.

"It was my money. Not yours. Why would I give it to you?"

"I don't know. Maybe because he intended it to be for keeping your children fed and clothed, that's why. What'd you actually do with it?"

For one heart-stopping moment, as confusion and pain and finally anger chased across June's face, Hailey thought her mother might actually apologize.

Instead, June jumped to her feet so quickly her drink sloshed out of her cup. "None of your business, chick."

Chick? Chick? "So this is what betrayal feels like." Hailey didn't even try to hide her despair. "I don't think you have a clue how difficult this is. I'm trying to keep all of us fed and clothed, and to pay for this roof over our head. Do you have any idea how much three hundred a month would have helped?"

The corners of June's mouth turned down. "I needed it more," she mumbled.

"Mom, what you need is help." Hailey took a step closer. "Your addiction is destroying not only your life, but your children's, too."

"I...I can't." Tears welling in her eyes, June shook her head and backed away. "Please, stop judging me. You're not the one who lost a child."

"Ten years ago, Mom. Ten years. I understand you still mourn, but you have other children who depend on you. You need to be there for them—for us. Please."

Mouth working soundlessly, June stumbled toward her room. "Leave me alone," she said, closing the door hard behind her.

Staring at the door, Hailey wanted to cry. She also considered storming in there and demanding June do something, get help and be there for her family. But

Hailey had tried that in the past and been met with either stony silence or empty beer bottles being thrown at her. No, asking her mother to step up and at least try to beat her disease would accomplish nothing. Instead, desperately needing to talk to someone, Hailey pulled out her phone and called the one person she felt comfortable confiding in. Mac.

The instant Mac heard Hailey's voice, he could hear the upset. Years might have passed since they'd been together as a couple, but he still could read the emotion reverberating in her words.

"I need to talk to you," she said. And that simple request was enough to make him drop everything.

"I'll be right there," he told her.

"Not here. Can I come to your place? We could sit on the front porch and talk. Or maybe take a walk, I don't know. Anywhere but here. I've got to get away for a while. I left a note for the kids to eat leftovers."

"Okay," he agreed, slightly worried. "But promise me you'll drive carefully. Don't let whatever it is you're going through make you reckless."

Silence, as if it took her a moment to understand that someone actually cared what happened to her. Either that, or she found it odd that he did. Either way, after promising she would, she told him she'd see him in fifteen minutes and hung up.

Hailey. Suddenly, the world seemed brighter, more interesting. She'd had some trouble, and the first person she'd thought of was him.

While he waited, he wandered in to check on his father. Gus slept soundly, the television on with the volume low. Something the anchorwoman said caught

Mac's attention. Another girl had gone missing. Though as of yet, there was no indication of foul play, in view of the recent murder, the police were taking this disappearance very seriously.

When a photograph of the fourteen-year-old girl flashed up on the screen, Mac couldn't believe his eyes. Emily McNair could have been Lola Lundgren's twin. And both of them bore a startling resemblance to Brenda Green.

No wonder Hailey wanted to talk to him. His stomach roiled. Taking care not to wake Gus, Mac went outside to wait.

Too restless to sit on the porch swing, he settled for prowling the front landscaping, pulling the weeds he hadn't yet gotten around to removing. Staying busy helped pass the time while he tried to consider the potential ramifications of another girl missing.

The sound of a car coming down the street had him straightening. Eyeing his small pile of weeds, he wiped his hands off on the front of his jeans.

Once she'd parked and killed the engine, she opened her door and rushed up the sidewalk toward him.

For one, heart-stopping moment, he thought she might fling herself into his arms. Instead, she stopped a few feet from him, her gaze locked on his. Her mouth worked, but no words came out.

"Hailey?" Taking a step toward her, he reached out and squeezed her shoulder. "Are you all right?"

"No," she managed, and then she bowed her head. "You know what? I'm thinking this was a mistake. I shouldn't have come here." Her voice wobbled, catching on the last few words.

He knew that sound, too. She was fighting to keep

from crying. The hell with attempting to keep his distance. Even friends hugged when offering comfort. Pulling her close, he tucked her head under his chin and simply held her while she wept.

Tears of pain or anger or frustration, it didn't matter. She'd talk when she was ready, tell him what had hurt her when she could. Meanwhile, he'd let her dampen the front of his shirt and try not to let his desire for her overrule his common sense.

"Not a mistake at all," he told her fiercely. "I'll do whatever I can to help."

Finally, her quiet sobs eased enough that he loosened his grip. "Do you want to sit on the porch swing?" he asked. "Or would a walk around the farm feel better?"

"I…" Swiping angrily at her eyes, she exhaled. "Swing, I think. I just needed to talk to someone before I explode."

He took her hand and led her up the porch to the swing. The crepe myrtle would soon begin blooming, the fragrant blossoms providing a colorful screen between them and the street.

She took a seat, gently tugging her hand free. "Sorry about that." Her rueful smile let him know how much her emotional outburst had embarrassed her. His heart squeezed.

"Don't be," he said and nothing more. Instead, he waited, having learned a long time ago how important silence could be when someone needed to unburden themselves.

"I ran into Rod Bowers today at the grocery store," she said. "While I was there trying to figure out the best way to stretch my paycheck. I don't know if you remember, but he and my stepfather, Aaron, were good friends. Anyway, he confronted me about something he'd heard. Gossip. Rumors. You know how it can be around here."

Whatever he'd thought she'd come to say, he hadn't expected this. Still, he nodded and waited for her to continue.

"He heard I was taking care of your father, and he took exception to it. Considering how he was helping support my family and all."

"What?" He reared back, though not enough to let her go. "How is that any of his concern?"

"That's what I said." She heaved a sigh. "I told him where I worked was none of his business. He insisted it was. Turns out he's been giving my mother three hundred dollars a month to help out. For nearly the entire ten years. Can you guess what she did with that money?"

Closing his eyes, he swore. "I hope you set Rod straight."

"Oh, I did." Anger and pain mingled in her voice. "Believe me, I did. I told him if he wanted to help our family out, not to give any more money to Mom."

Mac for sure knew he didn't like the idea of Rod Bowers thinking his money gave him the right to tell Hailey what to do. He opened his mouth to say so, and then changed his mind. Clearly, Hailey had taken care of that misconception herself.

"On top of that, I got home and found out another teenage girl is missing," Hailey continued. "She's one of Tara's little friends. Emily McNair. She's been over my house several times. I'm hoping she's just run away or shopping or doing some typical, careless, fourteen-year-old stunt. Because the alternative—"

"Isn't acceptable," he finished for her. With one kick

of his foot, he started the swing moving, bringing back memories of the hours they'd spent here, doing exactly this. Back then, he'd battled the urge to kiss her, contenting himself with small touches—her hair, the curve of her cheek, her hand.

And now, a decade letter, he realized nothing had changed on that front.

"Does Gus know?" she asked, breaking his train of thought. "About the missing girl?"

"I don't think so. I found him asleep with the TV on when the story aired, so I doubt it." He debated his next words, and then decided the hell with it, because they needed to be said. "You know, more people in town might give you a hard time about working to take care of my father. It could get ugly."

She moved her head in a small nod. "I know. But it's really none of their business."

"That won't stop them. I remember, believe me."

She regarded him steadily, curiosity lighting up her face. "What do you mean, you remember? Remember what?"

Though he hated to dredge up the ancient past, he figured she already knew and just needed to be reminded. "After my dad was arrested, my mother and I became outcasts within the hour. No one would speak to us or sell us anything or even wait on us. Not at the gas station or the convenience store and the café." He made a sound that was supposed to be a humorless laugh but came out more like a chuff of pain. "It got so bad someone threw a brick through our window. Mom worried I'd be attacked or our house would be set on fire. That's why we snuck out and left in the middle of the night."

Hailey stared, her expression stunned. "I...I didn't know. I thought..." She looked down at her hands.

Cupping her chin, he raised her face to make her look at him. "You thought what?"

"I was seventeen." She swallowed hard. "I'd just lost my sister. My mother howled with pain, and I had three young kids to shield. When you disappeared without even saying goodbye, I thought that was your way of breaking up."

"My mother made me promise not to call you. She was terrified that someone would find out where we'd gone and follow us. But I left you a note explaining everything. That should have helped, right?"

"A note." Her frown told him she'd never seen it. "Where did you leave it?"

Again he cursed, low and furious. "I gave it to your stepdad. He promised to make sure you got it."

Another betrayal. "He ran off a few days after you did. He left Mom and the twins and Eli without even a note. He's never touched base, not on their birthdays or Christmas or anything."

"I'm guessing he doesn't pay child support either."

"Nope. Despite contacting the Texas Attorney General's office, we haven't been able to track him down to collect a single dime in child support."

He could understand her bitterness. She'd been trying to take care of her entire family since she'd been seventeen years old, with no help from anyone. And there was nothing, not one damn thing, he could do to make things right.

They continued to swing in companionable silence. He felt a glow of warmth when she snuggled closer and put her head on his shoulder.

"I didn't know," she finally said, her voice low. "About what happened to you, about any of it. There was too much going on, too much pain and craziness and tears. I feel like I owe you an apology for not being there for you."

His chest felt tight, the bone-deep ache mingled with wonder and shock. "Hailey, you can't take care of everybody. You could barely take care of yourself. I didn't expect you to help me. If anything, I wanted to figure out a way to help you. Don't ever apologize for that. Ever."

Head still on his shoulder, she cut her eyes up at him. One corner of her mouth quirked in the beginning of a smile. "I guess it's all water under the bridge now, isn't it?"

Lost in the softness of her gaze, he struggled to formulate a reply. Before he could, her phone rang. "It's Tara," she said, sitting up straight.

He listened while she spoke with her sister, hoping she hadn't called to give them the worst kind of news.

"Really?" Hailey sounded upbeat. "That's fantastic. Thanks so much for letting me know. Yes, I'll be back soon. No, there are leftovers in the fridge for dinner. Just finish your homework, okay?"

When she hung up, she shoved her phone back into her pocket before looking at him. "Tara's friend Emily has been found," she said, grinning with joy. "Alive."

And then, she reached up, pulled him close and kissed the hell out of him.

Celebratory kiss. That was what Hailey told herself all the way home. Certainly, she'd been fighting the urge to touch him, eerily reminiscent of her teenage self. But it had felt good to unburden herself to him, and as they'd shared truths, they'd had that same click of connection as before.

Sure, her mother's betrayal for ten long years would sting for the foreseeable future. It hurt, knowing how hard Hailey had struggled to keep food on the table and the kids clothed, knowing that all along June could have helped. And, yes, her mother still needed help, still needed to want to get it. But little Emily hadn't been murdered, and that happy news went a long way in balancing out the rotten beginning to the day.

That, and the way she and Mac still came together with such passionate ease.

She thought of what her younger siblings had said. To them, she didn't seem happy. Maybe they were right, but she couldn't honestly say she considered herself unhappy. More like existing, coasting along on day-to-day life, doing what needed to be done to keep everyone safe.

Including herself. Since losing Mac—and the life she'd once known—she'd locked her heart away deep inside, ensuring it wouldn't get broken again. Sadly, she hadn't even realized it until Mac's return. The kids had pegged it perfectly—she felt as if she'd come alive again.

Still, there was too much to consider before allowing herself to rush headfirst into a *thing* with Mac. Her life no longer belonged only to her. Tom, Tara and Eli depended on her. She couldn't make rash choices that might endanger the lifestyle she worked so hard to ensure they had.

Despite her pragmatic thoughts, that night she went to bed with longing for Mac filling her heart.

The next morning, everything returned to normal.

The mad rush to get the kids up, make sure they were clean and dressed, and eating breakfast. She helped them pack their lunches, herded them all out to the car and took them to school.

When she returned home from chauffeuring children, Hailey always made herself a cup of coffee—her first of the day—and carried it out into the backyard to drink before leaving to go to work over at Mac's. Whenever possible, she tried to take a small slice of her day for herself before heading out to the Morrison farm.

Her mother still slept, not unusual, even though June hadn't gone out last night. No doubt when Hailey went to tidy up her mother's room later in the afternoon, she'd find an empty wine bottle or two. Or worse, rum, gin, vodka or scotch.

The rumble of a motorcycle making its way down the driveway alerted Hailey of the arrival of company. Hopefully, not some new "friend" her mother had made at a bar in town coming over to visit. June had done this before, stayed in for the night and gotten bored or drunk or both, and started making calls inviting people over.

The last time this had happened, every single one of the five people who'd shown up at the front door had been drunk—at eight thirty in the morning. Luckily, the kids had been in school and hadn't witnessed the fistfight that had broken out when Hailey had turned them away. She'd had to call the police, who'd shown up and had to cart most of the invitees to jail. Hailey had barely gotten June into her bedroom and closed the door. They couldn't afford bail money.

She only hoped this wasn't going to be a repeat of that. She didn't want to be late for work.

Resigned, Hailey set down her coffee cup and headed out front to intercept whoever before he woke her mom.

As she stepped out the front door, the motorcycle pulled up. Gleaming and black, with high chrome handlebars and an intricate painted design on the tank, it brought the word *wicked* to mind. The bike's rider wore a helmet, but she recognized the wide width of his shoulders and his tanned, muscular arms.

Mac. Her heart did a complete somersault in her chest.

He cut off the engine, the rumble's abrupt stilling startling in its silence. She waited while he removed the helmet, her blood singing through her veins.

"Mornin'," he drawled, grinning at her.

Friends, she reminded herself, even as her stomach did a flip-flop. "Good morning. When did you get a—"

"Harley? I've had her a couple years now. She's been where all my spare time and money have gone." He cocked his head, looking dangerous and sexy. "Want to go for a ride? I can take you to work if you want. You can wear my helmet."

"Which would mean you'd go without? No thanks. I'd rather you were safe."

He studied her, his gray eyes shuttered. "Another time, then? I have a spare helmet at home."

About to automatically decline, she made herself reconsider. Maybe every once in a while she should try something new, let herself be bold and daring and adventurous. A motorcycle ride might be the best possible place to start.

"Sure," she answered, smiling at him. "I'd really like that."

He blinked, which let her know she'd surprised him.

"Great!" Once he'd climbed off the bike, he stopped a few feet from her, his gaze intense. "I need your help."

Friends. "Of course," she responded. "What's going on?"

"I need the police to reopen your sister's murder case." His expression softened. "I know we talked about this before, I get that it's all in the past, but with this latest murder, there's a chance I can get my father exonerated before he dies."

Of anything he might have asked... But then what had she expected? He'd always maintained his father's innocence. "Why?" Her voice came out much smaller than she would have liked. "Why dredge up something so painful?"

Instead of answering right away, he put his arm around her and pulled her close. She kept herself rigid, resisting him, but he paid this no mind. He hugged her. Once, she would have melted into the comfort of his arms. Now, all she could think about was ulterior motive. How could one be friends in a situation like that?

"I can't," she began, pushing him away and herself out of his arms. "All that will do is bring everything up again. The kids were so young then—they don't remember much, if anything, of that time. My mother..." Swallowing, she glanced back at the house before forcing herself to continue. "She's become an alcoholic. You don't know what making her relive her daughter's death would do to her."

"No one would be reliving anything. There wouldn't be any court hearing or testimony or any of that. I just want the police to reopen the investigation. My father was arrested on circumstantial evidence. No DNA, no proof." His voice caught, and he stopped to clear his throat.

Her heart ached for him—for both of them—in fact, for everyone whose lives had been destroyed by the murder. "I'm not sure that's a good idea."

"What harm could it do?" He moved closer, towering over her. Once, his height had made her feel safe. Now she only noticed how he blocked the sun.

"If they again find all evidence leads to my father," he continued, "then nothing will have changed. But if they learn that maybe someone else might have been the killer, can't you see what such a thing would mean? If someone else murdered your sister, that person has gone free. Until now, when for whatever reason they were compelled to kill again."

She looked from him to her house, unable to keep from wondering how different her life might have been if Brenda hadn't died. Or if Mac's father hadn't been the killer. Now, it was too late. For her mother, for her. But not for Mac. Or Gus.

"I'll talk to the police," she said abruptly. "I'll ask them to reopen the case. But that's all. No one else can know. No press, no gossip, none of it."

Chapter 8

Hailey crossed her arms as she finished her statement, mentally daring him to agree to her terms.

"You got it." He smiled then, his eyes warm. "Thank you, Hailey. I'll need you to come up to the police station with me next time Dolores is with my dad."

Before she could respond, the front door flew open, and her mother came out. Wearing a badly wrinkled T-shirt and faded jeans, she squinted at the sunlight before sauntering over toward them.

"Have you been holding out on me?" she demanded, batting her lashes at Mac before taking Hailey's arm. "When did you get a boyfriend? You know how much I like bikers. Introduce me."

Oh, crud. Hailey shifted uneasily, her heart in her throat. If her mother realized who Mac actually was, all hell would break loose.

Mac stepped forward, grabbing June's hand and shaking it. "Nice to meet you, ma'am."

Frowning, June studied him. Hailey knew how much she hated being called ma'am and hoped she was focusing on that instead of trying to figure out why he seemed so familiar.

No such luck.

"You!" Snatching her hand away, June glared. "You've got balls coming around here."

From the way Mac's mouth quirked, Hailey knew he was fighting not to laugh. "Those I do have, yes, ma'am."

Heck, if the situation hadn't had the potential to explode, Hailey might have laughed, too. She looked down instead.

"What do you want?" June demanded. "How dare you come sniffing around my daughter after all this time?"

"It's okay. He's my boss, sort of. And we're friends, Mom." Putting her arm around her mother's slender shoulders, Hailey tried to diffuse things.

But June was having none of it. Her bloodshot eyes widened. "You're back in town, and now there's been another girl murdered," she rasped, taking a step back. "Hailey, get away from him."

Hailey didn't move. "It's okay. Mac didn't kill anyone."

"You don't know that. Like father, like son."

If anything, June's words drove Mac's earlier point home. Clearing his father's name would change everything. Even if she wasn't sure she believed in Gus's innocence, she had to at least get the police to try. If they proved he'd killed Brenda, once and for all, then that would be that. And if they found otherwise…then a good man had been sent to prison for a crime he hadn't committed.

When no one responded, June huffed and crossed her arms. "You need to get off my property."

"Mom," Hailey protested. "Maybe you didn't hear me. He's my boss. I work for him now."

A look of confusion clouded June's face, making Hailey wonder if her mother even remembered. Then the older woman's expression cleared, the bewilderment replaced again with anger. "I don't care. You're not on the clock. He needs to go."

Mac's easy smile made Hailey's chest hurt. "Sure thing. I'm leaving." He met Hailey's gaze. "About that motorcycle ride? Tomorrow morning, same time? I can take you to work and then bring you home in time to pick up the kids at school."

"Sure." She held his gaze, avoiding looking at her mother. "As long as you bring that second helmet."

"Will do." Grabbing his own helmet, he put it on before climbing on the bike. The engine roared to life. Inclining his head in a nod of farewell, he took off. Hailey stood looking after him until the sound had completely faded.

Then, and only then, did she reluctantly turn to face her mother. As she'd expected, June's furious expression left no doubt as to how she felt about Mac's visit.

"Please." Hailey held up her hand to forestall a torrent of invective. "Not now. Mac's a good man. You can't hold him responsible for what happened."

Some of the hot air left June. Uncrossing her arms, she rubbed her palms together. "True. But, honey, you're letting yourself in for a world of hurt."

It had been so long since her mother had called her honey—or any endearment—that Hailey was momentarily speechless. When she found her voice, she pushed past the absurd ache. "It'll be fine. Since I work for him now, seeing him is unavoidable. We've decided we're only going to be friends."

June snorted at that. "I saw how he used to look at you. I doubt that boy could ever only be friends."

"That was then, this is now. He's not a boy, he's a man." Taking her mother's arm, Hailey steered her back toward the house. This close, she could smell the alcohol from the night before. "How about you let me fix you some breakfast?"

Allowing herself to be directed, June sniffed. "I could go for a cup of coffee," she allowed. "And maybe a few pieces of toast. I'm not sure my stomach could handle much more than that."

"Maybe just a couple of eggs, too, hmm?" Once she had June seated at the kitchen table, Hailey got her the coffee, cream and sweetener, before cooking up fried eggs and toast. When she slid the plate in front of her mother, the older woman leaned over and inhaled the scent.

"I don't know…" Her complexion appeared to have turned slightly green. "This might be too much."

"Well, why don't you just try a bite or two?" Hailey began. But June jumped up from the table, knocking over her coffee in her haste, and ran for the bathroom. A moment later, the sound of violent retching echoed down the hall.

If this kept up much longer, June was going to drink herself into the grave. Though she'd tried without success in the past, Hailey knew she had to keep on her mother and see if she could convince her she needed to get help.

All the way home, Mac thought about Hailey's situation. When she'd said her mother had a drinking problem, he hadn't really understood the impact on Hailey and her siblings. That is, until her mother had appeared, stinking of alcohol and stale cigarettes and looking like she hadn't slept in days. Her sallow skin and bloodshot eyes made her appear way older than he knew she actually was. He wondered if June Green was capable of functioning much at all. Probably not, since Hailey had explained she took care of the kids and the house as well as her mother.

Had June ever considered rehab? Or, if that wasn't possible, joining AA? He'd have to be careful mentioning this to Hailey. In fact, he decided he'd wait and let her bring it up first.

When Hailey arrived twenty minutes later, he made himself scarce. Dolores with hospice would be there around eleven. That was when he and Hailey would head into town to talk to Detective Logan.

Since Mac didn't want to get all sweaty, he spent most of the morning working in the shade, installing a new outdoor ceiling fan on the covered back patio. The old one had been in horrible shape, so he'd removed it and headed to the local Home Depot store to purchase another.

The work was simple but engrossing. When he saw Dolores's gray Buick pull into the yard, he was surprised how quickly time had gone by.

Heading into the kitchen, he washed his hands and

gulped down a glass of water. In the other room, he heard Hailey greeting Dolores and then Gus cracking a joke.

Hailey's smile faltered when Mac walked into the room. He hated that. If he had one wish, he'd hope the sight of him would always bring her happiness. Maybe someday.

"I'll take over from here," Dolores said, her cheerful voice making Hailey smile.

"Are you ready?" Mac sidled up next to Hailey, trying to keep his voice low. He didn't want Gus to know what they were doing until after the fact, and only then if they were able to accomplish anything.

She blinked. "Sure. Let me get my purse."

"We'll be back in a couple hours," Mac told Dolores. "I'm taking Dad's helper out for lunch."

Dolores grinned. "Sounds great. I've got to help Mr. Gus here take a bath and a few other things. Take your time."

Grumbling, Gus seconded her statement. "Buy that sweet girl something good, you hear me?" he told Mac. "She deserves it for taking such great care of me."

Mac nodded, taking Hailey's arm and helping her out the door. They were halfway to his truck before she pulled her arm free. "Are we really going to lunch?"

"I don't see why not. After we visit the police station, we can eat. I was hoping you could recommend someplace good. All the restaurants I remember from before seem to be gone."

Clearly preoccupied, she flashed him half a smile before climbing up in his truck. Though the year and make had changed, he couldn't help but flash back to the many times she'd done exactly that. Though instead of buckling in her seat, she'd scooted over on the bench seat to ride right next to him. He actually found himself regretting that they no longer made bench seats in the newer pickups.

At the sideways look Hailey gave him, he would have thought she'd read his mind.

"Let's run by and see if we can catch Detective Logan. After we talk to him, we'll grab a bite."

She nodded. "Okay. I've been wanting to try that Mexican restaurant on Main Street."

Driving downtown felt like a trip back in time. When he'd first pulled into Legacy after a decade away, he'd been stunned to see how little the place had changed. Sure, most of the restaurant names were different, one or two of the stores had been replaced with something else, but by and large Main Street was like a snapshot into the past. With newer cars, of course.

When they pulled into the police station and parked, Hailey fidgeted with her seat belt.

"What's wrong?" he asked.

"Nothing, really," she began, and then shook her head. "I'm just dreading going in there. They'll probably think I've gone crazy."

"You don't have to do this if you don't want to." Though it killed him to say it, he meant every word. He'd never want Hailey to feel as if he'd forced her to do anything.

She frowned. "Oh, I want to. It's just going to be unpleasant, that's all. But I'll survive."

More relieved than she could ever know, he leaned over and kissed her cheek. "I'll be right there with you. Let's go and get this over with."

"I might want a margarita afterward," she said, smiling. He felt the force of that smile all the way to his heart.

Side by side, they walked up the sidewalk. The single-story, painted brick building could have been a police station in any town, any state. It had that homogenous look from the fifties or sixties, which was when he'd guess it had been built.

Inside, the worn linoleum and light-colored wood reception desk came from the same era.

"Can I help you?" An older woman, her gray hair chopped in a hair style close to a crew cut, glared at him.

"Hey, Ruth Ann," Hailey said, smiling. "I haven't seen you in a while."

"Hailey Green." Ruth looked from her to Mac and back again. "What can I help you with?"

"We're here to see Detective Logan. Is he in?" Hailey continued to use a sweet, friendly tone. Meanwhile, Mac tried to relax. He'd tensed up the second they'd stepped inside the door. Even though he'd always been a law-abiding citizen, what had happened to his father had given him a bone-deep distrust of law enforcement.

Ruth's brown eyes widened as she again scoped out Mac. "Let me go get him," she said, her abrupt tone and rigid spine letting them both know she disapproved.

"Wow," Hailey whispered, after Ruth disappeared into the back. "I wonder what's going through her head right now."

"Nothing pleasant, I'm sure," he whispered back, flashing a quick grin.

A moment later, Ruth Ann reappeared. "He'll see you now," she announced. "Right this way."

As they followed her into the busy squad room, the bustling noise died down somewhat as people stared.

Officers and civilians alike. Mac could well imagine how the tongues would wag around town this evening.

Hailey shot him a glance that plainly said I told you so, one corner of her mouth quirking in the beginning of a smile. He smiled back, broadly, in order to make sure everyone watching saw it.

Detective Logan stood when they entered his office. He wore thick glasses and had his dark hair cut in military style. "Hailey Green," he said, holding out his hand. "It's been a long time."

After shaking his hand, Hailey introduced him to Mac. They shook also.

"What can I help you with?" the detective asked, his gaze on Mac.

Hailey spoke. "I'd like you to consider reopening my sister's murder case."

"Why?" Swiveling his head to look at her, he didn't miss a beat. "That case is closed. We got a conviction."

"Because I think it's related to the latest murder," Hailey continued. Mac admired her courage. "And it's entirely possible you got the wrong man."

Now Detective Logan looked back at Mac, his gaze decidedly unfriendly. "Did he put you up to this?" he asked Hailey. "Because if he did—"

"I'm a grown woman," she interrupted smoothly. "I can assure you I'm fully capable of making my own decisions. So no, he didn't put me up to anything."

"Then why's he here?"

Now Mac spoke. "I'm here because I promised my father I'd do my best to clear his name before he passes away. And he's dying. I'm also here because I'm worried if you don't find the actual killer, another young girl will lose her life."

"Is that a threat?" the detective barked.

Mac exchanged a glance with Hailey. "I don't follow," Mac finally said. Though actually, he did. The Detective had made a veiled reference to the possibility that he still considered Mac a suspect.

"I fail to see the need to reopen the case," the police officer reiterated, effectively dodging Mac's question.

"Then who is your superior?" Chin up, Hailey stared the other man down. "I'm a family member and I'm making a request."

"And I'm taking your request under consideration."

If Detective Logan wasn't backing down, neither was Hailey. Mac watched, full of admiration as she shook her head. "I don't feel like you are. If I have to, I'll contact the other girl's family and tell them my suspicions. And the press. Just think what a field day they'll have with that. Especially when everyone learns you outright refused to even review the old case for similarities."

"We already have," the detective told her quietly. "I have people working on that as we speak." He shot Mac a warning look. "But that doesn't mean your father will be exonerated."

"Unless you catch Lola Lundgren's killer and he confesses to both murders," Mac said. "I get it. Thank you for your time."

On the way to the door, Hailey kept her face expressionless. Outside, she grinned. "So they have already reopened the case. I don't get why he wouldn't just say that from the beginning."

"He might just be saying that to get you to back off," Mac pointed out, his tone dark.

"Yeah, I know." Waiting until he hit the remote to unlock the truck door, she climbed in. "I've just got to figure out a way to find out. I might be taking that all to his supervisor after all."

More grateful than he could express, he started the engine. "Are you ready for lunch? We've got plenty of time, since visiting the police station didn't take nearly as long as I expected."

"When do we have to be back?" she asked, her expression pensive.

"Dolores said a couple of hours. She has a lot to do today with Dad."

"How about we go for a drive, and then grab a bite to eat?"

Hands on the steering wheel, he froze. "A drive? Where'd you want to go?"

Before she even spoke, he knew.

"Up by the lake," she said. "I haven't been up there in ages. It'd be nice to climb the rocks and sit and look at the water. Maybe fish."

The way they'd used to. Blinking, he realized he was tired of living in the past. He wanted to focus on the here and now, where there was still the possibility of a future.

"Sure." He kept his tone easy. "It'll be nice to get away from everything for a while."

Since most people were at work in the middle of the day, they only passed a few other cars on the way to the lake. The summer houses were still mostly closed up, since the influx of people didn't really begin until after Memorial Day.

He pulled up to the bluff where they'd always gone, satisfied to see it, too, remained unchanged by time. They got out at the same time and climbed the rock, all without exchanging a single word. When they reached the top, she settled into her old place and he to his, so close their hips and knees bumped.

Just like old times, he wanted to say, but when he turned his head to look at her, the words caught in his throat. Teenage Hailey had been pretty, but this Hailey, adult Hailey, glowed with a special kind of beauty.

Despite the glittering water of the lake below, he couldn't tear his gaze away from her.

When she glanced up and caught his staring, he didn't look away. He couldn't.

"Mac?" She reached up and cupped the side of his face with her hand. Turning his head ever so slightly, he breathed a kiss into her palm.

The sound she made—a low, throaty hum of pleasure—sent his pulse leaping.

He didn't know who moved first, didn't actually care. They came together, both certain. The kiss, urgent, moist and hot, made his entire body burn as if a blaze of lightning had seared them together.

With her curling into his side, he wanted to tear away the clothes that separated his skin from hers. Instead, he slid his hand down the curve of her hip, across her thighs and stroked her through her jeans. Even with the barrier of denim, he could feel the heat of her desire.

"I want," she began, boldly cupping the swell of his own arousal, "I want you to make love to me."

His younger self wouldn't have even hesitated, not caring about the fact that anyone could come across them and see. Even now, as aroused as Mac was at that moment, he almost said the hell with it.

"Not here," he choked out. "Too risky."

To his disbelief, a sensual smile curved her mouth. "You're probably right. In your truck or in the woods?"

Though he'd kick himself later, he had to know. "Hailey? What are you doing?"

Her expression clouded. "Never mind," she said briskly, her gaze already gone distant. "Let's go get lunch. I'm starving."

Jumping to her feet, she climbed down from the rock as nimbly as any teenager, and hurried toward his truck.

Since his arousal made moving a bit more difficult, he followed much more slowly. When he reached the truck, he used his remote to unlock the doors, and Hailey climbed inside so fast one would have thought a swarm of bees chased her.

His chest tight, he walked around to the driver's side and got in. Instead of starting the truck, he turned to face her. "What's going on, Hailey?"

When she looked at him, he saw pain and bewilderment and, yes, anger in her eyes. She swallowed hard. "I thought you wanted me the same way I want you. Clearly, I was wrong. I should have listened when you said you wanted to be friends."

"I do want you," he told her. "More than you can ever believe. But as weird as this sounds, I want it to mean something."

She made a strangled sound. "You're a guy. You're not supposed to say things like that."

"I mean it." Unable to resist, he leaned over and pressed his mouth against the hollow in her throat, where her heart beat so frantically. "You and I were meant to be together. I want you, Hailey. But not just for a one-time thing, not for an hour, or a day."

"Stop." Leaning away, she held up a hand as if to ward him off. "Please, don't say things like that. I have my own life and you have yours. Too much time has passed, too much craziness. I can't be what you want. Not now, maybe not ever." Her attempt at a careless shrug fell flat.

"I see," he said. Oddly enough, he did. "But I don't understand why you wanted…"

Her skin bloomed red. "You don't?" Bitterness darkened her tone. "I'm guessing for you, it isn't possible that I might want to be touched, that I might need to be desired. I remember how great the sex was between the two of us, Mac. It's been a long time since anyone's touched me. How is it wrong that I want the person touching me to be you?"

Shocked, he saw she was on the verge of tears. Somehow, in trying to do the right thing, she'd managed to make him feel like an utter ass.

"I want to be the person touching you. The only person," he said fiercely. "On your terms, I promise." Because in that moment, he realized he'd be whatever she wanted him to be, and for however long, as long as he could be with her.

Chapter 9

Hailey's efforts to regain her composure weren't working. For one thing, she could feel the blush turning her face a vivid scarlet. For another, her absolute, bone-deep humiliation had her eyes filling with tears.

If she cried in front of him, she'd never be able to look herself in the mirror again. She'd offered him all that she had to give, and he'd turned her down, wanting it to mean something more than she was capable of right now. How could she come back from that?

If he pitied her, so help her God, she'd get out of his truck and walk the seven miles back to town on foot.

And then, and then he'd said the one thing that could guarantee to break her heart. The one desire she couldn't have and didn't dare dream of. That he wanted a permanent relationship with her. As if, despite all that life had thrown at them in the years they'd been apart, they could pick right back up where they'd left off.

She wasn't seventeen anymore. All the dreams and hopes of that younger, more innocent Hailey had been crushed and ground into the dirt. She knew exactly what she could hope for. Life had taught her that she could have no illusions about what her future held.

Damn him for giving her even the tiniest sliver of hope.

Despite all that, she hadn't been too proud to tell him what she wanted, what she could allow herself to have. She'd expected him to refuse her, but instead he'd managed to shatter her heart one more time.

He'd agreed to her terms. Simultaneously thrilled and dismayed, she'd waited to see what he'd do next. When he'd slipped the key into the ignition and driven them back to town for lunch, she'd been shocked. Truth be told, she'd been looking forward to some fast and furious lovemaking in the cab of his truck.

She'd powered through her lunch, tasting nothing except her own confusion. Her entire body throbbed and ached with unfulfilled desire. While he chowed down, teasing and acting generally unaffected.

After the quick lunch, they headed back to the house where Dolores was just finishing up. Glancing at the clock, Hailey was stunned to notice she had less than an hour left before finishing for the day.

Mac immediately made himself scarce. Smart move. Meanwhile, the time with Dolores had exhausted Gus, and all he wanted to do was sleep. Which left Hailey with little to do besides tidy up.

When two o'clock came, Hailey debated simply getting into her car and heading home without informing Mac. But in good conscience, she knew how he could lose track of time, and she didn't want to leave Gus alone.

As she opened the door to go look for him, she saw him heading back toward the house from the barn. She stepped outside, car keys in hand, unaccountably nervous.

"Are you taking off?" His broad, friendly smile made her feel better.

"Yes. I'll see you tomorrow." She managed to dredge up something close to a smile. "Have a good night."

"You, too." He waved, and then disappeared inside the house, leaving her staring after him. She wasn't sure which was worse—too much emotional insight, or pretending that everything was just hunky-dory.

After picking up the kids from school, she made a quick stop for gas. When she went in to pay, she got each of them a special treat. A candy bar—dark chocolate for Tara, nuts and chocolate for Tom, and peanut butter and chocolate for Eli. Their favorites.

Their squeals of delight as she passed them out lifted her mood. Everything would be all right. It had to be.

When they got home, the house was quiet. June's bedroom door was closed, which wasn't unusual. She had the master bedroom, with its own bath. She'd put in an appearance on her own time, which usually was when she got hungry.

Normalcy reigned for the rest of the afternoon, which was just how Hailey liked it. The kids did their homework, then fought over which TV show they were going to watch. Hailey sighed and hoped they'd work it out among themselves. She prepared dinner, one of the kids' favorites—hamburger tacos—and waited for her mother to stomp into the kitchen and demand to be fed.

Instead, when dinner was done and the table set, Hailey told her siblings to go ahead and start while she fetched their mother. A quick knock on the bedroom door produced no response. Dread coiling in her stomach—she hated finding June passed out drunk—Hailey tried the knob. It turned easily. Taking a deep breath, Hailey stepped inside.

The messy bed looked normal, but empty. Hailey walked around to the other side, just to make sure her mother wasn't lying on the floor. The door to June's bathroom was closed, but no sounds of water running came from inside.

"Mom?" Hailey tapped sharply. "Are you in there? Is everything all right?"

No answer.

Trying the door and finding this one locked, Hailey clenched her teeth so tightly her jaw hurt. "Please, open the door. If there's any way you can. Please."

Nothing.

Tara peeked around the corner. "What's going on? Is Mom all right?"

"I don't know." Hailey tried to keep her voice calm. "She's apparently locked herself in the bathroom."

At those words, Tom and Eli joined Tara. Exchanging apprehensive looks, they tentatively entered the master bedroom.

Hailey reached up and felt along the top of the door frame for the spare key they always kept there. Except it was gone.

Great. Biting back a curse, she turned to face the others. "I guess I'm going to have to try to pick the lock." Which she had no idea how to do.

"Let me try." Tom ran off and returned carrying a

paper clip. He unbent it and, working with such intense concentration his tongue poked out of his mouth, began using it on the lock.

Criminal in training? Or merely the result of curiosity and experimenting? Hailey made a mental note to ask him later where he'd learned to do that.

A few seconds later, they heard a click.

"Here we go." Raising his hands in victory, Tom stepped back. Way back, nearly all the way to the bedroom door. So did his brother and sister. Hailey couldn't blame them. Who knew what they might find inside the bathroom? Hopefully, there wouldn't be blood, and June would be at least partially dressed.

"You all wait here," Hailey ordered. Then she turned the doorknob and stepped inside.

Her mother sat in the bathtub, head lolling against the side doors. An empty bottle of vodka and a prescription pill bottle sat on the side of the tub.

Horrible accident or on purpose?

Later, after 911 had been called and their mother taken away to the hospital, Hailey pushed away her fears about money and sat down on the couch with her arms around all three of her badly shaken siblings.

"Was it an accident?" Eli asked, his blue eyes round.

"Of course it was," Hailey said, shooting the two teenagers a warning look over Eli's head. "I'm fixing to drive to the hospital, and I want you all to promise me you'll stay right here."

"We promise," they all chorused.

"Good. Tara, I'm putting you in charge. Boys, do what your sister says."

It was a measure of how shell-shocked they were that no one argued. Their mother needed help. This was the first time she'd done anything like this, but now Hailey worried it wouldn't be the last. She was lucky to be alive.

She needed treatment. Counseling. Once again, not something she had money for, but maybe there were some state agencies or something that could assist. For now, once they'd pumped her stomach, the hospital would keep her under observation. At least June had Medicaid due to a career-ending back injury she'd had shortly after Brenda died. They wouldn't have to worry too much about those bills. She'd work out some kind of payment plan if she had to.

Stomach burning, chest tight with worry, Hailey told herself she'd deal with this minute by minute. No problem was too big not to have a solution. Her belief in this mantra had been instrumental in helping her make it through the last ten years.

After kissing each of them on the cheek, Hailey got in her car and headed to the hospital. The Check Engine light had come on a few days ago, but she didn't have the money to find out what might be wrong. She'd added a quart of oil since that always seemed to help and hoped that would hold the jalopy together for a bit longer. She didn't know what she would do once the car died. They didn't have money to buy another, that's for sure.

On the way, every time she thought of finding her mother in the tub, her heart flip-flopped in her chest. The day had been rather eventful. But this…

She thought back to the past, remembering what life had been like after Brenda's murder. Mac's father. She remembered how shocked she'd been when she'd learned he'd been arrested for her sister's murder. The withered, gaunt shell of a man in the hospital bed bore no resemblance to the jovial giant she remembered. She'd spent that day—in fact, the next several days—locked in her room. Her mother and stepfather, Aaron, had started fighting, horrible, vicious battles, taking out their shock and grief on each other.

That day, Mac had called numerous times. Unable to talk to anyone, she'd never answered, finally turning the phone off.

She shook her head. Even thinking of those dark days made her feel ill. They'd all done their best to continue with their lives—everyone except June. Hailey realized she'd been fooling herself that her mother would ever get better. What had happened today had shifted everything into a different perspective. And she couldn't deal with this alone.

Pulling into the hospital lot, Hailey parked. Then she took a deep breath and dialed Mac's number.

When Mac saw Hailey's number come up on the screen of his phone, his heart stuttered in his chest. After he answered, when she began speaking in a shaky rush of words, he had to struggle to understand. One thing he did get was the word *hospital*.

"Slow down," he told her. "Take a deep breath." He listened while she did. "Now tell me what happened."

Her mother's bathtub incident—whether actual suicide attempt or horrible accident—stunned him. Hailey was so distraught, he knew he had to go to her. "I'll meet you at the hospital," he said and ended the call.

After asking his father if he'd be all right for an hour alone, Mac jumped on his motorcycle and raced off into town.

When he arrived and parked, he hurried into the ER. The triage nurse pursed her lips but buzzed him into the back. "Her daughter's with her now. Room 17."

He found the room with no difficulty. The door sat slightly ajar, so he pushed it open and entered. Hailey sat in a chair next to the unconscious woman in the bed, hunched over, her head in her hands. She looked up when he entered. The agonized expression on her face had him crossing the room quickly and pulling her into his arms.

He held her, saying nothing, breathing the fresh, clean scent of her hair and wishing things could have been different. The fact that Hailey had called him gave him hope. Given enough time, he thought there might be a chance to change things.

When she finally broke away, he saw from the tear tracks on her face that she'd been silently crying.

Wiping the back of her hand across her face, she looked at him. "She needs help, Mac."

He nodded. "Is she going to be all right?"

"The doctor seems to think so. They pumped her stomach." Angrily, she swiped again at her eyes. "She took a bunch of pills with booze."

"On purpose?"

Her defeated shrug tore at his heart. "I don't know."

"Has she ever done this before?"

"No. But she's been drinking more and more." She took a deep breath. "This might be all my fault. I confronted her about the money Rod Bowers has been giving her."

"This is not your fault." He kept his voice firm. "None of this is. You are the only thing holding your family together. Stop blaming yourself and start pointing your finger right where it belongs." He jerked his chin toward the unconscious woman in the bed. "Her."

"She's sick, Mac," Hailey protested. "I'm hoping when she regains consciousness, she'll agree to go to some sort of treatment. The only problem is I don't know how we'll pay for it."

"What about your stepfather?" he asked. "Is there any way he'd be willing to help?"

Slowly she shook her head. "We haven't heard from him in years. Not since he took off shortly after Brenda was murdered."

This surprised him. He'd guessed June and Aaron had divorced. But the three youngest children were his. "He never tries to see the kids?"

Her mouth tightened. "No. I guess since he doesn't pay child support, he's too scared to put in an appearance."

Mac thought of the money he'd put aside. There was more than enough to get him through this rough patch with his dad, even if it lasted for a couple of months. Though Gus's doctors hadn't been that optimistic, he knew his father was a fighter. If anyone could prolong his life, Gus could.

Objectively, he knew he had enough funds to take care of things with his dad. And, with Hailey helping look after his father, he would be able to take on the occasional job if he wanted to, making more money.

Just like that, he reached a decision.

"Let me help," he said. "I have some money set aside."

Before he'd even finished speaking, she shook her head. "I can't take charity. I'm sorry, but I can't."

"You can pay me back. A little at a time, if you need

to." Though he had no intention of ever asking her for a dime. He considered this a gift—to Hailey, to her family. To himself.

The faint spark of hope in her beautiful blue eyes broke his heart. "She has Medicaid. Maybe they'll help pay for treatment."

"You check into that. While you're doing that, I'll find a facility with openings."

"It has to be close by," she said.

"I understand." He took a deep breath, hating to be the one to tell her, but knowing he had to. "There's one more thing, Hailey. Your mother has to agree to treatment. No place will admit her without her consent since it's not court-ordered."

Hailey frowned. "Are you sure?"

When he nodded, she sighed. "Okay. I'll talk to her when she wakes up."

He checked his watch. "Do you need anything before I go? I've got to get back to my dad."

"I don't think so." Her tremulous smile stopped him in his tracks. "But thank you for coming up here. You'll never know how much I appreciate it."

He let himself out, aware how difficult—and expensive—it could be to get into an inpatient alcohol treatment facility. He might have to pull a few strings to make it happen, but it would happen.

After Mac left, Hailey sat with her mother, not sure what to do now. When the nurse came in, she gave Hailey a sympathetic look. "Why don't you go home, hon? Now that her stomach has been pumped, she'll be out for a while."

"What will happen next?"

The woman eyed her. "Once she's healthy enough to leave, she can go home."

Stomach clenching, Hailey nodded. "I'm hoping to convince her to check into rehab. My friend is working on finding a place where she can go."

"Good." Coming closer, the nurse squeezed Hailey's shoulder. "For both your sakes, I hope she agrees."

Exhausted, Hailey nodded. "I'll be back in the morning. Do you think she'll be awake by then?"

"Hopefully."

Once Hailey got home, all the kids met her at the door. Wide-eyed, Tara asked how June was doing. Hailey noticed she called their mother by her first name rather than Mom.

"She's asleep, right now." Hailey led them all into the kitchen and asked them to take a seat. Once they had, she had a frank discussion with them about alcoholism, one she probably should have had long before.

Except she'd totally underestimated her siblings. "We already know about all that," Tom said, his arms crossed. "What we really need to know is if she's going to get help."

He sounded so much older than fourteen it made Hailey's throat ache. "I hope so," she answered quietly. "Mac is going to see if he can locate a nearby facility that has a vacancy. I'm going to talk to her in the morning."

"I wouldn't," little Eli put in, his expression solemn. "Just take her there and let them fix her. I wouldn't give her a choice."

Now all three of them nodded. "We agree." Tara's fierce voice matched her frown.

"Unfortunately, it's not that easy." Hailey hated to

break the news to them, but she had to. "Mom's got to agree she needs help. Otherwise, they won't admit her without a court order. We don't have one of those."

"Then get one," Tara began. The other two had similar sentiments, and they all began speaking at once. Hailey let them, eyeing them one at a time, her heart both heavy and full.

"I love you guys," she finally said, once a pause crept into the conversation. Her eyes filled. "I hope you all understand how much."

Eli squinted up at her. "You're crying?" Expression anguished, he jumped up and threw himself at her. "Oh, please, don't cry."

Of course this only made the waterworks start in earnest. The heck with blinking back the tears. Hailey let them fall, holding out her other arm to invite Tom and Tara to join in.

Only once all four of them stood united, arms around each other, was Hailey able to smile. "We're in this together. As long as we have each other, everything will turn out fine." Even if their mother refused to get help.

"We know," Tom and Tara said in unison.

"I know," Eli got in. "We did the dishes and cleaned up while you were gone. We even made you a plate."

Which reminded her that she hadn't eaten.

Suddenly starving, she thanked them. Tom made her take a seat while Tara nuked the hamburger meat. Tara actually assembled three tacos on a plate, with lettuce and tomato and cheese, before carrying the meal over to Hailey.

Eli brought her a glass of ice water. All three took seats at the table and watched while Hailey ate. When she'd finished, the twins cleaned up, insisting she go sit on the couch and relax.

Her cell phone rang while they were watching some silly talent show. Mac. Hailey jumped up and went into the kitchen to answer.

"I think I've found a place," Mac told her, his voice low and exhausted.

She glanced at the clock. Seven thirty. "How?" she asked. "It was after hours when we found my mother. I'm surprised you could even get someone to answer the phone."

"I called Dolores."

"The hospice nurse?" Hailey asked. "I don't understand."

"She has connections," he said. "Once I told her what happened, she called a friend, who called another friend, and so on. Long story short, there's a facility near Kingston that has an opening. The admissions director—a lovely woman, according to Dolores—has agreed to hold it until noon tomorrow. It's actually affordable. And it looks like they accept Medicaid."

Stunned and relieved, Hailey briefly closed her eyes. "Which means my mother has to make a decision quickly."

"Exactly." He hesitated. "Hailey, do you want me to go with you to talk to her?"

"No." She didn't even have to think about that one. "That would only make her more agitated. I'll run over there right after I take the kids to school. Let Gus know I'm going to be late."

"Late?" Mac snorted. "I'm going to tell Gus you won't be here at all. Take the day off. Heck, since tomorrow's Thursday, I don't expect to see you until Monday. You'll need that time to get your mother moved and settled."

And here came the tears again. She cleared her throat before speaking, hoping he wouldn't notice. "Thank you," she said. "I appreciate it more than you know."

"No problem. And, Hailey?"

"Yes?"

"I'll miss you. If you need company, anytime, day or night, call me. I'll be there as quick as I can."

"You can't leave Gus," she pointed out. "I'd feel terrible if something happened to him because of me."

"He wouldn't be alone. Like I said, I called Dolores. She told me she'd be willing to sit with Gus if I needed to be with you. In fact, she insisted."

Suddenly, irrationally, Hailey wanted nothing more than to ask Mac to come over and hold her in his arms. Of course, she didn't.

"That's really nice of her," she said. "And I promise I'll keep that in mind."

"You do that. And, Hailey, don't forget to call me."

After finishing the call, she wandered back into the living room. The talent show was just wrapping up. All three young faces swiveled to look at her.

"Well?" Tara demanded, when it became clear Hailey wasn't going to volunteer information.

"Mac thinks he's found Mother a rehab place she can go to. I'm going to discuss it with her in the morning."

Though they all nodded, Tara especially looked disappointed.

"What's wrong?" Hailey asked.

"I was hoping you had a date." The wistfulness in her younger sister's expression was the only thing that kept Hailey from laughing.

"Now's not the right time," she said instead.

"But it is," Tara responded. "It's exactly the right time. You need someone to take you out, distract you from all this and treat you like a princess."

Tom snorted. Eli looked from one sister to the other, his eyes huge.

"What I need is Mom to agree to go to rehab. Nothing more, nothing less." Stifling a yawn, Hailey glanced longingly toward her bedroom. But she couldn't go to bed before her siblings. If she did, they'd stay up until midnight and not understand why they couldn't get up in the morning.

Settling back into her spot on the couch, she prayed she could stay awake until ten.

Chapter 10

When Hailey walked into her mother's hospital room in the morning, June had just finished breakfast. The yellow cast to her pale skin and the dark shadows under her eyes testified to the beating her body had taken due to the combination of pills and alcohol she'd consumed the day before.

"Good morning," Hailey said, trying for cheerful.

June winced. "I feel like death."

"You should. You're lucky to be alive."

"Don't be so dramatic." After picking up her juice, June took a couple of deep swallows. "That would be so much better if they'd spike it with vodka."

Grimly determined, Hailey pulled up a chair. "Mom, we need to talk."

"Not about that money again. I'm tired of hearing you whine about that."

Ignoring the flash of anger that shot through her at her mother's words was hard. But Hailey did it. She reminded herself to focus. "No, not about the money. You almost killed yourself yesterday. Your children—all of them—walked in and saw their mother almost lifeless in the bathtub."

June pursed her lips but didn't speak.

Taking this as encouragement, Hailey rushed on. "You need help. Treatment."

"Like rehab?"

"Yes." Bracing herself for the protest, Hailey couldn't believe it when June nodded.

"I've looked into it, you know," June said, her voice soft and sad. "It's too expensive. People like us can't afford that."

"Actually, it looks like your Medicaid might cover most of it."

June's mouth fell open. "Seriously?" At Hailey's nod, she shook her head. "I never even thought of that being a possibility. I'll have to consider it."

"We don't have time." Biting back rising panic, Hailey struggled to sound cool and collected. "Openings in these places are hard to come by. They've agreed to keep this one open until noon. They're doing it as a special favor to me through a friend of mine."

"I'd really like a couple of days to decide."

Which meant no. Suddenly, Hailey realized she'd had enough. "They're going to discharge you from the hospital today, Mother. If you come back home, everything is going to go right back to the way it was."

June shrugged. "That's my choice. My life. My rules."

"No. Not anymore." Hailey took a deep breath. "I'm changing all the locks on the house. If you don't get treatment, you're not welcome there anymore. You'll have to find somewhere else to live."

If looks could kill. "You can't do that."

She was right, but she didn't need to know that.

"I can and I will." Crossing her arms, Hailey glared right back. "You can't continue to do this to Tom, Tara and Eli. And me. You need help."

"So you keep saying." June's mocking smile felt like the final straw.

Pushing to her feet, jaw clenched, Hailey turned to go. "Have a nice life, Mother."

She made it all the way to the door, before June stopped her.

"Wait."

Slowly, Hailey turned.

"Fine. I'll go to rehab."

Hailey didn't move. "You can't change your mind. Once I make the call, that's it. Do you understand this?"

"You don't have to speak to me like I'm a child." June's petulant tone was back. "Yes, of course I get it."

Going with impulse, Hailey stepped over and gave her mother a quick hug. "Thank you for this," she whispered. Then she stepped away and got out her phone to make the call.

Things moved fast after that. The facility had already gotten preapproval and just needed the paperwork signed when they arrived. Hailey helped her mother pack, and drove her there herself.

By the time Hailey finished signing paperwork and making sure June was settled in her new room, it was time to pick the kids up from school. June had been assigned a small living area, which she shared with a roommate. She'd griped about this at first, until Hailey gently reminded her of the, no doubt, much greater expense of a private room. She hurried out, stopped by the director on the way, who reminded her no phone calls or visits for at least two weeks. They wanted to get her acclimated, the woman said.

Bone tired after picking up all three kids from school, Hailey drove them through the drive-through of the local fast food restaurant. The kids were excited at the unexpected treat, so she didn't tell them the true reason they were having burgers and fries was because she was too exhausted to cook.

She fell asleep on the couch watching the news.

Anxiously waiting to hear from Hailey was torture. Mac had given up pretending to be unaffected, which meant Gus saw and teased him mercilessly.

Finally, after checking his watch for the twentieth time, Mac gave up and decided to get out his phone.

Before he could, Gus called him. "Hey, Mac, you got a minute?"

"Sure." Hurrying in, Mac was pleasantly surprised to see Gus sipping on a can of vegetable juice.

"What's up?" Mac asked. Then he looked at his father, really looked. Gus's complexion actually had color, and his eyes were clear, revealing no hint of any pain. "Dad, you look really good."

"Thanks." Grinning, Gus finished off the rest of his drink. "I feel pretty great. Must be all the great care I'm getting from that pretty girlfriend of yours."

"She's not my girlfriend." His automatic reply made Mac briefly feel like a teenager again. "Though not from lack of trying."

"Have you?" Gus's piercing gaze was that of the man

he'd been before prison and illness had taken so much from him. "Been trying, that is. Because from where I sit, I haven't seen much of that at all."

"Seriously?" Mac shook his head. "Dad, you have no idea."

"Oh, but I do." Gus's expression turned pensive. "You forget, I was married to your mother for a long time. Believe me, I know what courting looks like, and you ain't doing it, son."

Courting. The old-fashioned term made Mac smile. "I actually don't think Hailey would let me court her."

"Ah, but that's where you're wrong. You don't give her a choice. Swoop in and sweep her off her feet."

Mac grimaced. "That's what I'd like to do. I really would. But I'm afraid to make the wrong move. I feel like I have one shot at getting her back, and I don't want to blow it."

Gus snorted. "So you're playing it safe? That's not like you. Go big or go home. If you want her badly enough, you should give it everything you've got."

"Thanks, Dad." Maybe his father was right. Giving Hailey time so far hadn't accomplished anything but a tentative sort of friendship. They were meant for each other, and he knew she realized this, too—even if the knowledge was buried somewhere deep inside of her.

"Right now she's got a lot going on." He explained to his father everything that had happened with Hailey's mother. "I was just about to call her and check on her."

"Go ahead." Gus waved him away. "The evening news is coming on in a few. I'll be fine."

Walking outside, Mac dialed Hailey's number. A second later, a young girl answered. When he asked for Hailey, she told him her sister was asleep.

"But I'm really glad you called," she continued. "My name is Tara, and I've been wanting to talk to you." Barely pausing for breath, she rushed on. "So when are you going to take my sister out on a real date?"

Mac laughed—he couldn't help it. Her question and his father's statement about courting Hailey had come too close to each other to be only coincidence. "Soon," he answered.

"That's not good enough." He swore he could hear her tapping her foot. "What about Saturday?"

"This Saturday?"

"Yes. That gives you all day tomorrow to plan something. That should be more than enough time, don't you think?"

He did, but still. "Are you always this bossy?"

Now she laughed. "Nope. Only when something is really important. This is. Should I tell Hailey you'll be picking her up at six?"

"Sure. Why not? And, Tara, please, tell her to dress nicely."

He was still grinning when he walked into the living room to tell his father. But Gus was asleep, so Mac took a seat to watch the news alone.

A knock on the door made Mac jump. He hurried to answer before the sound woke Gus.

Detective Logan stood on the front porch, expression grave. "There's been another murder," he said, and then filled Mac in on the details.

The next girl's body was discovered by an elderly man walking his dog. She'd been killed in an empty lot, not far from where Lora Lundgren and, a decade earlier, Brenda Green had been found. She, too, had only been fourteen. Due to the possibility that they might have a serial killer at work, the FBI had been called in.

Mac swore. Softly, almost under his breath. He debated inviting the other man in but decided against it. After all, he wasn't exactly sure why Logan was here.

"I just have a few questions," the detective said, pushing his thick glasses up with one finger. "First, I need to know your whereabouts last night between five and seven."

Mac didn't even have to think. "I was here, with my father." But then he realized he hadn't been, not the entire time. "I also was with Hailey Green, up at the hospital. Her mother was brought in by ambulance. She was in Room 17. I'm sure one of the nurses can verify that for you."

"How long were you there?"

"I'm not sure. Twenty or thirty minutes, probably."

"And what time was this?"

It had been dinnertime, Mac thought. "Five thirty or six."

"And the rest of the time you were with your father, except for driving time."

Driving time. The way Logan said that sounded like he thought Mac had made a detour to murder a teenager before coming home for the night.

"That's right." Mac couldn't help it; a cold, hard lump settled in his stomach. "I can't leave him alone for very long."

"Is there anyone else who can corroborate that story?"

"My father."

Expression skeptical, Logan cleared his throat. "Anyone besides him?"

"No." Mac crossed his arms. "I'm guessing his word isn't good enough for you?"

The other man sighed. "May I speak with him?"

"Of course." Mac stepped aside. "I might have to wake him."

As he followed Mac into the house, Logan's next question made Mac tense up, though he struggled to hide it. "He sleeps a lot, does he?"

"Of course. He's very ill." Now Mac turned to give the other man a warning look. "And please, try not to upset him."

"I'm just doing my job."

"Of course." Mac sighed. "Dad, we have company," he called out, hoping to give his father some warning.

But Gus had already managed to sit up, at least on his elbows. He looked grumpy and disoriented. Mac hurried over and helped him get settled in a more stable, upright position.

Gus's questioning expression hardened when he saw Detective Logan's uniform. "What now?" he barked.

"Another victim," the detective answered. "We just found the body, but the coroner thinks it happened last night. We're not making this information available to the media until tomorrow. We've just notified her family."

"Oh, no." As he closed his eyes briefly, Gus's stony expression crumbled. When he opened them a second later, he fixed Detective Logan with an intense glare. "You've got to find out who's doing this. That's why I wanted you to reopen the Brenda Green case. I just know they're all related."

"Related how?"

"I don't know." Gus's frustration came across in his

voice. "There are similarities in the victim's looks, for one thing."

The detective pulled up a chair next to Gus and sat down. "True. And both victims are roughly the same age as Brenda Green was." He took a deep breath, glancing up at Mac before refocusing on Gus. "And their bodies were arranged the same way, with a bottle of Guinness in their hand."

Gus gasped. "You've reopened the old case." Only a few people knew that the killer had put the empty bottle of Irish beer in Brenda Green's hand. Gus knew because they'd told him, in their numerous and aggressive attempts to make him confess to a crime he hadn't committed. And everyone in Legacy knew Guinness was Gus's favorite beer.

"Yes. And we've been careful not to leak that particular information to the media, so keep it under your hat."

"Will do." The fierceness in Gus's tone made Mac look twice. His father's eyes were shiny with unshed tears.

So help him, if this Detective Logan was just playing with the older man… No. Mac knew he couldn't allow himself to think like that. Surely not everyone was out to get his father. Maybe Gus's time had finally come. Perhaps exoneration might actually be a possibility.

Hope. Such a fragile thing, so easily destroyed. He pushed it away, back in the furthest recess of his mind, where it couldn't hurt him.

"We've got a lead on some Irish Travellers," Logan continued. "The Irish version of a Romani. There were a couple involved in an alleged murder up near Fort

Worth a few years ago. Apparently one or two have been hanging around Legacy. Maybe the Guinness is a clue."

Too easy was Mac's first thought. But then again, who knew what went through a killer's brain. "What about the ten-year gap?"

"This particular group hasn't settled anywhere. They keep moving. We're still checking, but there's a distinct possibility that they came through town a decade ago."

When the phone rang and caller ID showed it was the rehab facility, Hailey's stomach dropped. Several scenarios ran though her mind, each of them horrible, before she made herself stop and answer the phone.

"How's my beautiful daughter?" June asked. She sounded cheerful and upbeat and, most important of all, sober.

"I'm fine," Hailey answered cautiously. "I thought you weren't allowed to have any contact with us for two weeks."

"Visitation. That's true. But I was able to get a hold of a cell phone. They don't know I'm calling you, but if they find out, surely they wouldn't object. How could they fault a mother wanting to phone home to check on my kids?"

Something…a trace of nervousness in her mother's voice, put Hailey on alert. She'd gotten a hold of a cell phone? How? And why? June wouldn't dare ask for liquor, right? Still, she had to have a powerful reason to phone her. In the past, June had never worried about the kids at all. Why would she? Hailey took excellent care of them. "We're all fine. Now tell me why you really called."

The little fake trill of laughter from June was another telltale sign. "Well, I heard from Aaron."

"Your ex-husband, Aaron?"

Another little laugh. "Your adoptive father, Aaron. And you know good and well that we never actually divorced. I still love him, and I'd like to have him back in my life. In our lives."

Reeling, all Hailey could do was shake her head. "Mom, he never sent a dime of support for his three kids."

"Is money all you think about?" June chided. "He had a valid reason."

"Really? I'd love to hear it."

"He's been in prison."

Though she knew she probably shouldn't, Hailey said the first thing that came to her head. "Now there's a shocker. What'd he do, rob a bank?"

Silence. When June spoke again, she sounded genuinely hurt. "He was always good to all of you kids. I don't know why you'd say such a thing."

Was June reinventing history? Even back when he'd lived with them, Aaron had been a low-level criminal. He'd worked for a foundation company, and stole as much as he could without anyone noticing. He'd loved to brag about stealing cars and selling them to chop shops for cash.

However, June knew all this. Hailey saw no reason to repeat it. "What'd he do, Mom?"

June sighed. "He was driving drunk and almost killed someone. With all that was going on at home, he didn't want to call and bring any more trouble into our lives. He went to prison. Now, he's done his time and wants his family back."

Over her dead body. Still, Hailey knew if what her mother said was true, Aaron probably had every right to his kids, at least the ones he'd physically sired. Especially since her mother was in rehab.

"He's not a bad man," June continued. "He's just had his issues like I do. While he was in prison, he got clean and sober. You can't hold that against him."

Hailey didn't know what to think or how to respond. When she finally did speak, she could only say what was in her heart. "I won't let Tom, Tara and Eli be hurt."

"Hailey! He'd never hurt them. They're his children. He loves them."

Sure he did. "All that time and not one card, one letter or one phone call? That doesn't sound like someone who missed their kids to me."

"He was ashamed." Now June's voice was sad and tired. "You've had a lot of responsibility thrust on you since you were seventeen. Maybe now you can take a step back and enjoy your life."

As if. There was no way Hailey planned to abandon her siblings to a father they barely remembered. Eli had been so young, he wouldn't even recognize Aaron. In fact, Hailey doubted Tom and Tara would either.

"How about we leave that up to them? If the kids want to meet Aaron, then fine. If not, he needs to stay away until we can give them time to get used to the idea of having a father again."

When June spoke again, a thread of steel rang in her tone. "That's a great idea, but it won't work in this situation. Aaron has nowhere to go. The house is still in his name, so he'll be moving into my old bedroom. His parole officer has already approved it. You're going to have to adjust, Hailey. I'm sorry."

She hung up before Hailey could respond.

For the first time in her life, Hailey contemplated throwing her phone against the wall. Of course, being the practical soul she was, she didn't. After all, she couldn't afford to buy another.

So Aaron would be moving back in. Damned if Hailey would be supporting him, too. Or cooking for him. Her mood dark, she wondered when her stepfather would be showing up. Hopefully, she'd have time to prepare the kids.

As fate would have it, she didn't. As she left her room to head to the twins', the front doorbell rang, making her jump.

Her first thought was not to answer it, but Eli opened his door and came flying out into the hall. He stopped when he saw his oldest sister.

"Are you going to get it?" he asked. The excitement in his high-pitched voice made her realize how seldom they got visitors. She nodded, praying it wouldn't be Aaron. But then, who else could it be? Reluctantly, she pulled open the door. Her stomach twisted. Yep. Aaron.

Shorter than she remembered, the tanned skin she recalled now pale, Aaron flashed her an uncertain smile. "Hailey?"

Swallowing hard, she nodded. "I just got off the phone with Mom."

"I'm so glad she got help." He sounded earnest; she'd give him points for that. He shifted his weight from foot to foot, clearly waiting for her to ask him inside the house.

She studied him, still uneasy. Dressed in clean, if faded, clothing, he looked relatively normal. Not like the villain she'd built up in her mind for years. At least he had a valid excuse for not visiting or paying child support. She might not understand why he hadn't attempted to contact anyone and explain, but she supposed that was between him and June.

Eli, apparently remembering the stranger-danger she'd drilled into him, remained hidden behind her.

"I'd really like a little more time," Hailey said. "Mom just sort of sprung this on me, and I haven't had a chance even to talk to the kids. Could you possibly come back in a couple of days?"

Unsmiling, he shook his head. "I have nowhere else to go. All I own are the clothes on my back. As soon as I can, I'll get a job and help out. This is my home, Hailey. Please, don't forget that. I really want everyone to get along."

Resigned and hopefully hiding her resentment, Hailey stepped aside and gestured. "Come on in."

Eli waited until Aaron had stepped inside and the door had closed before walking up to stand in front of him. "Hello," he said, sticking out his hand politely. "I'm Eli."

Expression part shocked, part amazed, Aaron shook the little boy's hand. "I'm Aaron. I used to live here, a long time ago. Back when you were a baby." He took a deep, shaky breath. "I can't believe how much you've grown."

"You used to live here?" Eli looked to Hailey for confirmation.

She might as well get this over with. "Eli, go find your brother and sister. Tell them we have a visitor."

"But—"

"No arguments." She pointed. "Go now."

Eli sped off, taking the stairs two steps at a time.

She turned back to face Aaron, trying to squelch her resentment. "I'd rather tell them all at once. No one knew what happened to you." She couldn't keep the disdain from her voice.

"Did they ever ask about me?"

Heaven help her, she actually felt a twinge of pity. "When they were younger. We just said you'd moved away."

He nodded. "I guess I deserved that. For the first few years, I was so angry. Losing Brenda, seeing the pain your mother was in and then almost killing someone with my car…" Expression grim, he shook his head. "It wasn't until later when I fully understood how much I'd truly lost."

Though she still felt agitated, some of her trepidation eased. Aaron seemed exactly what her mother had said he was. Maybe she'd been wrong to make a snap judgment. Maybe she needed to give him a chance.

A moment later, Tom and Eli thundered down the stairs, Tara following more slowly. When they entered the room, they were uncharacteristically silent, eyeing Aaron with interest.

"He says he used to live here," Eli said loudly.

The twins swiveled to look at Hailey for confirmation. Since she couldn't see any other way around it, she knew she had to tell them the truth. "Kids, this is your father, Aaron. Aaron, meet your children."

Chapter 11

After Detective Logan left, Gus's exuberance quickly turned to exhaustion. "He's a good guy, Mac," Gus said. "I really think he might be the one to figure out who the real killer is. Especially since the FBI is going to be helping."

His father's eyes were already drifting closed. Mack fluffed his pillow and helped him lie back down. "I hope so, Dad. Get some rest."

Wandering outside, Mac considered calling Hailey. Though Detective Logan had said the media hadn't yet been informed, Mac knew how this small town worked. Once the parents had been notified, the news would spread like wildfire. With two of her siblings attending the same school, Hailey might have heard already, and, even more important, she or the twins could have known the murdered girl. Right now, the idea of taking her on a date seemed ludicrous.

He took a deep breath and called her. After a couple of rings, her voice mail picked up. He left a message asking her to return his call, before wandering back into the house.

Gus had turned on the evening news. "Looks like Logan wasn't able to keep a lid on the story," he said, pointing toward the TV. "Of course, that's an FBI spokesman who made the statement. The reporter is wrapping it up now. Listen."

"Police—in conjunction with the FBI—are investigating every possible lead. But people in the town want to know why Gus Morrison, convicted of killing Brenda Green ten years ago, was released from prison. His return to town coincided with another murder, ten years ago to the day. And now another young life has been snuffed out."

Feeling sick, Mac glanced at his father. Silent tears streamed down the older man's cheeks. "Dad," Mac began.

But there was more, and Gus shushed him with a gesture.

"Police have stated that Gus Morrison is terminally ill and too weak to have killed the second victim. They've turned their attention to his son, Mac Morrison, who returned to the tiny east Texas town of Legacy with his father."

Mac couldn't help it—he gasped out loud. Holy hell.

"There you have it," Gus said, his voice defeated. He swiped at his face with the back of his hand. "It wasn't enough to convict one innocent man. Now they're after you."

"Don't worry." Reaching out, Mac squeezed his dad's

too-thin shoulder. "I didn't do it. They won't have anything to say otherwise."

"Really?" His dad coughed, trying to clear his throat. This took him several attempts, during which Mac waited, his chest aching for his father.

Finally, Gus took a swallow of water and continued. "One reporter already used the phrase, 'like father, like son.' That'd be my worst nightmare," he whispered.

"Mine, too."

Gus's eyed widened. "There's no way they could do to you what they did to me. No way. Our family doesn't have that much bad luck."

"Luck doesn't have anything to do with it, I'm afraid. There's a serial killer out there. I don't know why he started killing again as soon as we came back to town, but I'm sure the police are working on it. Detective Logan certainly is."

His cell phone rang. "Hailey," he said. "I've got to take this." He walked outside to the front porch before answering.

"Have you heard?" Voice shaky, Hailey could barely hide her panic. "This time, the murdered girl is fifteen. My sister knows her from school. Tara's beside herself. I got a call from the detective in charge of the case himself, assuring me that he has this under control."

"Detective Logan?"

"That's him."

"Yeah, he stopped by here a little while ago. He claimed they were not going to release information to the press, but it was on the evening news."

"That's where I saw it. It doesn't sound under control to me," Hailey said.

As usual, the sound of Hailey's voice felt like cool

water on fevered skin. His fears receded enough for him to be able to think. "I'm wondering if they even have a suspect. Beside me, that is." Might as well put it all out there in the open.

"I heard that foolish reporter. But they can't be serious, can they?" The shock in her voice felt gratifying. "They can't think you had anything to do with this?"

He considered keeping the hateful words to himself, but they were etched too deeply on his soul. "Like father, like son," he repeated bitterly. "Or so I've been told. Trudy Blevins stopped by a few weeks ago."

The deafening silence made him reconsider. He wondered if her silence was because Hailey still believed his father might be responsible for her sister's death.

"That's wrong," she finally said. "You'd never do anything like that."

Relief flooded through him. "Thank you for that," he said quietly. "Right before you called, I'd just finished watching the news with my father."

"That must have been rough. How'd he take it?"

"Not well." He swallowed.

"Things aren't too great over here either." The quaver in her voice, so unlike her, had him tensing up again. "Aaron's back. My mother got a hold of a cell phone and called to tell me not only are they still married, but his name is still on the deed to our house. He's moved back in."

Stunned, at first Mac wasn't sure how to react. "Where has he been for the last ten years?"

She told him everything her mother had told her. When she'd finished, she let him have a moment for everything to sink in before continuing. "The kids are all in shock. As for myself, I'm resentful and angry and afraid to leave him alone in the house. He's acting like he has every right to be there, but I'm not comfortable at all."

"Not comfortable how?" What little he remembered about Hailey's adoptive stepfather wasn't good. The guy had been kind of shady, a small-time, petty criminal. He actually wasn't surprised to learn that Aaron had gone to prison.

"I don't know." She sounded annoyed. "I guess I got used to thinking of this place as *my* house. Now he's taking over, acting like it's been his all along. He seems to think he can just walk in, and we can all become one happy family. The kids are hiding up in their rooms. It's awful."

"Mac." Gus called him from inside.

"My dad needs me. Are you going to be all right?"

"I think so." She sighed. "What a crazy mess. It makes me wish we could all just pack up and get in the car and drive as far away from here as we could."

Gratified that she'd included him, he smiled. "I know the feeling. Call or text me if you need anything, okay?"

She promised she would and ended the call.

Only after he'd put his phone in his pocket did he realize he'd forgotten to ask her about going on a date. Ah well, it was probably for the best. The timing couldn't be worse.

Since Hailey didn't work at Mac's on weekends, with everything at home in upheaval, she knew it would be a long two days. She decided to keep the kids busy—take them into town, maybe pretend to shop at the mall or go to the budget matinee.

Friday night, while Aaron hogged the TV to watch

some crime drama, she gathered all three in her room and told them her plan.

"I'd rather hang out at Sarah's house," Tara immediately protested. Since her friend had been killed, she'd been subdued and clingy with her friends, always wanting to be with one of them.

"No." Hailey didn't even have to consider. "I want you with me—all of you. I need to know everyone is safe, especially now."

Chastised, Tara nodded. "Sorry."

Tom and Eli exchanged glances and shrugged. "Cool. A movie sounds better than the mall."

"Unless you have money for video games," Eli put in. He grimaced when Hailey shook her head no.

"All right, then. That's our plan. Y'all meet me in the kitchen at ten. Make sure you eat breakfast. We'll leave right after that."

The next morning, Hailey rose at her usual time and went downstairs to make a breakfast casserole. She'd learned how to stretch six eggs by mixing in milk, onions, a couple handfuls of hash browns and some seasonings. She'd just popped it into the oven and poured herself some coffee when Aaron wandered into the kitchen, hair still wet from his shower.

"Mornin'," he said, smiling. "I hope you don't mind if I have some cereal or oatmeal or something. As soon as I find work, I'll restock your cupboard."

She started to say okay, but relented. After all, she wasn't a petty person. "I just put a breakfast casserole in the oven. When June was here, it was enough to feed all five of us. If you don't mind waiting, you're welcome to have her portion."

Clearly surprised, he blinked. "That would be great. Thank you."

Pouring himself a cup of coffee, he took a seat at the kitchen table. "I'm looking forward to spending time with the kids now that I'm home. I was thinking about taking them to the park or maybe the lake today. I'll need to use your mother's car. What do you think?"

She had to struggle to hide her dismay. While she appreciated the consideration he showed by asking her opinion, she didn't know what he'd do when she told them she and her siblings already had plans. Would he ask to tag along? Or worse, tell her he was their father and they were coming with him in her mother's car?

Watching her, he shook his head. "I understand how you must be feeling," he began.

"Do you?" This time, her cool tone left no doubt what she thought of that comment.

"Yes. You've been struggling, trying to raise three young 'uns when you're just a youngster yourself. I have no doubt it's been hard, and I'm sorry I wasn't able to help you or your mother at all."

Heaven help her, now she actually felt *bad* for thinking such unkind thoughts about him.

"Hailey, please. Give me a chance to get to know my kids. I'm the only father they've got. How about we at least ask them and see what they think?"

Before she could respond, Eli came barreling into the kitchen, stopping short when he caught sight of Aaron. "Uh, hello," he said, his subdued tone so unlike him that Hailey took a second look.

"Hello to you, too." Aaron smiled. "Your sister and I were just talking."

"About me?" Squinting at him, Eli went over to the refrigerator and poured a glass of orange juice.

"No, not about you." Hailey ruffled his hair. A second later, Tom and Tara arrived, jostling each other with their elbows, each trying to get through the doorway first. Hailey was glad to see a little bit of spark in Tara.

It didn't last for long. The instant the twins saw Aaron, their expressions identically shut down. Some of the tightness in Hailey's chest eased when she saw that.

"Hey, kids." Aaron cleared his throat. "I know you don't really know me, and I don't really know you, but I'd like to try to change that. How would you feel about hanging out with me today? I thought we could go to the lake and fish or—" he cast Tara a sideways look "—lay out. Or whatever. Just take it easy and get reacquainted."

All three of the kids looked at Hailey in unison. "We sort of have plans," Tara stammered.

"I know." Aaron's smile remained steady and even. "Hailey told me. She said she'd let you decide."

While Hailey actually had said no such thing, she didn't see the point in protesting. Not now. She already had a pretty good idea which way this was going to go.

"I'd like that," Tom said, surprising everyone. He shot Hailey a defiant look. "All the other kids have dads. I've been sad not having my own."

Hailey's heart wrenched. She hadn't thought of what it must be like to be a boy, missing a masculine influence. But that said, was Aaron really the kind of person she wanted influencing Tom and Eli?

It appeared she wasn't going to have a choice, at least not right now.

"I'd like that, too," Eli piped in hesitantly. He idealized his older brother, and whatever Tom wanted, Eli wanted, too.

"Great!" Aaron's smile widened. "What about you, Tara?"

Making a show out of studying her fingernails, Tara shrugged. "I don't know. I guess. As long as you take us out for lunch."

At that, Aaron's smile slipped a little. "I don't have money for that," he said apologetically. "I'm sorry."

"I can pack you all a picnic lunch," Hailey heard herself offer. "Nothing fancy, just sandwiches and chips and drinks."

"Wonderful." Raising his hand as if he were about to high-five her, Aaron thought better of it and lowered his arm. "Thank you so very much. As soon as I can, I'll make it up to you."

"Sure," she said, knowing better. She'd heard that all her life from her mother.

"In fact," he continued, watching her closely. "I'm going to need to borrow the car to look for work. I've got a lead on a janitor position. They don't mind that I'm an ex-con."

A paying job? Now, that would be something. For as long as Hailey could remember, neither June nor Aaron had held down steady work. She murmured something about how they could probably work out a schedule.

After breakfast, everyone went off to their own rooms to get ready. Hailey stayed in the kitchen, cleaning up before she got started fixing lunch for four people.

Movement caught her eye. She looked up to see Tara hovering in the doorway. Clearly something was bothering her, but Hailey knew from experience not to ask.

When her baby sister was ready, she'd talk. Not a moment before.

Finally, just after Hailey finished making the sandwiches for the kids' picnic with their father, Tara finally sidled in, arms crossed. Pretending to just now notice her, Hailey started. "Tara. What are you doing? If you don't want to go, you don't have to."

"It's not that. I might as well go. Maybe we all need to give Aaron a chance."

Hailey noticed she, like the others, didn't call him dad. Not yet anyway. "Then what is it?"

Expression serious, Tara swallowed. "Look, I just want to say something to you."

Crap. Now what? Pushing back the shiver of misgiving, Hailey kept her face expressionless and nodded. "Okay. What's up?"

"I know your life sucks. We all do. But we want you to know how much we—Tom, Eli and I—appreciate all you do for this family. You give so much to us. Everything. And we know it's got to be hard. But we love you. Okay?" Finishing up, her voice wavering on the edge of tears, Tara scrubbed at her eyes with her fists. "That's it." Now she sounded angry. "Okay?"

Touched and stunned, Hailey nodded. "Thank you. I think. What do you mean, my life sucks?"

Tara had the grace to blush. "Come on, Hailey. You have to know. You do everything for us. Nothing for yourself. You have no life." Outrage made her voice rise.

Then, while Hailey still struggled with what to say, Tara launched herself at her and wrapped her in a hug.

Hailey hugged her back, still perplexed. When Tara finally released her, the young girl smiled through her tears.

"Honey?" Hailey studied her, a little unsure how to handle this. "Why are you crying? Is everything okay?"

"I think so." Expression changing in the mercurial way of a teenager, now Tara appeared grimly determined. "But I want to tell you, all of us talked about this, and you've got to take some for yourself."

Still confused, Hailey eyed her. "Take some what?"

"Happiness, silly." Tara mocked punched her in the upper arm. "Don't let second chances pass you by. That's all I'm sayin', okay?"

Second chances. Now Hailey understood. Tara had her eye on a romance for her big sister. In the uncomplicated world of a fourteen-year-old, this concept seemed simple and straightforward, without all of the crazy emotional undertones.

Hailey managed to nod. "Thanks," she said dryly. "I appreciate you thinking of me."

"You're welcome!" Tara gave that particularly sly smile that meant she was up to something. "Have fun on your day off, okay?" With that, Tara dashed out of the room.

With all the sandwiches made, Hailey bagged them in one brown paper sack, added a large bag of generic potato chips and got out four bottles of store brand water. These were an indulgence since they usually just drank tap, and she kept them in the pantry in case a spring storm knocked out their water supply. Now she was glad she'd gotten them. Putting them in a small Styrofoam cooler, she added ice and then, lastly, put the sack with the food in it on top.

That done, Hailey eyed the clean kitchen, poured herself a glass of lemonade and wandered outside to sit in one of the old chairs on her front porch.

Her younger sister's words rang in her ears.

Happiness. The idea made her dizzy. Mac. He embodied her idea of happiness. If she closed her eyes, she could see him, his rugged features and broad shoulders the epitome of masculine strength. More than that, more than the physical sum of his body and hair and eyes, she knew him. Deep inside, she understood every dream and wish and desire. Still.

As he did her. Ten years had barely been a blink in the timeline of their lives. Mac. Just like that, she swore she could feel him next to her, his muscular arm heavy on her shoulders, his warm breath caressing her cheek.

Mac. Dizzy with need, she could hardly catch her breath. Take some happiness for herself, Tara had said. No one would ever know how deeply this tempted her. But at what cost?

She wasn't entirely sure she trusted Aaron. But he was the kids' father, and they were all old enough to know right from wrong. Shaking her head, she wasn't sure what she imagined he'd do—try to recruit them as accomplices to rob a bank or commit petty crime? Surely not. And worrying about it would accomplish nothing but make herself ill.

Daydreaming about Mac was much more fun. Smiling, she settled back in her chair to do exactly that.

As if thinking about him had worked some sort of magic, her cell phone rang, Mac's number on the screen. Taking a deep, shaky breath, she answered.

"A little birdy just called and told me you have the day off. How about a ride?" he asked, the husky timbre if his deep voice skittering along her nerve endings, bringing them to life.

"A ride?"

"On my motorcycle."

She swallowed. "Oh. I don't know." *Take some happiness for yourself.*

His quiet chuckle elicited a reluctant smile from her. "Are you afraid?"

Maybe she was, just a little. But her sister's words came back to her again and dammit if Hailey didn't realize she really wanted to feel the thrum of that powerful motor under her, to press her body up against Mac's and hold on while the road whizzed past.

"Yes," she said, quickly, before she could change her mind. "When?"

"How about now?"

"Now?" she squeaked, secretly thrilled.

"Why not? You have the day off. We'll head up to Mineola and grab lunch."

"What about Gus?" she asked, responsible as always.

"I called Dolores before I called you. She told me sometimes she takes private caregiver jobs. It just so happens she's available and on her way over. We have the entire day to ourselves."

Her heart skipped a beat as she realized she needed to change, put on some makeup and fix her hair. *And put on my earrings, of course.* "Give me thirty minutes, okay?"

"Sure. I'll see you then."

As dates went, Mac thought this would be pretty damn perfect. Casual and close, or at least he hoped.

Just being in the same vicinity as Hailey made desire uncoil and rise up inside him. He wanted to touch her so badly he shook with it. Even more, he wanted to taste her—her mouth, her creamy smooth skin, her womanly essence. There had never been anyone else for him; none of the women he'd known in the past decade had even come close to making him feel what he felt for her.

He hadn't been surprised to realize his emotions had never abated. Being with her felt right. Now, for the first time since they'd split up, for the first time in ten long years, he felt complete. As if the missing half of himself had snapped back into place.

If only she felt the same way.

He got his bike out, glad he'd washed it earlier. The sky had clouded up, but the weather forecast hadn't said anything about rain. Spring in Texas brought unpredictable weather, but he had the weather app on his phone and knew it would alert him if anything changed.

Too impatient to wait, he started the engine, grabbed his extra helmet and, after securing it, he took off. If he got there too early, he'd wait outside until Hailey was ready. He didn't want to waste one second of precious time when they could be spending it together.

Turning down her long and winding driveway, he rounded the last corner, and her house came into view. His heart gave a quick leap as he caught sight of her waiting on her front porch.

Engine rumbling, he pulled up and stopped. "Do you want to hop on?" he asked. Slowly, she shook her head, motioning to him to kill the motor. Once he had, he removed his helmet and eyed her. She gave him a slow, unintentionally seductive smile and saluted him with a glass of lemonade.

"Do you realize this is the first time I've had the entire house to myself?"

He blinked. "Ever?"

"Ever. Well, a long time anyway. It seems like for-ever. Come here?"

Though she'd phrased it as a question, damned if he could resist. Putting the kickstand down, he climbed off and crossed the short distance between them.

"Pull up a chair," she said, still smiling.

Instead, he took the porch steps two at a time and went to stand in front of her. He wanted to touch her so badly he shook with it. A touch. Just one, he thought, giving in to the urge to caress the silky smooth skin on her shoulder. But the instant his fingers connected, he knew he was lost.

Unless she shrugged him away. But, no, she didn't. Instead, she held herself still, watching his face, her eyes huge and the dark blue of a sky before a storm. Emboldened, he took a step closer. As he did, she stood and embraced him.

Dizzy, he thought his heart might pound right out of his chest. Holding her, breathing in the clean sham-poo scent—strawberry—of her hair, his body became instantly aroused. Because this was the first time she'd reached out to him, he didn't want to rush things or push too hard. He closed his eyes and prayed for strength.

"Mac?" Her lips moved against his skin, sending a lightning bolt of raw need straight to his groin.

Though he didn't want to, he drew back slightly, so he could look down at her upturned face. Right then, he would have given her anything. All she had to do was ask.

"Everything has been crazy, I know. And we should try to get a little distance so we can consider the con-sequences of our actions."

Jerking his head in a nod, he fought to keep his disappointment from showing.

"I know we should…" she whispered.

He waited, unable now to focus on anything but the heady temptation of her parted lips.

"But I don't want to. I want you." Standing up on tiptoe, she pressed her mouth to his. That first contact, and he was lost.

Chapter 12

His. The way it used to be, the way it should have always been.

Mac deepened the kiss. She opened her mouth to him, warm and moist, kissing him back, her tongue claiming his. This. He felt himself drowning, going under, not even caring that he might never find his way back.

A clap of thunder sounded, so loud the ground shook.

Hailey gave a self-conscious laugh and stepped back, her hand automatically going to her hair. "Wow. Nature is sending us a hint."

"Or an invitation." He bit the words out, the savageness of his need making his voice sharper than he intended.

She looked down, shifting from one foot to the other. Apparently suddenly remembering the lemonade, she

reached for it the way a shipwreck victim grabs at a
buoy. Two long swallows and she finally raised her gaze
to his again. Her enlarged pupils showed her desire.

His own arousal had to be obvious to her, straining
the front of his jeans. He was so hard he could barely
walk. And then she shifted against him, aligning their
bodies up perfectly, so that his desire nestled right into
her softness.

Aware the decision belonged to her, he couldn't
move. He'd clenched his hands into fists to keep from
touching her. He vowed she'd never know how badly
he wanted to back her up against the wall and kiss her
until she melted against him.

Then he decided what the hell. Maybe she needed to
understand. "When you kiss me like that, do you know
what that does to me?"

Eyes wide, she shook her head. But then a small
smile played around the edges of her mouth, and he
realized she did. Maybe she wanted to hear him say
it anyway.

"I want to make love to you, to bury myself deep inside you. I want to move together with you, slow as hell,
until you beg me to go faster. And then, I want to take
you so hard and so deep, the walls shake."

At his words, she caught her breath. He could see
her pulse beating like a trapped butterfly at the base
of her neck.

Every muscle quivering, he waited on her response.
She only licked her lips, her gaze dark, eating him up
with her eyes.

"Say something," he groaned.

"Yes," she replied. "Yes, yes and yes."

They came together like two storms in the middle of

the plains. Locked as one, she fumbled with the door, and they fell inside. They barely made it to her bedroom before shedding their clothes, each of them helping the other, shaking with the desire to come together again, skin to skin.

Except for one necessary impediment. He located the condom he always kept in his wallet and, fingers shaking, tried to fit his engorged body inside. Hailey finally helped, each touch of her slender fingers pushing him closer and closer to losing control.

After what seemed an eternity, it was on.

"Fits like a glove," she chuckled, the throaty sound of her voice making him shudder with need.

"Come here," he ordered. And she did.

Back onto the bed they fell, still locked together. Breaking the kissing off long enough to meet and hold his gaze, she helped guide him inside of her. The instant he felt the moist heat of her sheathing him perfectly, his entire insides settled, no longer alone, no longer apart. This was where he belonged.

Finally.

Bodies slickened by desire, they moved together in that perfect unison he remembered. She'd been a virgin the first time they'd made love, yet because they'd come together in more than just a physical need, there'd been no awkwardness or hesitation. They simply were, and so it was again, two people becoming one.

As her body clenched around him, signaling her release, she clutched him to her and cried out. In that instant, one second before his own release claimed him, he knew he could never let her go. Not ever again.

They held each other, bodies still locked together, while their heart rates slowed and their breathing went back to normal. Finally, she gave him a small shove, and he rolled over onto his back. There was no need for words, neither needed to tell the other how incredible their lovemaking had been. Each already knew.

"Now," she said, pushing herself up off the bed and standing, completely unself-conscious in her nakedness. "Let me get cleaned up, and we can go on the motorcycle ride you promised me."

Once inside the bathroom, Hailey eyed herself in the mirror. Yep. She looked exactly the way she felt—like a woman who'd been thoroughly made love to.

She felt slightly sore but very well-loved. Hurriedly, she cleaned up, wondering how her newly tender body would feel on a motorcycle seat but willing to try.

Spending the rest of the day with Mac was a gift she wasn't going to pass up.

Just as she emerged from the bathroom, another clap of thunder sounded, so loud the entire house shook. She hurried back to her bedroom to find Mac at the window, peering outside.

"Looks like a storm's rolled in," he said quietly.

Immediately she thought of the kids, out at the lake with Aaron. She reached for her phone and called the number of the cell phone Tom and Tara shared. The call went straight to voice mail. "Great, just great."

Mac put his arm around her. "Don't worry. I'm sure Aaron's got enough sense to head home with a storm coming. They're probably on their way right now."

Though she nodded, telling herself it was just a little rain, she jumped two feet in the air when her cell phone tornado alarm sounded.

Tornado Warning! A Tornado Warning has been issued for your area. Take shelter immediately!

"Oh, no." After silencing the alarm, which came from the app Tornado, she hit redial to try the twins again.

Once more, the call went straight to voice mail.

Heart in her throat, she swallowed.

"Cell phone service might be messed up due to the storm," Mac said.

Outside, a loud shrill wail sounded. The tornado sirens.

"I've got to find them." Though she tried to keep back the panic, it took over. "Let's go. In my car."

"Shh." He turned her into his chest, stroking her hair. "Aaron has your car, remember. We've got to take shelter. Now."

"Not without them," she began, wrenching out of his grasp.

"Come on." Half carrying, half dragging her, he pulled her along the hallway to the bathroom. It was their designated "safe" room since it was interior with no windows.

She allowed herself to be led along, mechanically, while very fiber of her insides screamed for her sister and brothers.

"I can't…" she gasped.

"Hailey, they need you. What good will you be to them if you're dead? In the tub. Now. Tell me where I can find a radio."

"In the kitchen."

"Thanks. Now get in the tub, please. It's the safest place right now."

Once she'd climbed inside, Mac retrieved the old radio, plugged it in and turned it on. Then he grabbed one of the kids' twin mattresses and pulled it over them.

Huddled together, she couldn't stop shaking. Several imaginary scenarios—each more awful than the one before—flashed through her head. The kids could be in danger, and she couldn't help them. She said this out loud.

"Or they could be perfectly safe," Mac put in, his voice dry. "What's the point of worrying about something before you know it's even happened?"

"You have a point," she conceded. "But I can't help myself."

"A tornado has been spotted on the ground five miles northeast of Mineola, moving east," the reporter said on the radio. "Everyone in that vicinity should take immediate shelter."

Hailey winced. "It's heading right toward us."

"And nowhere near the lake," he pointed out. "I'm sure they're fine."

The tightness in her chest eased somewhat. She could handle being in danger, as long as the kids were okay.

Then she remembered Gus and Dolores. "What about your dad? Your house is in the path, too."

He nodded. "Dolores is an experienced caregiver. The hospital bed has wheels. I'm sure she got him into the main bathroom."

Some of his calm penetrated through her haze of fear. He kissed the side of her neck. "Everything's going to be fine."

They stayed huddled in the bathtub for thirty more minutes, just to be safe. Periodically, Mac pushed up the mattress, told her to stay put and went outside to check the sky.

The second time he returned, he told her that the sirens had stopped blaring. The radio station had gone back to playing music and only interrupted one other time to talk about damage to another small town west of them.

When he removed the mattress and carried it back to the bed from where it had come, Hailey stood and stretched. Immediately, she called the twins' phone. This time, Tara answered, sounding worried.

"Is everything okay?" Tara asked. "We heard there was a tornado out by the house."

"We're all fine. What about you?"

"Oh, we're good. We've been fishing. Tom and Eli both caught catfish. Aaron says there's enough to feed all of us for dinner tonight."

The note of happiness in her baby sister's voice wasn't lost on Hailey. "Are you having a good time?"

"We were, until it started raining. But Aaron got us back to the car, so we only got a little bit wet. He borrowed money from Eli to buy some ice for his Styrofoam ice chest. He has this really cool knife he used to cut up the fish. He called it filleting it or something."

"Borrowed money from Eli?" Appalled, Hailed swallowed.

"Only two dollars. Chill out. We're fine, you're fine, and the storm's gone. We're going back out to fish some more. Eli and Tom really like it."

"What about you?"

Hailey could almost see Tara rolling her eyes. "It's okay. I brought a book, so I'm good."

"When will you be home?"

Tara sighed. "I guess when we get done. Aaron seems okay. Stop worrying and go have fun yourself. Call Mac or something."

"He's here with me right now."

The high-pitched squeal coming from Tara made Hailey wince and hold the phone away from her ear. "There you go," Tara exclaimed. "You enjoy your date. We'll spend our time getting to know Aaron. Everything worked out in the end, right? It's a good day."

How was it possible that her fourteen-year-old sister sounded as if she was the oldest one? Shaking her head, Hailey agreed that it had been a good day and hung up. When she looked up, she saw Mac watching her.

"Hailey thinks we're on a date," she said, smiling.

He raised a brow. "Aren't we?"

Though she didn't answer, the thought sent a little thrill of pleasure through her. Was this a date? She didn't have enough experience to even realize what a date should be like. "How are things at your place?" she asked.

"I checked on Gus. Dolores says everything there is good. They just got a little rain and wind. Nothing to worry about." His smile sent warmth through her. "How about we continue on our date?"

"Is that what this is?"

He went still. "If you want it to be."

She couldn't help but laugh. "We just made love. If that constitutes a date, then by all means let's continue."

At that, he came over and kissed her. Slow and deep and long and moist, until she could barely even remember what they'd been talking about.

When he came up for air, his gaze gleamed with wickedness. "It's the best kind of date, Hailey. But we've got more to do before this day is over. Let's not waste any more time."

Riding on the back of Mac's motorcycle was exactly how she'd imagined it would be. The rumble of the powerful engine underneath her, holding on to Mac's muscular body and having a reason to sit as close as possible. Even wearing her helmet, the wind in her hair. She found it exhilarating, fun and sexy as all get-out.

As they rode the winding back roads through the woods, she saw her home with fresh eyes. Sometimes, when one lives so long among great beauty, it's taken for granted and no longer appreciated.

Now, without the metal walls of a car separating her from the landscape, she saw this had happened to her. She felt more alive than she had in years, more present. Happy.

She thought of what her too-wise-for-her-years sister had told her. *Grab some happiness for yourself.*

And so she had. Even though Mac couldn't hear her, she threw her head back and laughed out loud.

While he drove, Hailey molded against his back, Mac thought of all the places he wanted to take her. His heart felt full. Surely now, after the way they'd come together, body to body, combusting when they touched, Hailey would finally understand what Mac had known ever since he'd come back to town.

They never should have let each other go.

Ahead he knew of a popular fruit and vegetable stand. He'd never been able to forget Hailey telling him that day in the grocery store that she couldn't afford to buy much fresh produce. Today, it would be his treat.

At least as much as he could fit in his saddlebags, which he knew from experience would be a good-sized bag.

As they rounded the curve in the road, he saw the sign up ahead. After pulling into the parking lot and killing the engine, he took off his helmet and waited while Hailey did the same.

"What's this?" she asked, looking around.

"A local farmer's market." Once he'd dismounted, he held out his hand. "They have amazing produce and reasonable prices."

Anything and everything Hailey even remotely appeared interested in, Mac bought. He never told her any of this was for her and the kids, just gathered it up in bags and placed it in the little basket. By the time they'd finished walking the rows, he had a basketful of perfectly curved yellow squash and zucchini, plump red tomatoes, apples, carrots, lettuce, onions and red potatoes. He'd added a nice cantaloupe, too, wishing he had room for a watermelon but knowing that would never fit in his saddlebag.

Once he'd paid, he'd stowed everything away, still not telling her that all of it was for her family. After that, they drove into Mineola, stopping at East Texas Burger Company and chowing down on juicy burgers and fries for a late lunch.

Watching Hailey eat brought him pleasure. She took dainty bites at first, almost as if she was afraid to get her lips dirty. Then, after that first taste, she dug in with gusto, devouring half her burger with an intensity that made him think of sex.

When she looked up to find him watching, she blushed. "I was hungry," she said.

"Me, too." He indicated his clean plate. "I beat you."

His comment made her grin. "Just barely." And she finished off her meal, leaving only a handful of fries on the plate.

After he'd paid the check, they wandered outside. "What's next?" she asked, glancing up the colorful main street with its numerous shops.

"We can ride the back roads some more," he told her. "Or we can walk around here and shop. It's up to you."

Her beautiful blue eyes lit up. "Do we have time to do both?"

Offering her his arm, he smiled. "We do."

After they'd spent a couple of hours roaming through the stores, Hailey only looking but not buying of course, she proclaimed herself all shopped out. They got back on the motorcycle, and Mac glanced at his watch. The day had gone by too quickly.

"We still have time to do a little riding around, if you want," he told her. "I thought we might stop for a drink at that bar on the way to your house."

She nodded. "Let's go ride. After we're done, we'll see."

So he took her down roads where the houses were few and far between, where huge leafy live oaks made canopies over the road and the pine trees filled in the spaces between them. He took her past the old cemetery where his father's parents had been buried, and his mother in a little plot decorated with a headstone. Gus Morrison's name had already been inscribed there. All that needed to be added was the date of death.

Since the thought definitely brought a black cloud to the day, he pushed it away.

Finally, he judged it time to head back to Legacy. He knew just the place he wanted to take Hailey for a drink. Whether or not she remembered it, as teenagers they'd often eyed the elegant Trinity Room. They'd made plans to go there after their senior prom. But when Brenda died, neither of them had gone to prom. Heck, Mac had barely graduated at all. Luckily, even though his mother had dragged him away to Huntsville before the end of the school year, he'd had enough credits to get his diploma.

But he'd never forgotten his promise to take Hailey to the Trinity Room. He'd even scoped it out a week or so ago, noting the decor had changed, probably out of necessity. Though the place had kept the name, the interior of the restaurant and bar had been remodeled sometime in the last decade. To his regret and relief, the atmosphere was now casual. Since he'd seen a row of motorcycles parked there once or twice, he figured he and Hailey would go unnoticed.

When they pulled up and parked, he stood, removed his helmet and turned to give Hailey a hand with hers. She got off the bike slowly, her gaze trained on the old building. When she finally faced him, she had tears in her eyes.

"Do you remember?" she asked.

He held out his hand. "Yes. I've spent ten years regretting that we never got our evening here. Now we will."

Looking down at her jeans, she grimaced. "We're not dressed for the Trinity Room. Maybe we could come back another time."

"It's changed." Gently, he tugged her toward the door. "They've redone the place. It's more of a sports bar now."

She dug in her heels. "Seriously? That would be a shame."

"Maybe," he allowed. "But places and people change. We certainly have. We can still have our moment here, if you're open to it."

A ghost of a smile flitted around her mouth. "I so wanted to be wearing a formal gown. And see you in a tux."

"Maybe someday." Keeping his tone light so he didn't frighten her, he led the way toward the door. "One drink, your choice, and then we'll head home. You can even have some frothy frozen concoction if that's what you want."

Inside, the dimly lit atmosphere was broken up by several strategically placed TVs, all tuned to various sporting events. The back corner booth was empty, so he took her there.

Once they were seated, the waitress brought menus. Though he was still full from the earlier burger, he asked Hailey if she wanted to share an appetizer. She shook her head no. "I'm looking to see what kind of mixed drinks they have."

"Right there," the waitress said, pointing to a long list on the back side of the menu. "I'll leave you alone to decide."

Once the waitress was gone, Hailey looked up from the menu. "I don't normally drink alcohol. What kind of drink is sweet and fruity, where you can't taste the liquor?"

"Those are the kind you have to be careful of," he told her, grinning. "They go down smooth and way too easy."

She snorted. "I'm only going to have one. Now, which ones would I like?"

Turning his own menu over, he read through the selections. "Texas Tea, Bahama Breeze, Pina Colada. All of those should meet your criteria."

When the waitress returned, Hailey ordered the Bahama Breeze. Still grinning, Mac ordered a beer.

"Nothing to eat?"

After he declined, the server gathered up the menus and promised to bring their drinks shortly.

Mac leaned across the table and took Hailey's hand. "So we finally get to have our drink here."

She nodded, about to speak. But instead, something across the room caught her eye. Her smile slipped, and she swallowed, hard. "Brace yourself," she murmured. "A group of the PTA ladies from the twins' school is headed this way."

PTA ladies? He didn't even have time to question this statement before they arrived. Five women, two of them unsteady on their feet. A tall, stocky woman with short dark hair, clearly the leader, stepped up to their table. Carefully avoiding Mac's gaze, she locked on Hailey.

"What are you doing here with him?" she demanded, her small, close-set eyes going from Hailey to Mac and back again. "I would think even you would have more pride than to be seen around here with a murderer!"

No doubt bewildered, Hailey could feel her mouth fall open in shock. Then, she made a show of looking around, standing to peer past the group of women as if searching for someone in the bar. "Where?" she gasped, putting her hand to her chest for dramatic effect. "I don't see a murderer, but if you say he's here, maybe you all should leave before someone gets hurt."

It took every ounce of restraint Mac possessed to keep from laughing out loud. Of course the beady-eyed woman found no humor in this whatsoever. Pale skin mottled, she glared at Hailey. "I'm serious. I personally find it insulting that you—of all people—are hanging around this man."

Hailey shot Mac a look that clearly told him to stay out of it. Facing the larger woman, she shook her head. "Stop it, Betty Sue. Mac's not a murderer, and I think you know it."

"I heard he—"

"Stop it." Cool, calm and collected, Hailey interrupted. "You should know better than anyone how untrue gossip can be. Now I'll kindly ask you to leave me and my friend alone to enjoy our drinks."

Which had just arrived. "Excuse me," the waitress said, shouldering in between the women. Placing Hailey's drink in front of her, she winked at her before delivering Mac's beer to him. "Enjoy," she said. "Let me know if you need anything, you hear me? Anything at all."

After she'd left, the leader of the women appeared uncertain. But one of her friends, one of the ones who had clearly been drinking, pushed her way in front of the others. "You can't talk to Betty like that," she said, huffing. "Who do you think you are?"

Before Hailey could respond, the woman grabbed Hailey's drink and splashed it in her face.

Chapter 13

In retrospect, Hailey knew she should have seen it coming. But she'd always found it difficult to believe the ugliness that resided in some people's souls.

Sputtering, eyes burning, she grabbed for a paper napkin off the table and wiped her eyes. Black mascara showed on the white paper. She spotted Mac's beer. Without taking the time to think through her actions, she grabbed it and dashed it at the other woman.

Except said woman was now doubled over, overcome with a fit of the giggles. The beer went over her, making a direct hit right between Betty Sue's eyes.

With a bellow of rage, Betty launched her considerable bulk at Hailey.

She never made it. Mac grabbed her and lifted her up and back as effortlessly as if she were Eli's size.

"That's enough," he said, his voice cutting through

the group, a double-sided knife backed by a large, muscular man. "Unless you want her to press charges for assault, I suggest you all leave and go home. Right. Now. And make sure the two who are drunk have someone to drive them home."

When he released Betty Sue, she shook herself like a dog shaking off water. For a heartbeat, Hailey wondered if she would defy Mac and see how much more trouble she could cause.

But then she snarled, "Let's go." Her friends followed her away.

"Wow." Still mopping up the sticky mess, Hailey wondered how much mascara she had under her eyes. No doubt she looked like a raccoon. A particularly bedraggled one.

"Here, honey." The waitress appeared, holding a wet bar rag and a dry towel. "These are clean. The restroom is over there if you want to go get cleaned up. I'll take care of the table. And two new drinks are on their way, on the house."

Though the last thing she felt like doing was sipping a drink, Hailey thanked her. Grabbing her purse, she made it to the ladies' room. As soon as she caught sight of herself in the mirror, she knew it was just as bad as she'd feared. Luckily, she carried a few makeup items with her, and after washing her face with hand soap, she did her best to repair the damage. Her hair had mostly escaped unscathed.

Her sodden shirt was another story. She didn't have a change of clothes. She blotted as much as she could with paper towels. Nothing to do but march back to the table and sit back down. Poor Mac. He'd tried so hard to make this a date she'd never forget. And she wouldn't, though for all the wrong reasons.

When she got back to the table, Mac held up a brand-new T-shirt. "I got this for you," he said. "Now you have something dry to change into."

She stared. The purple T-shirt had The Trinity Room emblazoned across the front of it. "They sell T-shirts now?"

"Yep. And they're a steal at only twelve dollars."

Accepting the shirt, she eyed him. "Thank you."

Though he shrugged, his pleased smile sent warmth through her. "I didn't want you to have to ride home on the bike, with all that wind. A wet top will make you feel cold."

Sweet. Nodding, she returned to the bathroom and changed. After taking off the soaked blouse, she used more paper towels to help dry her bra, then slipped on the new shirt. Much better. She rinsed out her other blouse and wrung it out over the sink. After drying it as best she could with paper towels, she returned to the table.

"Even though they comped our drinks," Mac said. "They wanted me to relay their sincere apologies for the terrible misunderstanding in their establishment."

Though Hailey nodded again, she thought of the couple other situations she'd witnessed when with Mac. "Are people awful to you everywhere you go?" she asked, not even attempting to stifle her outrage.

"Some are, some aren't. It's a lot better than it was right after Dad was arrested." His rueful smile was, she knew, an attempt to tell her not to worry. "Of course, I was only a kid then and not so good at defending myself. At least that part has changed."

Still… She hated that people felt they had the right to judge him. And her, for being with him. Her family had been the one wronged; her family—and his—had suffered. She wished she could figure out a way to publicly let the entire town know how hurtful their actions were.

"Are you ready?" Gray eyes flashing with humor, Mac stood and held out his hand. As she took it, again she felt that click of recognition, of connection.

"What would you like to do now?" he asked as they walked outside to his bike. "We still have a little bit of time left before I need to get back so Dolores can go home."

She thought of the kids, wondering if Aaron had yet brought them to the house. "It's been an eventful day," she told him, barely stifling a yawn. "I think I need to get back."

Clearly disappointed, he nodded. "Maybe we can do this again sometime."

"I'm sure we can."

He took her directly home. As they pulled up to her house, she felt relieved to see her car parked in front of the garage. When Mac cut the engine, she climbed off and handed him her helmet. "Thank you for a memorable day," she began.

Unsmiling, he regarded her. "Aren't you going to invite me in?"

"Aaron and the kids are home," she began, and then stopped.

His gaze locked with hers. "Are you ashamed of me, Hailey?" he asked, his quiet voice letting her know how important her answer was to him.

"No, of course not." She bit her lip, finally deciding

he was right. "You know the kids are going to tease me, don't you? Please, I'd love for you to come in and meet the rest of my family."

His grin made her entire body heat. "I'd like that," he said. "Lead the way."

Inside the house, it seemed awfully quiet. Usually, the kids would be parked in front of the television watching whatever show they could find, but the TV was silent. The door to Aaron's bedroom was closed.

"Wait here," she told Mac. Heading up stairs, she found all the other bedroom doors closed, as well. Knocking first on Tara's, she peeked in and found her sister cross-legged on the bed, earbuds in place, listening to music. When she caught sight of Hailey, Tara pulled the buds from her ears and jumped down to envelope her in a fierce hug.

"How was your day?" Hailey got out. "Did you catch any more fish?"

"Yes. But, oh, my gosh, I heard about how close that tornado came. I'm so glad you're all right."

They chatted for a few more minutes. "Where are the boys?" Hailey finally asked. "And where's Aaron?"

"I don't know. Last I heard, everyone went to their own rooms. Have you checked there?"

"No." Not wanting to make a big deal out of it, but unable to figure out any other way to handle things, Hailey blurted out the news. "Mac's here."

"Here?" Tara squealed. "In the house? Where?"

"In the living room." Hailey barely got out the first word before Tara squealed again.

"I can't wait to meet him." She tore off, clattering down the stairs.

Resigned, Hailey went to fetch the boys. At least Eli had already met him.

Once everyone—except Aaron, still in his room—had clustered around Mac, peppering him with questions and talking over one another in their attempts to be heard, Hailey went in the kitchen. Might as well start dinner. Since Mac was already here, she figured he could eat.

While she sautéed chicken and veggies and cooked rice in the microwave, everyone migrated into the kitchen. Though the kids were still talking a mile a minute, Mac handled himself well. They showed him the fish they'd caught, now filleted and bagged in the refrigerator. They'd made Hailey promise to cook it for their dinner tomorrow. Once or twice, Mac caught her eye, grinning. Her heart swelled with joy. Maybe, just maybe, the two of them might have a chance at a future together after all.

And then Aaron wandered into the kitchen. One look at him and Hailey could see he'd been drinking heavily. Hadn't June said he was sober? Hailey was shocked June had lied to her, but hopefully, he hadn't gotten started until long after he'd brought the kids home.

"I got the job," he proclaimed, grinning. "I only had to interview over the phone. I start work Monday."

"Really?" Hailey couldn't help but wonder if he was telling the truth. "They do their hiring on Saturday?"

"Apparently, this company does." He narrowed his eyes. "Janitors have work weekends, too, you know."

She nodded, aware that everyone watched them silently. "Where will you be working?"

"I think they said the elementary school. But first

I've got to check in at the headquarters to fill out paperwork."

Since when did elementary schools allow convicted felons? She made a mental note to check on that. So help her if he was lying. She'd had enough lies to last a lifetime. "Well, congratulations then."

"Thank you." He leaned over to see what she'd made. "Why didn't you cook the fish?" he asked Hailey, slurring only slightly. When he moved closer to her, too close, as far as she was concerned, she could smell the strong odor of rum. She knew it well, as it was one of her mother's preferred libations.

He also didn't appear to notice Mac, sitting quietly at the table with his back against the wall. She felt safer with him there, aware he'd jump to her defense if need be.

"I'd already planned to do the chicken," she answered, turning back to the stove. "We'll fry up the fish tomorrow."

"No. I want fish tonight." He moved even closer, not touching her, but close enough that she could feel his breath on the back of her neck. She knew enough from dealing with her mother that he was spoiling for a fight.

The kids' eyes went huge and round, clearly sensing trouble. She hid a shudder, not wanting Aaron to know how badly he was creeping her out.

And then Mac cleared his throat and stood, the sound of his chair scraping back loud in the too-quiet room. "You must be Aaron," he said, his voice pleasant. "I don't know if you remember me from back when Hailey was in high school. I'm Mac. Hailey's…friend."

Clearly startled, Aaron jerked away, his mouth falling open before he snapped it back into place. "Who... what?"

Mac stuck out his hand. Aaron blinked, belatedly realizing perhaps he'd better move farther away from Hailey. After sizing Mac up and no doubt noting that Mac had a good six inches on him, Aaron walked forward to shake it. Only Hailey noticed the muscle working in Mac's jaw.

Somehow, Mac got everyone settled and seated at the table, perfectly playing the host even though it wasn't his house. Keeping an eye on Aaron, who sat cradling his face in his hands, Hailey dished up the food. This chicken was one of the kids' favorite meals, and they all dug in. Even Aaron, who kept shooting longing looks toward his room, but sipped the tall glass of ice water Mac had gotten him.

After dinner, she sent the kids off to do their own things. When Aaron started to get up, she motioned him back to his seat. She pulled up a chair across from him, glad to have Mac's solid and reassuring presence there to back her up.

"Aaron, we need to talk." She kept her back straight, her chin up and her gaze firm. Across from her, Aaron slouched in his seat, looking for all the world like an aging, disgruntled teenager. "I've dealt with Mom's alcoholism for ten years. I can't—I won't—deal with it with you now. Do you understand me?"

"I don't think you're in the position to make any rules," Aaron responded. "You live in my house, drive my wife's car."

Suppressing a flare of anger, Hailey calmly nodded. "That may be true, but I'm the only one around here with a job. I keep your children fed, and I've taken care of them for most of their lives. So believe me when I say I make the rules around here."

"I just told you. I got a job." Yawning, the gesture sent a nauseating wave of alcohol breath her way. "And I'm going to be needing the car to get to work."

"Or I can drive you. Unless of course, you want to start taking the kids to school every day and picking them up."

She held her breath, hoping her bluff would work. Actually, there was no way she'd let Aaron drive the kids anywhere every day. Not until she was 100 percent certain he wouldn't drive drunk. With that thought, something else occurred to her. "Do you even have a driver's license?"

Narrow-eyed, Aaron stared her down. "No, but I plan to try to renew it next week. Give me a break. I'm trying to get back on my feet and earn a paycheck."

"You're not touching the car again until you're legal to drive," she pronounced. "I'll be happy to drop you off at work every morning and possibly pick you up at night."

Without repeating herself, she again let him know she intended to continue making the rules. As far as she was concerned, he hadn't proven himself yet. Behind her, Mac stood silently, her own personal bodyguard. She briefly wondered if Aaron would be so amendable once Mac was gone. One thing was for sure, she'd find out soon enough.

"Fine," Aaron finally said, dragging his hand across his bloodshot eyes. "Look, I'm sorry. Getting out of prison and coming home ten years later is hard. Everything has changed. And with June gone…"

Hailey exchanged a quick look with Mac. Aaron

sounded sincere. Maybe, just maybe, everything would work out okay.

"I understand." Hailey too softened her tone. "But the kids have seen enough drunkenness in their young lives. I get that you might occasionally feel the need to drink. But, please, don't let the children see you drunk again."

After a moment, Aaron nodded. "I don't have a drinking problem, you know. Once June gets out and comes home, I probably won't drink at all."

The *probably* in that sentence worried her.

When she didn't respond, Aaron pushed to his feet. "Thanks for the meal," he said. "And for letting me have the kids to myself all day. We'll talk before Monday once I know where and when I have to report for work." Then he headed toward his bedroom, closing the door behind him.

Hailey let out a breath she hadn't even realized she was holding. "That was weird," she said, still unsettled. "I sure hope he doesn't drink around Mom once she's recovered."

"Me, too." Putting his arm around her, Mac pulled her close. "But, Hailey, you can't take the weight of all the world on your shoulders. You'll never survive. Your mother—and Aaron, too—is an adult. They're responsible for their own choices."

Standing in the comforting circle of his muscular arms, Hailey nodded. She knew he was right. "I know. But I have to protect the kids. If I don't look out for them, no one will."

And therein lay the crux of everything. Sometimes, she allowed herself to pretend she and Mac could start a life together. In fact, she was only deluding herself.

She could never leave here, not until the last of her siblings was grown. Eli was only eleven. She'd be living in this house a long, long time.

The next day had long been her favorite day of the week. On Sundays, she always let the kids sleep in, allowing Hailey to enjoy a little quiet time with the Sunday paper and a cup or two of coffee. From what she'd seen of Aaron in the past few days, he wasn't an early riser, so she should be free to enjoy her Sunday morning like she usually did.

At ten, she always cooked a huge breakfast, something different than the usual. Today, she made biscuits and sausage gravy, which she hadn't fixed in a while. This meal had the benefits of being inexpensive, easy to prepare and tasty. A win-win, as far as she was concerned.

As usual, Tom, Tara and Eli appeared right at ten. She'd just removed the fluffy biscuits from the oven and the sausage had already been cooked and crumbled in the white gravy. They all sat, and she poured them each a glass of orange juice. Then, eyeing Aaron's still closed door, she shrugged and served her siblings their breakfast before finally sitting down to eat her own.

Aaron finally wandered in from outside just as she'd finished washing the dishes. "I walked to town," he told her. "I've been walking a lot lately, to get my strength back up."

"You have?" She eyed him, not sure he was telling the truth. "When?"

"Early mornings. I know you think I sleep in, but I'm usually gone when you take the kids to school. I also walk at night, after everyone goes to sleep. I can already feel myself getting stronger."

Impressed, she wasn't sure how to respond. "That's great," she said finally. "Healthy, too."

"I'm thinking I can walk to work as long as it's on this side of town."

Again he'd managed to surprise her. Maybe, just maybe, she needed to give him more credit than she had until now. Slowly, she nodded. "If that's what you want to do. That's your choice. Just remember to let me know if you need a ride."

"I will. Is there anything left from breakfast? I've worked up an appetite."

She'd made sure to save him some and quietly made him a plate before retreating to her room.

The rest of the day passed uneventfully. She caught up on housework, enlisting all three of her siblings' help by assigning them rotating chores. When they'd been younger, they'd complained, but these days they did what she asked without a single word.

Lunch consisted of peanut butter and jelly sandwiches. Aaron didn't move from in front of the TV, and she didn't offer him one.

She couldn't help but wonder if this would be the new normal. The idea depressed her, but when Eli came running in to show her the frog he'd found outside, she banished that thought. Always, she had to focus on the kids.

Despite falling into her comfortable routine, Hailey thought often of Mac, considered calling him, but in the end she decided against it. They'd shared a fun Saturday along with some crazy-good sex, but since it could never be more than that, she knew she needed to have a long conversation with Mac before continuing anything else.

Right after dinner, Hailey's phone rang. Her first thought as her heart leaped was Mac, but caller ID showed the rehab facility. This meant either her mother was making another illicit phone call, or something had happened.

"Hailey!" It was June. "How is everything?"

Glancing across into the den where Aaron and all three of his kids were engrossed in a television show, Hailey swallowed. "Just fine. How's everything going with you?"

"I'm doing wonderful. I admit, the first few days in detox were hard. I thought I was going to die." June took a deep breath. "I'll be honest, I almost paid someone to sneak a small bottle of vodka in to me."

"Almost?"

June laughed. "That's right. Almost. I didn't. I stuck it out."

Her mother sounded like the mom Hailey remembered, from before Brenda's death. Happy, full of life. For the first time since June had gone into rehab, Hailey felt cautiously optimistic.

"How are Aaron and the kids getting along?"

"So far, so good. He took them fishing Saturday. They seemed to have a good time."

"Oh, I'm so relieved. I really think the boys especially need a father figure in their life."

"Maybe so," Hailey allowed. "It still seems kind of weird having him live here in the house."

"Give it time, honey. He lived there before. I'm sure you remember."

"I do." Hailey didn't mention to her mother how

much she remembered. Aaron had always seemed kind of shady to her, but June loved him. And he had given Hailey her three siblings, so there was that.

"What else is new?" June asked.

Hailey told her about the tornado almost touching down too close to home. She also briefly discussed the fact that she still had a job with a regular paycheck. She didn't mention Mac at all.

"Good for you!" June exclaimed. "As for me, guess what? Now I've actually earned the right to make phone calls and have visitors!"

Stunned, Hailey eyed the calendar that hung on the pantry door. It seemed awfully quick to her, but what did she know? She'd never known anyone who'd gone to rehab before. "That's great! When would be a good time for me to bring the kids to see you?"

"I'm not sure. Soon." The hesitation in June's voice perplexed Hailey. But then again, maybe her mom needed to feel stronger before she'd be up to seeing her children.

"Do you want to talk to them?"

The small silence that followed that question was telling. "Not just yet."

Frowning, Hailey shook her head, even though her mother couldn't see. She wasn't sure she understood what June was thinking, but she tried to be charitable. Maybe this was part of her recovery. Perhaps she didn't want to talk to her own kids until she was certain all of this would take.

"Hailey?" June asked, a new, plaintive note in her voice. "Would you put Aaron on?"

"Of course." Even though June had called Hailey's cell phone. But then, Aaron didn't have one of his own.

Hailey wasn't sure why that rankled, but it did. "Hold on," she said, and then hollered for Aaron. Because no way did she intend to bring it to him and then possibly have to let the kids hear that their mother was on the phone and didn't want to speak to them.

Still staring at the TV, Aaron didn't respond. Hailey tried again, louder.

"What?" He swiveled his head to look at her, but didn't get up.

"Can you please come here?"

Expression slightly annoyed, he heaved himself up off the couch and stomped into the kitchen. She waited until he was maybe three feet away from her before holding out her phone. "You have a call."

Looking bored rather than surprised, he answered. When he heard June's voice on the other end, he spun around and took the phone into his bedroom. A second later, Hailey heard the click of the door closing.

This all had the effect of making her feel queasy. Suddenly, she desperately wanted to talk to Mac. But she couldn't, because Aaron had her phone.

She glanced again at the kids, all engrossed in their television program. It was still early, not yet seven. If she hopped in the car now, she could be at Mac's in fifteen minutes. And she badly needed to get out of the house—almost as badly as she needed to see him. Yes, they still needed to have a talk, and maybe now would be as good a time as any.

Decision made, she walked into the den and announced she was going to run an errand. Since Aaron was still there, she knew they'd be fine, but just in case, she put Tara in charge.

"Again?" Tom groaned, rolling his eyes. "Why is it

always her? We're the same age. You should put me in charge once in a while."

Grinning, Hailey blew him a kiss. "Eli, you be good, okay?"

Barely looking up from the TV, he nodded. Then, after shooting her a quick, mischievous glance, he grinned. "Tell Mac hi for me."

"Mac?" Hailey tried to pretend, but she'd always been horrible at hiding the truth. Her face colored, which made all three of the kids crack up laughing. Finally, she gave up. "When Aaron comes out, one of you please get my phone back from him. If anyone needs me, Mac's number is programmed in there."

Head held high, she sailed out the door to the sound of their delighted laughter, her heart lighter than it had been in a long time.

Chapter 14

After dinner, Mac sat in the chair next to Gus's hospital bed and turned on one of his father's favorite shows. Usually, Gus paid avid attention to the engrossing story line, but tonight he could scarcely keep his eyes open. After ten minutes, he'd fallen soundly asleep.

Gus was failing fast. Mac could see it—his father seemed to shrink, as if the illness made him smaller, more and more with each passing day. Though Mac knew each man's death was a personal thing, he didn't understand why Gus didn't even want to try to fight it. But Gus had said he'd done some reading, conferred with a couple of doctors and then made his decision. He'd declined chemotherapy, declaring he valued quality of life over quantity. There was no cure for his particular type of cancer, and all chemo would do was buy him a few more months.

Selfishly, Mac wanted more time. The clock kept ticking, and neither Mac nor the police had gotten any closer to learning the identity of the murderer.

The FBI had set up offices in town. They were all over this thing since the last murder, bringing in people for questioning. Detective Logan had brought out one of the agents to talk with Mac and Gus, though everyone knew the focus was more on Mac than his clearly seriously ill father.

Mac hoped he had no reason to be worried, and by the time Logan and the FBI agent had left, they knew it, too. He and Gus had talked about it after, and they both agreed that the FBI didn't appear to have a single lead. The odds of falsely accusing and convicting Mac of a crime after doing that exact thing to his father seemed unlikely.

Everyone in town seemed to be holding their breath, praying no other girls were killed. Parents kept a closer eye on their children, especially those with thirteen or fourteen-year-old daughters.

Eyeing his sleeping father, Mac went to the fridge and grabbed a six-pack of beers. Then he went outside to the half-restored barn, sat down in the hay and drank one. So much had changed in his life since he'd last lived in Legacy. It seemed there'd been one loss after another.

He'd lost Gus years ago—ten, to be exact—though he and his mother had continued to visit. And then his mother had been killed in a car crash. It had torn Gus up that he wasn't able to attend his own wife's funeral. It had destroyed him to see his son handling all the arrangements and grieving alone.

Therefore, this time Mac took great pains to conceal

his anguish over Gus's cancer from his father. When he'd heard the news, he'd raged in private. And then he'd gotten busy, fighting to have Gus released, wincing inside each time he used the term *come home to die.* When he'd finally won after months of fighting, he hadn't been able to celebrate the fact that he'd regained his father. Gus's early release from prison only meant he could be with his son again, for far too short a time. Mac had vowed to do everything within his power to ease his father's gradual transition from life to death, well aware when it was over, he'd lose him again, far sooner than either of them wanted.

Here, in the old barn, Mac allowed himself to reminisce. The beer went down cold, the yeasty taste on his tongue just right. He and his father had spent many hours in the same barn when the place had been an active farm. Gus had taught Mac how to milk cows and goats, to assist in the birth of a calf and, most important for Mac's future livelihood, how to build things with his hands.

His childhood had been idyllic, though at the time he hadn't appreciated it as much as he did now. His parents' marriage had been a good one, and there'd been lots of laughter and love between them with plenty to spare for their only child.

Letting his mind wander, Mac sipped his beer as he remembered. He and Hailey had played hide-and-seek in and around this barn. They'd shared their first kiss in the hayloft, and right then and there, Mac had known she was the girl he'd someday marry. That certainty had wavered somewhat, with time and distance between them, but from the moment Mac had learned he'd be bringing his father home, he'd known he had to see Hailey again. Now that he had, he felt exactly the same way he had when he'd been younger.

He finished the first beer and popped the top on the second can. He'd often wondered what his life would be like now if Brenda Green had lived. Would he and Hailey be married, with a couple of kids of their own?

Outside, darkness had begun to fall. He had a small battery-powered camping lantern, which he switched on. The small pool of light kept at bay the dark shadows that had begun to take over the already dim interior of the barn. Since he'd left the double doors open, the breeze kept him cool, and he could still see the night sky and make out the presence of thousands of stars.

From around near the house, he thought he heard the sound of car tires on gravel. Listening intently, he realized someone had pulled up and parked in front of the garage. He heard a car door close, debated getting up to see who might be visiting so late and decided against it. If Detective Logan had come calling unannounced, well he could just come back later.

"Are you okay?" a soft voice asked from outside his circle of light. Hailey. His heart skipped a beat in his chest, and just like that, his dark mood lifted.

"I'm fine," he lied, taking another deep slug of his beer. To his relief, his voice sounded steady. "Just hunky-dory. What are you doing here? Is everything okay?"

"Yes. I just…" She stopped talking and came closer. "I just wanted to be with you. That's all."

Something tight in his chest loosened. She wanted to be with him. And he wanted to be with her. He just needed a moment to recover, to shove his hurt and pain back inside of himself and lock it away.

Throat aching, eyes stinging, he silently willed his voice not to crack, though it did. "Want a beer?"

"Sure." She moved closer, tilting her head as she peered at him. "Are you sure you're all right?"

Handing her a can, he listened as she popped the top and waited until she'd taken a sip and swallowed.

"Yep. I'm absolutely fine," he repeated. And he would be, he swore. He just needed to get his emotions back under control. This was why he'd come out here, to let some of what he kept locked inside out.

"Really?" She moved around his side, circling and then stopping just a few feet behind him. "Because you forget. I've known you a long time, Mac Morrison. And you don't sound fine to me."

He couldn't speak to save his life, not without giving away the depths of his sorrow. So he sat, hunched over his beer, nearly broken, afraid to turn and face the one person who might be able to heal him. He didn't fully understand why—maybe because it would destroy him if she turned away.

"You haven't lost him yet," she said, proving the bond he'd once thought unbreakable miraculously still remained intact.

"I know," he muttered, and that was all he got out before she set her beer can down. She knelt on the hay bale right next to him and wrapped him tight in her arms. She held on tight, refusing to let him go, even when he made a halfhearted attempt to shake her off.

Emotion swelled in him, all the pain and confusion and sorrow he'd tried to bury deep inside. Men weren't supposed to cry, at least in the world he'd been raised in. He hadn't intended to, at least not with anyone there to bear witness. But Hailey wasn't just anyone. There wasn't a single other person he trusted more.

So he let the tears flow. Silently, at first. And then, when he could no longer contain it, the dam burst, and he turned his head into her shoulder and let it all out.

And still she held on. Her silent presence gave him strength. She didn't comment, didn't try to question him. She just supported him, her tight embrace letting him know she was there for him.

Spent—and quietly ashamed, because old habits and beliefs died hard—he managed to get himself back under control. Swiping at his wet face with the back of his hands, he gradually registered the feminine scent of her, something fruity and floral and pure Hailey.

"Sorry about that," he muttered, his voice hoarse.

"Don't be." Her simple response made him raise his head to look at her. What he saw in the muted light of his old lantern filled him with wonder.

"Hailey?" Reaching out, he stroked her cheek with his fingers. "Are you crying?"

She attempted a smile, and then lifted one shoulder in a halfhearted shrug. "Maybe," she allowed. "Just a little."

Perplexed, he leaned in and kissed her. One soft kiss, the salt of her tears mixing with the salt of his own. "Why?"

"Because I can't bear it when you're in so much pain." The fierceness of her tone let him know she would go to battle for him if she could. "But don't you be sorry, ever. You're a good man, Mac Morrison."

And then she let him go, leaning to pick up her beer and taking a sip.

They sat side by side and talked, hips bumping. She

told him about her mother calling, and he told her about Detective Logan's frequent phone calls, the way he and Gus would talk for half an hour. And the fact that even with the FBI helping, they didn't have one solid lead on who the murderer might be.

"Maybe whoever it is has moved on," Hailey said. "Like they did after they killed Brenda."

"Moved on and returned. Detective Logan said they're investigating the transient population. There are a group of Irish Travellers who come through town every couple of years. He feels it might be one of their people due to the Irish beer left at the murder scene."

"Irish Travellers?"

"Modern-day Romani. They've settled in the Dallas-Fort Worth area as well as Houston. But there are still groups of them who moved from town to town. There's been a pretty good-sized group that recently settled in Tyler." He shrugged. "I don't know much more than that."

Taking his hand, she twined her fingers in his. "I just hope they figure it out before anyone else gets hurt. And before Gus…"

She didn't finish the sentence. She didn't have to. Before Gus died. More than anything, Mac knew the greatest gift he could give his father was to clear his name before he passed.

Driving home from Mac's, Hailey knew there was no way she could have had the talk about their lack of a future with him. Not that night. Clearly, he'd gone into the barn to grieve alone, and then she'd shown up. He could have reacted several different ways, including asking her to leave. Instead, he'd bared himself to her, letting her see inside his soul. If anything, this made her realize she loved him even more.

Too bad she couldn't figure out a way to make a relationship between them work.

Monday dawned with a dreary sky and the air oppressive with humidity. She turned on the television to catch the morning news while the kids got ready for school.

A severe thunderstorm warning, flash flood warning and a tornado watch had been issued for Wood County. Nothing out of the ordinary. This was normal Texas spring weather.

Still, after the last incident with a tornado touching down awfully close to home, she couldn't help but be worried. Even before the other day, and despite having lived in Texas her entire life, she always felt a prickle of unease even at the thought of a tornado. Last time, she hadn't been paying attention to the weather. She wouldn't make that mistake again. For now, as long as the alert didn't change from watch to warning, the chances of dealing with a tornado again were slim to none.

She hoped.

Since she hated driving in rain and flash floods could be deadly, she rushed the kids a bit. As a result she got them off to school early, which left her with extra time on her hands before she had to report to work at Mac's.

Instead of going home to have her coffee, she impulsively stopped at the local coffee shop and purchased three coffees. She added cream and sweetener to hers, knowing Mac took his black and suspecting Gus did the same. She didn't want to examine her whim too closely.

All she knew was she wanted to have coffee with Mac rather than by herself. Plain and simple.

She arrived at the Morrison farm half an hour early. Luckily the coffee shop had given her a drink carrier, so she was able to carry all three at once.

"Hey." Mac raised a brow, clearly surprised to see her so early. He took the drink holder from her, setting it on the counter. "What's this?"

"I brought coffee," she said, inhaling deeply since he was standing so close. He smelled like soap and man, a clean, sexy scent that made her want to nuzzle up to him so she could inhale it for longer.

Dang. She blinked, aware she needed to get a grip.

Mac didn't appear to notice.

"Great." He glanced back at the counter. She followed his gaze to the full coffeepot there. "I didn't know. I just made some."

"Ah, but this is special coffee," she elaborated, feeling slightly reckless, wishing she was daring enough to push him back against the wall and kiss the tar out of him. "Not your everyday java, at least according to their sign. This is the Roasted Bean's best."

"I see." His gaze darkened from silver to burnished steel. The flash of his grin took her breath away. Again she had visions of him naked, on top of her, inside of her.

"Here you go." She busied herself removing a cup from the holder. "You still drink it black, right?"

His grin widened, clearly pleased she'd remembered such a small thing. "Thank you." Accepting the cup she handed him, he eyed the other two.

"One for me and one for Gus." She took a deep sip of hers, making a little sound of pleasure. "This is good."

"Gus can't really drink coffee." Dragging his hands through his thick, dark hair, Mac grimaced. "With his pancreatic issues, it's too much for him. Even if he could get it down, it'd make him sick."

"Crud. I didn't know."

"Come here." Putting his cup on the counter, he pulled her in close. She thrilled to the feel of his hard, muscular body, allowing herself to entertain a few racy fantasies.

"Mac?" Gus called, his voice thick and gravelly.

Hailey pulled away, and both she and Mac hurried into the next room. Just as they reached him, Gus began coughing, a thick, phlegmy sound. Immediately, Mac pushed a button on the hospital bed, raising it up.

"Dad? Are you all right?"

Gasping, Gus nodded violently, waving away Mac's attempt to hand him a glass of water. "Dang sinus," he finally growled. "I need to ask Dolores about some allergy meds."

"Are you hungry?" Hailey made her voice light and deliberately cheerful. These days, Gus ate less and less. Sometimes he'd ask for her to make something that he thought sounded good, but would only take one tiny bite before pronouncing himself done. Dolores had privately told Hailey this was his body's way of shutting down, and trying to force food on him would only make him sicker.

Hailey wondered if Mac knew this, too. She supposed he did, since he was in charge of his father from two o'clock on.

"I think I could eat a boiled egg," Gus told her, glancing sideways at Mac.

"I'll get it cooking," she said.

She fixed him one egg, soft-boiled the way he liked it. Though she knew he wouldn't eat it, she made one slice of toast with some peach jelly. She also added a small juice glass full of milk. If she could get Gus to take even a few sips, she considered it a victory.

After putting everything on a tray, she carried it out to him. Already he looked better than he had a few minutes ago—color had returned to his face. Mac had combed his hair for him, and helped him brush his teeth over a small tray.

Gus smiled as she set his breakfast on the hospital bed arm in front of him. "Looks good," he said. Then, as she'd known he would, he took a single, tiny bite of the boiled egg. Eyeing the toast and jelly, he shook his head. "I used to love peach preserves."

"Surely you can take one taste?" Hailey coaxed.

Slowly, Gus shook his head. When Hailey glanced at Mac, she surprised him watching her and his father, a look of such tenderness on his rugged face that she caught her breath. Telling herself that it had to be directed at his father, she busied herself getting everything ready for Dolores, who'd be coming later that day.

"Do you want any more of that egg?" Mac asked, gently trying to get Gus to take another bite.

"I'm full." Gus turned his head away. "How about you call Detective Logan? I want to find out if they've gotten any new leads."

Mac glanced at his watch. "I'm not sure he'll be in yet. It's still pretty early."

"Try anyway." Gus sounded almost desperate.

"Please," Hailey seconded. She wasn't sure why this issue was so important to Gus right this instant, but it was.

After dialing the number, Mac handed his cell to Gus. Listening, a look of expectation on his face, Gus waited. Eventually, without speaking, he handed the phone back to Mac. "Voice mail," he told him. "I didn't leave my name and number because I want to keep calling back until I reach him."

"What do you want to tell him?" Hailey asked.

"To hurry the hell up," Gus answered, his voice a rasp. "We're running out of time."

Watching Hailey interact so easily with his father brought another kind of tightness to his chest. Alone with her in the barn the previous night, he'd bared himself to her in a way he'd never done with any other human being.

After, he'd run a gamut of emotions, ranging from mortified to resigned. Though she certainly had acted sympathetic, he worried that secretly she'd despise him for giving in to emotions men weren't supposed to have.

And then he'd realized something else. He was only human. He laughed, he wept. He experienced grief and sorrow and love and ecstasy. Just like every other single person on this planet.

Once he'd been able to let the shame go, he acknowledged that he and Hailey had shared a defining moment. If anything, this proved to him that they belonged together.

Now he only needed to convince her.

Leaving her alone with Gus, he headed to town to pick up some materials for a custom kitchen cabinet job he was doing for an elderly couple the next town over. He'd gone over to do an estimate and submitted a bid, never thinking he'd actually get the job. Maybe because he hadn't done that kind of work in a while. But Mr. Smith had called him and asked when he could start. Best of all, he'd do most of the actual construction in his barn and then fit everything into their kitchen, after he'd ripped out their old stuff.

The creative challenge—they'd given him free rein design-wise—made him feel more alive than he had in months. Except for when he was with Hailey.

Who knew, maybe his life had finally started to come together. Either way, he had the feeling he was exactly where he was supposed to be.

The previously slate-gray sky had darkened, and the electricity in the air promised a coming storm. He checked his phone, still only a tornado watch, but along with the severe thunderstorm warning and the flash flood warning, he figured he'd better get his lumber and stash it in the barn as quickly as he could. He brought a tarp to cover it just in case. Wet lumber wasn't good for anything.

On the way to the lumberyard, his cell rang. Detective Logan. He felt a moment's disappointment that he wasn't with his dad and then answered.

"We think we have a lead," Logan began, without even saying hello. "Now we normally don't release this kind of info, but I'm going to make an exception in your case. A guy named Norman Toogood. We've had our eye on him for a long time, but didn't have anything concrete. And now we do. One of the local restaurants have him on security film talking to Lola Lundgren."

"That's not much," Mac said.

"No, but it's a start. A man of his age shouldn't be

chatting up a fourteen-year-old girl. There's definitely something going on there."

Mac's heart skipped a beat. Seeing that he had gripped his phone way too tightly, he forced himself to relax his fingers. "What's his story?"

"He's part of the Travellers. Except he hung out here in town when they moved on. He's working at one of the gas stations off the interstate. The FBI has sent men to bring him in for questioning. I just wanted to let you—and your father—know."

After thanking the detective, Mac pulled over and turned his truck around. A few drops of rain had begun to speckle his windshield. He'd go buy materials later. First he had to tell his father the good news. He knew he could call, but he wanted to deliver the information in person. He couldn't help but wonder what Hailey's reaction would be when she heard. Today might just be the day steps were actually taken, not only to clear Gus's name, but to bring closure to Hailey and her family.

By the time Mac pulled up in front of his house, the rain had started coming down in earnest. Wind blew sheets of moisture sideways, reducing visibility to only a few feet. Luckily his house and the rest of the farm sat up on a hill, so if the creek flooded, he'd be safe.

But Hailey needed to get home. He thought about the route she took to get to both schools and her house. He thought she'd be safe, but maybe he ought to let her borrow his four-wheel drive truck to be safe.

Grabbing the tarp from the passenger seat, he held it over his head and dashed into the house.

Exactly as Mac had expected, Gus heard the news with a whoop of celebration. He actually fist-bumped the air, and then dissolved into a fit of coughing. Hailey, who'd listened in silence, hurriedly rushed to plump up Gus's pillows and help him take a sip of water.

To his disappointment, she didn't seem the slightest bit interested in what Detective Logan had said. She smiled politely and nodded, but didn't make a single comment.

Later, when she was in the kitchen preparing Gus's lunch, he asked her about it.

"It's just a lead," she told him, leaning back against the kitchen counter, her bright blue gaze clear and untroubled. "I only want to know once they have either concrete evidence or a confession."

Though glad Gus hadn't heard, he had to admit she had a point. "It's raining pretty hard out there," he said, changing the subject. "Do you want to borrow my truck? You can bring it back tomorrow."

Considering, she frowned. "Let's see what it's doing when it's time for me to leave. To be honest, I've always hated driving in the rain."

"If you'd like, I can pick them up." He shrugged, to show her it wouldn't be a big deal. "If you stay with Gus, I can go get them and bring them back here."

"We'll see." Again, he got a sense of disconnect. As if she heard his words, but they didn't touch her. When she looked up, she caught him watching her. "Sorry," she said, waving one hand. "I can feel the atmospheric pressure or something. Storms always make me nervous. Even more so now that we had such a close call with the tornado the other day."

More relieved than he could say, he grabbed her and pulled her close for a quick kiss. "You know the chances of another tornado following the same path are slim to none, right?"

Smiling for the first time since that morning, she nodded. "That's what I keep telling myself."

She'd barely finished speaking when the lights went out.

Chapter 15

Hailey let out a little squeak and jumped into Mac's arms. Not only did she feel safe there, but the solid masculine feel of his body sent a jolt of longing straight through her core.

Her breath caught—or maybe that was his. Either way, when he claimed her mouth this time, the deep, possessive kiss completely took her mind off the storm.

"Mac! Hailey!" Gus, his voice agitated. "Where are you? I can't see a damn thing in here."

Sagging against him, Hailey stifled a giggle. "Come on," she said, taking Mac's hand. "We'd better get in there and make sure he's all right."

The rain stopped by one o'clock, and the sun came out. Hailey checked her phone and all the warnings and watches had been lifted. Radar showed all the storms had moved east into Louisiana.

At two, she checked one last time on Gus, and then went to find Mac to tell him goodbye. He was on the phone—with clients, from the sound of it—so she blew him a kiss and left.

The roads were wet but clear. After picking up Tom and Eli from school—Tara had stayed after for a drama club meeting—Hailey took them home and did some light cleaning for a few hours until it would be time to start dinner. Unaccountably on edge, especially since the FBI had taken a viable suspect, she turned on the TV in case anyone in law enforcement wanted to make an announcement. She also checked her watch frequently, waiting for Tara to get home. Even if this Traveller guy turned out to be the killer, with all the strange doings in town, she wouldn't be able to relax until Tara walked through the front door. Tara's friend Sasha's mother would be picking the girls up after practice.

Needing to focus on something, anything, else, Hailey got out the ingredients for the evening meal. Tonight she planned to make one of the kids' favorites—roasted chicken drumsticks. The dish was not only economical, but easy to make. She also planned macaroni and cheese and green beans—more favorites—to complete the meal. As usual, cooking soothed her jangled nerves, and she lost herself in the assembling of the various components.

When a car pulled up in front of the house, Hailey breathed a sigh of relief, even though she hadn't really expected her sister for another hour. She rolled her shoulders to release some of the tension and watched out the window as Tara exited the vehicle and ran up the front walk.

"Another girl has been taken." Wide-eyed and out

of breath, Tara rushed into the kitchen to give Hailey the news. "We found out at the end of drama rehearsal. Aimee Westerfield."

"What?" Hailey stared. "But the police have someone in custody."

Shaking her head so fast her long hair whipped around her face, Tara seemed to be struggling not to cry. "If they have someone, either he did this before they brought him in, or they have the wrong person."

"Or she took off on her own like Emily McNair did."

"Maybe. But I don't think so. She and her boyfriend had a big fight, and she went for a walk by herself. At eleven o'clock at night. No one has seen her since. Her mom called the police station this morning when they went to wake her up and she wasn't there. They called her boyfriend, and he told them what happened."

"Oh, no." Hailey's stomach twisted. "That poor girl. And her family. Do you know her, too?"

"Not really. I know of her." Tara plopped onto a bar stool, reaching for one of the apples Mac had given Hailey. She'd put them in a ceramic bowl to encourage healthy snacking. "She's in my third period history class."

"Her parents must be worried sick." Trying to figure out the best way to ask, Hailey decided to just go ahead and say it. "Is Aimee blond-haired and blue-eyed, too?"

Tara frowned, clearly not having considered this angle at all. "Yeah," she finally answered. "She is." Raising her troubled gaze to meet her older sister's, Tara swallowed hard. "So am I."

With her gut knotted, it took every ounce of self-restraint Hailey had to raise her head and reassure her sister. "I've thought of that," she began. "That's why I don't want you taking any unnecessary chances, okay? We've just got to keep you safe, always." Unable to help herself, Hailey went over and gave her sister a fierce, quick hug.

Tara hugged her back.

"What was that for?" Tara asked once Hailey released her.

"Just because I love you. I don't know what I'd do if something like that…" The thought was so awful that Hailey couldn't even finish the sentence.

Grimacing, Tara nodded. Though she pretended otherwise, the glint in her eyes told Hailey her sister was secretly pleased.

Tara caught sight of the chicken legs that Hailey had placed in the roasting pan. "Ooh. I'm starving. When do we eat?"

"When this gets done cooking." Spinning around, Hailey turned the oven on to get it preheated. "I'll get started right away."

Tara smiled, though her eyes remained troubled. "I sure hope Aimee is all right. But something inside me is telling me she isn't."

"How do you know about this?" Hailey asked. "Was it on the noon news?" She'd missed that one since she'd been making Gus's lunch. And of course after that, the power had gone out.

Tara shrugged. "Probably. I only know because they made an announcement at school. They asked if anyone had any information about where Aimee might be, to speak to one of the teachers immediately."

Heaven help her, but Hailey's first instinct was to call Mac. And she would, as soon as she got done talking to Tara. This was definitely something he needed to know.

"There's a vigil at the school tonight," Tara continued. "I was thinking I might go."

"A vigil?" Hailey frowned. "What about a search? I'd think that'd be a lot more productive. They shouldn't have a vigil yet. Not until she's found."

Taking a bite of her apple, Tara shrugged. Once she'd swallowed, she spoke. "I'm not the one in charge of that, but still I think I should go. All my friends are going. It's important that we all support one another."

Hailey stared. Her kid sister sounded so grown up. "We'll see," she finally allowed. "It's a school night, so a lot of that depends on if you finish your homework."

Tara groaned and rolled her eyes. "I don't have any homework. The teachers all felt bad about Aimee disappearing, so they didn't assign any. Tom doesn't have any either."

"Then go up and make sure Eli is done. Dinner will be ready in about forty-five minutes. I'll think about this vigil thing and let you know after we eat."

Tara nodded and took off up the stairs.

After everything had been placed in the oven, and the green beans were simmering in the electric skillet, Hailey called Mac. The call went straight to voice mail, which she figured meant he was on the phone. She left a message.

Aaron came wandering out of his room just in time for dinner. Hailey wondered if he planned to contribute any part of his paycheck once he got paid. They could all use the extra financial help.

When dinner was over, Aaron jumped up and mumbled some excuse about feeling ill so he could retreat to his room. Once the door had closed behind Aaron, Hailey looked at all three of her siblings and shook her head. She couldn't say what she wanted to—Aaron was their father after all—but she let some of her feelings show on her face.

"Since I cooked, you three can clean up," she said, smiling.

"But what about the vigil?" Tara asked.

Hailey's cell rang, saving her from answering her sister.

"Have you heard?" Mac asked, his voice pitched low, which meant he didn't want Gus to hear.

"Yes. Tara came home from school and told me. Apparently they're having some sort of vigil, hoping the girl will be found."

"That's been canceled," he said glumly. "At least, according to Detective Logan. They found Aimee Westerfield's body about a half hour ago. And Norman Toogood has been in police custody. Once the coroner figures out time of death, the police will know if there's any way he could have done this."

"In other words, if he killed her before they picked him up."

"Exactly." He paused. "I'm trying to decide whether or not to tell Gus. This will devastate him."

More than anything, she wished she could hug him, offering her embrace for comfort. Instead, all she could do would be to give him her thoughts. "It'll be better if he finds out from you. You know this is going to be all over the news. Plus, Detective Logan is sure to mention it. Just tell him exactly what you told me. There's still a chance this is Norman Toogood."

Mac sighed. "You're right. Thanks, Hailey. See you tomorrow."

"Definitely." She didn't dare blow a kiss through the phone, not with three younger ears listening in.

When she turned around, all three of the kids were staring.

"Did they find Aimee's body?" Tom asked. Tara, who'd gone awfully pale, gripped the kitchen counter as if she needed help to remain standing.

Slowly, Hailey nodded. "Yes. But they have someone in custody. There's a very strong possibility he might have been the one who did this."

"Did you say…" Tara swallowed hard. "Norman Toogood?"

Puzzled, Hailey eyed her baby sister. "Yes. Why?"

"Because everyone knows Norman. They've got the wrong guy," Tara protested. "Norman wouldn't hurt a fly."

Hailey was pretty sure her mouth fell open. It took her a second to collect herself enough to ask. "What do you mean everyone knows Norman?"

Picking up that something might be wrong from the tone of Hailey's voice, Tara cocked her head. "Sometimes he works as a janitor at school. He's a really nice guy. All the kids like him."

The police must be aware of this little fact, right? Hailey texted Mac, asking him to check with Detective Logan, just in case.

He texted right back. Will do.

Great. Returning her attention back to Tara, Hailey took a deep breath. She needed to sound calm. If she alarmed her sister, she knew from experience that teenage hysteria or angst would develop.

"This Norman Toogood. How often do you see him? Are you telling me he hangs out with the kids?" Which in itself was cause for alarm, as far as Hailey was concerned.

Evidently Tara picked up on that. "I don't know," she said, with a shrug. "But I can tell you Norman is not a bad guy."

"Really?" Hailey allowed a little of her worry and anger to show. "Was he friends with Lola Lundgren? What about Aimee Westerfield? Did it never occur to you—any of you—that a grown man has no business being friends with fourteen-year-old girls?"

From the stunned expression on Tara's face, it was clear that it hadn't.

Suddenly exhausted, Hailey shook her head. "The vigil's been canceled." And the middle school would most likely make grief counselors available to the students if they needed them. "Please, finish cleaning up the dishes. Maybe we can watch a movie before we go to bed."

Clearly subdued, Tom and Tara immediately got busy. Only Eli continued to stare. Hailey was just about to ask him what was going on when he walked over and put his thin little arms around her. "I'm scared," he whispered in her ear, casting worried looks at his two older siblings.

Smoothing his short hair with one hand, Hailey kissed his cheek. "It's all going to be okay. The FBI or the police will figure something out." Hopefully soon, she added in her head. If Norman Toogood turned out to be the killer, the girls in this town would be safe.

And if not… She didn't even want to think about it.

Mac watched Gus doze and thought about how he would tell him what had happened. Honestly, he'd hoped to wait until he had actual details about the time of death. Unfortunately, in a quick phone call, Detective Logan had informed him that could take a while. Unlike TV shows, there was always a backlog. Even with the FBI helping to work the case, it could be four to six weeks.

"Unfortunately, without more evidence to charge him, we can't hold Norman Toogood much longer," Logan continued.

Mac's heart sunk. "Don't you have something?"

"Only a video showing him with one of the murdered girls shortly before she was killed. That gives us a strong reason to suspect him, but not enough to charge him."

"Then we need to find something," Mac replied instantly. "Hailey texted me that Toogood sometimes worked as a janitor in the middle school. He was friendly with several of the students."

"Yeah, we heard that. The FBI is in the process of interviewing some of the students now. So far, we haven't turned up anything concrete."

Damn.

"I'll let you know if we learn anything else," Logan had concluded.

After ending the call, Mac wandered back into the living room. As he'd feared, the sound of his phone ringing had caused Gus to wake up.

"What's going on?" Gus asked. He appeared disoriented. Mac wasn't sure if that was because he was still asleep or due to the lingering effects of his medication.

"Do you need anything to drink?" Mac asked, part stalling technique, but also partly because his father's lips were cracked. "Or your lip balm?"

Gus fumbled around on his tray table, locating the tube of lip balm and applying it. "Much better." He sighed. Then, narrowing his eyes, he took a second look at Mac. "What exactly is going on now?"

Since there seemed no way to soften it, Mac told him everything. When he'd finished, Gus sat silently, eyes closed. "So they're letting this guy go."

"Yes. They don't have enough to hold him."

Gus sighed. "They didn't have enough to hold me either, you know. They simply trumped up enough bogus evidence to make my charges stick."

Mac asked the same question he and his mother had asked a thousand times in the past. "Why, Dad? Why would they do something like that?"

Every other time, Gus had answered, "I wish I knew."

This time, however, he sighed. "There's something I need to tell you, son."

Hearing those words, dread coiled around Mac's heart. What if, after a decade of believing his father innocent, Gus was now about to confess he wasn't? An instant after having this horrible, inconceivable thought, Mac pushed it away. Not possible. Whatever Gus had to say, Mac was certain it wasn't a confession.

"I have a pretty good idea why I was set up to take the fall for a murder I didn't commit. I had an affair with a police officer's spouse."

Mac stared in disbelief. "Did you mention this to your lawyer when you were on trial?"

"No. Not then."

"Why the hell not? You could have saved yourself ten years in prison."

"If it could have been proven." Gus scratched his balding head. "And back then, I didn't think it was related. How could it be? This person wasn't related to any of the detectives assigned to my case. And everything was so hush-hush. I didn't think word would ever have gotten out. She wouldn't have wanted her fellow officers to know this about her husband."

Confused, Mac wasn't sure he'd heard correctly. "Are you saying you…"

"Had an affair with another man?" Gus nodded. "Yes. I did. It's been more than eleven years ago now, and it was a one-time thing. Short-lived, but intense. I'll spare you the details about how I never intended for it to happen, and how it ended, but I think this may have been the reason the police put a bull's-eye on me for the crime."

"Did Mom know?" Mac finally asked.

"Of course not. There's no way I'd want her hurt like that. That's another part of the reason I never brought it up to my attorney."

Stunned and unsettled, Mac had no idea what to say. At least his mother had never known. When he didn't speak, Gus filled the silence with more words.

"I loved your mother," Gus said. "And other women before her. But there have been other men since, in prison."

"Stop." Mac held up his hand. "I don't want to know. Really. Your personal life is your business. If you told me this information because you want me to use it to try to clear your name, then I will." No matter how difficult doing so might be.

"Hell, no." Gus sounded shocked. "No one can ever know about that. Chief Brigham's husband has a good reputation in this town. If people were to learn about his past indiscretion…"

"The chief of police?" Mac asked faintly. He felt dizzy. Maybe he needed to sit down. He dropped into the chair next to his father's bed and put his head in his hands while he tried to clear his head. "You had an affair with her husband? Why are you telling me this, Dad?" he finally asked. "If there's no way I can use this information to help you, why bring it up now?"

Gus stared at his son, his mouth working. "Because I wanted you to understand why I was railroaded. I also wanted you to understand me. Me. I'm a complicated person. I know nowadays, people are all for coming out and telling the truth, but people my age… We're a little more buttoned up and private."

"I see," Mac said, not sure he did.

A moment or two passed quietly, neither man speaking, both lost in their thoughts.

Finally, it was Gus again who broke the silence. "May I ask you something, son?"

"Sure," Mac asked dully. "Go ahead."

"Do you think less of me now that I've told you what I did?"

The question hung out there, so heartbreakingly poignant it brought tears to Mac's eyes. He pushed to his feet and carefully, gently, enveloped his father in a hug. "Of course not. I love you and will always love you."

Gus nodded, wiping away the tears that leaked from his eyes. "But you acted so shocked. I thought…"

"I *am* shocked," Mac replied, patting his too-thin, dying father on the back. "You gave me a truth that I hadn't been able to see," he said, aware he had to choose his words carefully. "I'm grateful to you for feeling safe enough to share that extremely personal information with me." He took a deep breath. "But it's still going to take me a while to get used to that knowledge."

Gus sighed, his eyes drifting closed. "Take all the time you need," he mumbled. And then he was fast asleep. Mac stood for a moment or two, watching his father's chest rise and fall. He still wasn't sure how to take what Gus had told him. The complexity of his father made him wonder what secrets his mother had carried with her to her grave.

Wandering outside to look at the setting sun, Mac fought the urge to call Hailey. Though he desperately needed someone to talk to about what his father had told him, this wasn't his news to share. If Gus wanted Hailey to know, he'd either give Mac permission to tell her, or Gus would tell her himself.

Gus slept through dinner, waking up only once to tell Mac he needed to use the bathroom. Mac took care of him, cleaning him up after, and offered him some food—anything Gus might want. Gus declined, though Mac got him to take a couple of sips from a protein shake.

Afterward, turning the TV on, Mac sat through a show about people searching for a house in Ireland before clicking the set off. Again, he ached to call Hailey, if only to hear her voice. But aware he didn't entirely trust himself not to discuss his father's news, he decided not to. Instead, he went to bed early, positive he'd been in for a long night of tossing and turning. Instead, to his surprise, he closed his eyes and when he opened them again, morning had arrived.

After his shower, he turned on the morning news. Of course, all they could talk about was the newest murder in the small town of Legacy. No arrests had been made, and one of the anchors speculated there were not even any suspects. The other anchor immediately said there was always a suspect.

When the camera showed the middle school where both Tara and Tom attended, again he reached for his phone, wanting to call Hailey. But he knew she'd be busy getting the kids off to school, so he didn't. He'd be seeing her in a couple of hours after all.

When Hailey arrived, her usual sunny smile had gone missing. She'd pulled her hair back into a tight ponytail and wore a faded T-shirt and jeans with absolutely zero jewelry, not even the earrings he'd given her so long ago, which he'd never seen her without.

She walked into the kitchen, right past a dozing Gus, and stood in the doorway. Her slumped shoulders and tired eyes spoke of her dejection.

"Do you want to talk about it?" He ached to put his arm around her and pull her in close, but suspected this wasn't what she needed right now.

Swallowing, she started to shake her head, and then nodded instead. "I guess I do. This one hits too close to home. The girl that was killed also went to school with Tara. Not only are they the same age, but they resemble each other. A lot. Slender with blond hair, blue eyes and freckles."

Like Lola Lundgren had been. And a decade earlier, Brenda Green. He winced. "Since they had to let Norman Toogood go, I don't think the police or the FBI have any viable leads."

"Which is ridiculous. Tara got called in to talk to the FBI. I was glad, because she kept insisting that everyone knows Norman and that he's a good guy. She didn't seem to think there was anything wrong with a guy in his mid to late forties hanging around fourteen-year-old girls."

Mac winced. "If it's him, he's been careful not to leave any proof. Sooner or later, he's got to mess up."

"You'd think so." Exhaling out a little puff of air, she looked at him. Really looked at him. "How'd Gus do over the weekend? I know we're working against time here, but I'm so hoping he can hang in there until they capture the right killer."

"Me, too." Even thinking about it made Mac's chest hurt. He thought of the secret his father had revealed yesterday and wondered if that had been a sign that Gus felt he was getting close to the end.

"I hate that he's suffering so much. Are you sure there's nothing we can do for your dad to help him? I know you said you were trying supplements and juicing. Has any of that helped him?"

"No."

"You're positive there's no chance he can get better?"

Mac grimaced. "There's no cure for pancreatic cancer. By the time they learned about Dad's, it was too late to do the Whipple, which is an operation to remove part of the pancreas. People who are a candidate for that have a better chance. But Dad's cancer has spread. It's just a matter of time. I've researched it endlessly. Chemotherapy would only give him a few months, and he decided he didn't want that."

"Oh, Mac. That stinks." She crossed the few feet that separated them and hugged him. His breath caught. He brought his arms around her, and they clung together silently, each drawing comfort from the other. His body stirred, because at the first touch he wanted more. He might have held on a bit too long, but she didn't protest.

As they stepped apart, Mac's phone rang. "It's Detective Logan," he said. "I've got to take this."

Logan was brief and to the point. "We think we might have figured out another common denominator. After talking to several kids at the school, we learned some of the other janitors have been illegally providing the kids things like alcohol and cigarettes. The district contracts out to a service. We've got those people compiling a list of names. Once they get that to us, we'll be bringing them all in for questioning. We're hoping once we round up and charge that individual with that smaller crime, it'll have a ripple effect."

"Are you thinking you might get a confession?"

The detective sighed. "Either that, or cause the killer to finally make a mistake."

Chapter 16

After cleaning up Gus as best she could, Hailey rushed to find Mac. As usual, he was in the barn, working on the custom cabinets. He looked up when she came in.

"What's wrong?"

"Your dad." She bent over, struggling to catch her breath. "He's really sick. I think you need to call the hospice nurse. I've got to get back to the house. I don't dare leave him alone too long." She didn't tell Mac that his father's breathing had changed, taken on that rattle Dolores had warned her about. He'd hear it for himself soon enough.

As she ran back to the house, Mac ran with her. He took one look at his father before pulling out his phone to call Dolores. After he'd finished, he slid his cell into his back pocket and raised his gaze to meet Hailey's. The bleakness she saw there made her stomach churn.

"Dolores is packing up and coming over. She'll be here twenty-four hours a day from now on. Hospice offers that service toward the end." His voice broke on the last.

Of course she went to him, as if by the simple act of human contact she could ward off the despair and pain that was to come. "I'm sorry," she whispered, clinging to him.

"Me, too." And he kissed her, the movement of his mouth on hers that of a drowning man desperate for air.

Though heat immediately zinged through her, she tried only to give comfort, knowing that was what he needed in this particular instant in time.

When he finally released her, they both were breathing hard. "If you only knew how badly I want you right now," he said.

The low-voiced declaration made her go weak in the knees. "Bad timing." She managed to keep her voice light. "Right now, Gus needs all your attention."

Though she didn't want to, Hailey left at her usual time. She picked up the kids, the older twins first. Tara seemed quieter than normal, but Tom's exuberance more than made up for his sister's glumness.

"Guess what?" Tom asked, the instant he got in the car. "I made the basketball team! We have practice almost every night for an hour after school."

All Hailey could think about was the cost. Even though the team was a school-sponsored activity, parents were required to pay for uniforms and things like that. And the fact that his practice would mean another trip back to the school, using precious gasoline.

But she couldn't tell him no. Tom had never complained, all through the years when he'd asked to be on various leagues and she'd had to deny him because they couldn't afford it.

As if he'd read her mind, Tom continued, "And it doesn't cost anything. Maybe a little for the uniform, but that's it. I can't wait until you all can come watch me in my first official game!"

His excitement seemed contagious. Even Tara grinned, offering him a high five. As soon as they picked up Eli, Tom repeated his news. Eli appeared thrilled for his big brother and, she thought, a little envious.

"When's the first game?" Hailey asked.

"Friday," Tom answered promptly. "That gives us two nights of practice before we play."

"Is that long enough?" asked Hailey, even though she knew absolutely nothing about middle-school basketball.

"Coach says it has to be. It's more of a scrimmage than a full-on game. We're a pretty tight-knit team, so I think we'll do great!"

That night, Hailey fried the fish the kids had caught to celebrate. She was proud of her brother and overjoyed to see the way the rest of the kids supported him.

While she was cooking, she overheard Eli ask Tom if he planned to tell Aaron.

"I don't think so," Tom said. "I'm still not real sure about him. Right now, at least for my first couple of games, I just want my regular family there. Maybe I'll invite him later, maybe I won't."

His *regular* family. Some of the sadness she'd felt since Gus had taken a turn for the worse lifted.

Over the next two days, Gus appeared to get better. Whatever the reason, he seemed tremendously improved. He sat up, talked and laughed, made his usual attempts to choke down a bite or two and had Dolores grinning. By Friday afternoon, she declared he'd rallied.

Mac and Hailey exchanged relieved glances. Maybe, just maybe, they'd have a little more time.

In the kitchen gathering up her things to get ready to go, Hailey asked Mac how the police investigation was coming along.

"I talked to Logan earlier," he answered. "They're still rounding up janitors. Apparently that particular company rotates their workers between different school campuses. Also, they apparently have several workers who are on parole."

"What?" Hailey recoiled. "Why would the school distract let them do that? Don't they vet all their employees, even those from another service?"

"They're supposed to. My guess is that this either slipped through the cracks or someone was bribed to look the other way. If so, I imagine someone's head will roll."

"I'd hope so." She shook her head, her mind on everything she needed to do in order to get ready for that evening. "I wonder if Aaron gets moved around. From the way he talks, he's only worked at Eli's school."

"I don't know, but if he's ever worked at the middle school, he'll be getting called in."

"I'd better get going," she said, still on the fence about whether or not to invite him. She knew Tom had said he wanted his regular family only, but she took that more of a comment on his uncertainty about Aaron. If Mac was going to be in her life, even for a little while, she really needed to see where he stood on things like attending the kids' sporting activities.

"You don't want to be late picking up the kids," Mac

commented, glancing at his watch. "What are you doing later? It's Friday night, and I thought we might grab a bite to eat or something. Dolores will be here with Gus."

"Normally, I'd love to," Hailey responded. "But tonight, Tom has a basketball game after school."

"He made the team?" Mac sounded pleased.

"Yes, he did," she said. "Anyway, I'm not sure if you like this sort of thing, but I was wondering if you'd like to go. Of course, if you don't, I totally understand…"

Feeling slightly foolish, she let her words trail off.

Mac cocked his head, eyeing her. "I'd love to. What time should I be there?"

Giddy with happiness, she grinned. "The game starts at seven. But this is really important to Tom, so I'm planning to be there a little earlier. Tara and one of her friends are riding there together—her mom is picking Tara up after school. And Eli asked if he could spend the night with one of his little buddies. I told him yes, as long as they come to the game. Of course Eli said they would."

"Do you want me to pick you up?" Mac asked. "I can swing by around six thirty."

She didn't even have to think. "I'd love that." Impulsively, she stood on tiptoe and gave him a quick kiss. "I'll see you later."

When she got home, the house seemed eerily quiet without the kids. As usual, Aaron's door was closed. Since she didn't want to alert him that anything out of the ordinary was occurring, she hurried to her room and shut her own door. She had a little time before she needed to get ready and, since tomorrow was Saturday, she didn't have to get ingredients ready for the kids to make lunches to take school the next day. Given that they wouldn't be eating dinner together, she'd made sure all the kids had a five in case they needed to buy food. She planned to make a quick sandwich a few minutes before Mac picked her up.

Right now, all she wanted was a nap. She could rest for an hour or two, then shower and have plenty of time to get ready.

With a heartfelt sigh of relief, she pulled back her comforter and slipped between the sheets. Head on the pillow, she sighed again and closed her eyes.

Touched and honored that Hailey had asked him to attend her baby brother's first basketball game, Mac spent the next several hours trying to preplan the evening. He should have asked her to go to an early dinner before the game. Kicking himself, he debated calling her, but decided he'd simply show up early and surprise her. She was always so busy cooking for her siblings, she deserved to let someone else prepare her a meal. Nothing too heavy, so he ruled out Italian. A steak house sounded too formal, as did seafood. There were a few of the larger chain restaurants up on the interstate, but he wanted something a little more intimate. Sushi? Did Hailey even eat sushi?

Then he remembered a little mom-and-pop café he and Hailey had gone to a few times back in high school. It had been located on Main Street downtown. Was it still there?

A quick internet search on his phone revealed it was.

Once that was settled, he went to check on Gus. Dolores winked when he came in. Gus was sitting up in bed, watching television. He smiled when Mac walked in.

"Dolores tells me you and Hailey have a date to-night," Gus said, beaming. His color looked good, and his eyes even had a bit of a sparkle. Immensely cheered, Mac privately thought they'd all been wrong. Gus wasn't quite done with this earth just yet.

"We do. Hailey's kid brother made the middle school basketball team. We're going to grab a bite to eat and then watch his first game."

"Way to go!" In a gesture reminiscent of the old Gus, Mac's father raised his hand for a high five. Smiling, Mac complied.

They talked for a few minutes longer, about trivial things, since both men knew there hadn't been any news on the case. The custodial pool was apparently large, and workers were still being interviewed, according to Logan. He'd promised to call if they had any changes.

After visiting with his dad, Mac hurried to shower and get ready. He decided ninety minutes early would give them enough time to have a meal and still arrive at the game on time.

He couldn't get over how happy he felt. Not only was he going to spend the night with Hailey and her little family, but Gus had visibly improved.

Once he'd dressed in a comfortable pair of jeans, boots and a button-down shirt, Mac told his dad—who was still awake—and Dolores goodbye. He drove to the large grocery store and headed to their floral department, where he selected a beautiful, multicolored arrangement of daisies and carnations and roses.

Then, with his step light, Mac got in his truck and drove to Hailey's house, full of hope about the evening ahead.

* * *

The pressure of a body on the edge of her mattress woke Hailey from a particularly pleasant dream. At first, slightly confused and still groggy, she thought it must be one of the kids, before she remembered they were all with friends.

"Mac?" she said, delighted. Rubbing her eyes, she sat up to look.

Aaron sat on the edge of her bed.

She recoiled. And then, aware this might not be the best reaction to reveal, she managed what she hoped was a friendly smile. "Wow. What's up, Aaron? You startled me."

He didn't smile back. "Where's Tara?"

Though having Aaron in her bedroom creeped her out, something in his voice as he asked about his daughter sent a chill up her spine.

Her first reaction was to panic. She pushed herself up and out of bed, and away from him. Standing near her dresser, she eyed him, trying not to glance at the doorway. "What do you mean? Have you heard something? Is she all right?"

"I haven't heard anything." His dismissive tone along with his flat, unblinking stare sent off every warning instinct she possessed.

"Oh. All right." Taking a deep breath, she lifted her chin. "Do you mind meeting me in the kitchen? I need to shower and change."

He didn't move. "I do mind, actually. Until Tara gets here, you'll have to do."

Okay, now every instinct was screaming. Time to put some distance between her and him. Leaping away, she sprinted for the door.

Not quickly enough. He stuck out his leg, tripping her. As she went down, she tried to grab hold of the dresser or the door—anything. Instead, she only connected with Aaron as he moved to intercept her.

Instead of helping her, he pushed her down, hard. So hard her chin hit the floor. She cried out in pain, realizing for the first time she could be in actual physical danger.

Then, as he climbed on top of her, she had the horrifying thought that he meant to rape her.

"Stop," she cried out. "Aaron, just stop. I don't know what's wrong with you, but let me up. Right this instant."

"You're done ordering me around," he sneered. "As of right now, that's over." He used his knee to press down in the middle of her back. At any moment she fully expected one of her bones to snap in half.

In pain and stunned, she tried to process the situation. "What do you want from me?" she finally asked quietly, aware she might be opening up an entirely different and unwelcome can of worms.

To her relief, he got off her and hauled her up. One hand tight on her upper arm, he warned her not to try again to run away.

"The cops are calling in all the custodial staff for questioning," he told her. "Did you have something to do with that?"

"Of course not. How could I?"

He bared his teeth. Exactly like a rabid dog, she thought dimly. "What does that have to do with you?" she asked, aware pretending bravery would be better than cowering in abject fear.

"Are you really this stupid?" The contempt in his

voice made her stomach clench. "I'm a janitor, remember. The FBI is talking to every janitor I work with. Luckily for me, several of the other guys are on parole, too. Otherwise, they'd have noticed me right away. I imagine they'll figure it out soon enough."

She struggled to process his words. "You mean... But you work at Eli's school. I thought they were only interviewing the ones from the middle school."

"They rotate us," he gestured, an obscene move involving his middle finger. Who he was flipping off, she didn't know. "I've worked there, too."

"Oh. But I still don't understand." Except she was starting to. Hopefully her sudden suspicion would turn out to be wrong.

"Sit," he ordered, motioning toward the bed. "You and I have a lot to talk about, I think."

Limping, trying like hell not to clutch her aching side, she made it to her bed. She perched on the edge, afraid to take her eyes off him.

"I killed Brenda," he told her, his tone as casual as if he was discussing the weather. "I was driving home from the bar, and I saw her walking along the side of the road. She was happy to see me, your sister. Relieved that she wouldn't have to walk the four miles to make it home."

Hailey froze, unable to fully process what she was hearing. "No one ever suspected you," she whispered. "I don't believe this."

"Yeah, no one ever thought the grieving stepfather could do such a thing. Especially when I was able to provide enough evidence to implicate Gus Morrison."

"You?" Her voice shook. "You implicated Gus?"

Clearly pleased with himself, he chuckled. "Yes. It was pretty damn easy to do."

Heaven help her, but she had to know. "How?"

"Oh, it was genius, if I do say so myself." The lilt in his voice told her how much he enjoyed telling her what he'd done. More than distaste, she felt a quiet, simmering fury. Aaron didn't seem to care that he'd ruined an innocent man's life or that of his family.

At least now, she thought, she could finally clear Gus's name. Then she realized if Aaron was telling her the truth, he didn't intend to let her live long enough to do anything of the sort.

"I took pictures of Brenda. Lots of pictures, all without her knowing. And then I printed them off and put them in Gus Morrison's glove box. Man never did lock his car."

"That shouldn't be enough to get anyone arrested," she protested, without thinking.

Luckily, her words didn't appear to have an impact on Aaron. "Oh, there's more. I grabbed a pair of her panties from the clothes hamper and put those in his car, under the driver's seat. I grabbed one of his empty beer bottles out of his trash—Guinness, I think it was—and put it with her body. I used gloves, and I was careful not to erase his fingerprints. And then, after I killed her, I phoned in an anonymous tip that she'd been seen riding in his car."

Hiding her growing horror, Hailey nodded. "But why?" she asked. "Why would you kill Brenda?"

"Because I wanted to," he said, anger deepening his voice. "She rejected me, cold little bitch. I offered her my love. We were meant to be together. But she said no. Not only that, but she threatened to tell her mother. So she had to die."

June. Mouth dry, Hailey swallowed. "Did June know about any of this?"

"Of course not." Again, he looked at her as if he found her question idiotic. "Poor woman mourned the loss of her daughter. Once she started hitting the bottle, she wouldn't have noticed if I'd have started bringing dead girls' bodies here."

"Did you kill the others?" Hailey asked, trying to sound admiring but probably only sounding as ill as she felt. "Lola Lundgren and Aimee Westerfield?"

"What do you think?" He leered at her, and then broke into a spine-tingling laugh. "I look at them and think I see my Brenda, but I'm always wrong. And then…" Tilting his head, he let his gaze roam all over her, making her feel violated. "I realized Brenda would be just a few years younger than you right now. Odd how I never noticed the resemblance before. I bet if she'd lived, you and Brenda could have passed for twins. Tara, too."

What did that mean? Was he going to try to force himself on her? Kill her? Eyeing her nightstand clock, she realized Tom would think she'd skipped his game. And Mac. He'd be showing up soon to pick her up. Maybe she could signal him somehow, let him know she was in trouble.

Buoyed by the prospect of rescue, she and Aaron both froze as they heard the rumble of a truck's powerful engine. Mac. Way too early. She tensed, ready to spring for the door and begin screaming.

"Expecting someone?" he asked, grabbing her in a choke hold and covering her mouth so she couldn't scream. He held her tight while reaching around him and brandishing a cord of thick rope. Grabbing her, he deftly tied her hands together and then her feet. After he'd trussed her up like a deer on the way to the slaughterhouse, he tied her to one of her own bedposts. When he finished with that, he stuffed a rag into her mouth and tied it behind her head with a flourish. "I really am good at this," he said, his voice cheerful. "I'll be back once I get rid of our visitor."

When he left, he closed her bedroom door behind him. Wildly, she glanced around, wishing she hadn't closed her blinds. Aaron had tied the rope too tight, and she was already losing circulation in her hands and feet. She tried to wiggle her wrists, like she'd seen people do on TV, but all that accomplished was giving her painful rope burn.

Next she attempted to roll left or right, any kind of movement that might knock something to the ground or create a sound to warn Mac at the front door. But she could barely move.

A few moments later, her cell phone began to ring. She'd placed it on the dresser earlier while she'd napped, and couldn't get to it. Fervently, she hoped Mac would hear it ringing. Closing her eyes, she thought hard. Even though she knew it was crazy, she concentrated on sending him thoughts, trying to find a way to telepathically let him know how much trouble she was in.

Whistling as he parked his truck in front of Hailey's house, Mac grabbed the flowers and bounded up the front steps. He couldn't wait to see the look on her face when she saw the flowers. And he'd come a little earlier than he'd planned, just in case she needed more time to get ready.

He rapped on the door in a series of jaunty knocks. When the door swung open to reveal Aaron, appearing annoyed, Mac merely smiled and asked for Hailey.

"She left." Aaron shrugged, managing to look both disinterested and bored. "Said she had someplace she needed to be."

Perplexed, Mac shifted his weight from one foot to the other. Not only was the timing all wrong, but she wouldn't have blown off Mac without a phone call. Plus, her car sat parked in the driveway.

Not taking his eyes from Hailey's stepfather, Mac pulled out his phone and called her.

Though he could only hear it faintly, her phone rang from somewhere inside the house. He recognized her ringtone.

"That's her phone," Mac pointed out.

"Is it? She must have forgotten to take it with her."

"Where'd she go?"

"Damned if I know." Judging from the smirk on the older man's face, Aaron appeared to be enjoying himself.

"Mind if I come in and take a look?" Mac asked.

"Actually, I do mind."

With Aaron blocking the doorway, clearly having no intention of letting Mac inside, Mac considered his options.

"Look," Aaron finally said, "though I told Hailey I wouldn't get involved, she wanted me to give you a message. After I heard it, I told her that was the kind of thing a man needs to hear to his face, but she wouldn't listen.

She broke up with you, Mac. Her new boyfriend, one of those FBI fellers, picked her up to take her on a date."

Not sure how much of this obviously blatant lie, if any of it, was true, Mac decided to pretend to believe it. For now. What Aaron didn't realize was how well Mac knew Hailey. Not only would she never do something like that, but attending Tom's basketball game would be more important to her than anything else.

"Who was the guy?" Mac growled. "Which FBI agent is poaching on my woman?"

Now, this kind of language Aaron clearly understood. Grinning, barely able to contain his glee, he made up a description of a tall, muscular guy who looked like a cross between Brad Pitt and Channing Tatum.

Not sure what else to do but aware something had gone very wrong, Mac stormed back to his truck, started it and drove off with a loud screech of his wheels. Once he'd reached the end of Hailey's long, winding driveway, he parked and killed the engine.

Then he hiked back to the house.

Keeping to the trees on the edge of the lawn, he went around to the back. As he peered into one of the windows, he saw the empty living room. Nothing appeared disturbed. Worried, he debated breaking down the back door and confronting Aaron, but right now all he had to go on was instinct and the fact that the other man had told him a big, fat lie.

Where was Hailey? Was she in danger? He didn't for a moment think her recently paroled stepfather would harm her. But then why the lie?

Returning to his truck, Mac tried to decide what to do. Just as he was about to get out and head back to the house, his cell phone rang. Detective Logan.

"We've got a lead on the killer." The usually laconic officer sounded excited. "We have surveillance video taken near where the last girl was found. There was a car, though we couldn't get a good look at the driver. We were able to run the registration off the plates. The car is registered to a June Green, the mother of the first girl who was murdered."

Chapter 17

Mac's blood froze. "June's in rehab. Her daughter Hailey has been using the car while June is recovering. The only other person who might have been driving is June's husband, Aaron."

"Aaron Green?" Logan rustled some papers. "I wondered about the last name matching the first girl who died. He's a definite person of interest. He works part-time for the janitorial service we're investigating. Like some of the others, he has a criminal record, which is completely against the school district policy. He's been asked to come in for questioning, but so far he hasn't showed."

Suddenly, everything became crystal clear. Mac felt sick. "There's a genuine possibility he's the killer. He was here when Brenda Green was killed. He went to prison for ten years and came back, and the killings started again." Mac took a deep breath. "And I think his stepdaughter, Hailey, is in danger." He explained the situation, Hailey's unlikely disappearance and the fact that Aaron had told a bald-faced lie.

To his relief, Detective Logan took his suspicions seriously. "Stay put. Units have been dispatched. Do not—I repeat—do not—go back to the house or attempt to break in. This is definitely a serious situation."

Definitely?

Though every instinct urged him to rush in and save Hailey, Mac agreed to wait and ended the call. But while pacing outside his truck, he had second thoughts. If Hailey was alone with Aaron in the house and in danger, he'd never forgive himself for not acting. *Definitely?*

He checked his watch. Only two minutes had passed. How much longer until the police arrived?

More to the point, how much more time did Hailey have before Aaron hurt or killed her?

Waiting no longer seemed like an option. Decision made, he left his truck where he'd parked it and took off for the house at a dead run.

Rounding the last bend in the long drive, he dashed into the trees as soon as the front of the house came into view. With the garage door open, Aaron was outside and had the trunk of the car up. Mac watched while Aaron made several trips into the garage, loading the trunk up with some sort of supplies. Remaining hidden—for now—Mac told himself it was okay as long as he could see Aaron. And of course, as long as Aaron didn't load up a body.

When Aaron made his third trip into the garage, he continued on into the house. He left the trunk still up. A moment later, he returned pushing a tied and gagged

Hailey in front of him. Her eyes were wide and unfocused with terror.

In that instant, Mac knew he didn't have time to wait for reinforcements. He had to get to Hailey right now.

Every time she moved, the rough rope cut into her skin. As painful as it might be, Hailey knew that rope burns were the least of her worries. But her struggles to get free had no result. When Aaron finally returned and loosened the tie that tethered her to the bed, she thought he meant to kill her right then.

Instead, he yanked her up and forced her to shuffle with him toward the open garage door. Each move brought excruciating pain. Her legs had gone numb, and the rope continued to chafe.

When she saw her car with its large trunk door open, she balked. If she got in there, she knew he would take her to some remote location and kill her. The idea of being enclosed in such a small space filled her with panic.

No. If he was going to kill her anyway, she'd rather die here, in her own driveway. She knew she had to fight now, if she wanted to have even half a prayer of surviving.

As he reached to shove her into the truck, she headbutted him as hard as she could, catching him under the chin. He staggered backward, anger darkening his face. He raised his fist to hit her, but someone yelled a warning.

A dark shape moving fast came running from the woods. Straight at Aaron, still in the process of turning, and tackled him. As Aaron went down, Hailey saw

who her rescuer was. The very person she'd been praying would save her. Mac.

Joy blazed through the terror and pain. Her heart
pounded so hard she thought it would jump out of her
chest. With the gag still in her mouth, she concentrated on breathing through her nose. Still hobbled, she
struggled to move away from the car and out of Mac's
way. Somehow, by some miracle, Mac had come back.
Maybe her desperate mental plea had reached him, or
perhaps he just had good instincts.

Using a wrestling move she remembered seeing him
use back in high school, Mac twisted Aaron's arm behind him. One knee on his back, he held him in place
as police cars came racing up the driveway. They skid-
ded to a halt in front of Hailey's car.

Detective Logan was the first one out. He scowled
when he saw Mac on top of Aaron. "I told you to wait
for backup."

"And I would have, but he was loading her in the
trunk of the car," Mac responded. "Would you please
have a couple officers come take custody of this guy?"

While Aaron had his rights read to him and, hand-
cuffed, was led away to the back of a squad car, Mac
untied Hailey and removed the gag from her mouth.
"Are you all right?" he asked.

Eyes stinging, she looked at the bloody rope burns
on her wrists and ankles and nodded.

"Oh, honey, you don't look all right," Mac said, his
silver gaze dark with worry. He reached for her and
gathered her carefully into his arms. Until then, she'd
stood frozen, her throat closing up, struggling to process what had almost happened to her. And what had
happened ten years in the past.

Now, with Mac holding her, she began quivering. "I had a killer living in my house, around Tom, and Tara, and Eli. I let them go off *alone* with him," she cried out. "If something had happened to any one of them, I never would have been able to live with myself."

"But nothing did. They're safe," he murmured soothingly, using one hand to smooth back her hair. "You're safe."

"And now every other fourteen-year-old girl in this town is safe," Detective Logan put in, walking up and clapping Mac on the shoulder. "You're not going to believe this, but Aaron confessed everything a minute ago. He even asked for a pad of paper and a pen so he could write it all out."

"Why?" She could do nothing but stare. "Why would he suddenly confess?"

Logan shrugged. "He seems to think he's in the right here. Keeps saying he really loved Brenda, and wants us to understand his point of view. It's been a long time and maybe he's tired of his feelings being undetected."

Though this boggled her mind, she managed to nod. "And he also might subconsciously realize he needs to be punished. I don't know. I don't pretend to understand killers. All that matters is we've got him."

It was over. It was really over. Relief flooded through her, making her knees weak. Thankful for Mac holding her up, she looked up at him. "You need to let Gus know."

"I do." The smile that spread slowly over Mac's face warmed a bit of the chill from her. But the numbness came back, spreading fast.

"We'll need to get to work on having him officially

exonerated," Detective Logan said. "He's going to be so happy."

"He is," Mac agreed, his gaze swinging back to find Hailey. "I want to tell him in person. Maybe we can do it together."

Somehow, she managed to smile back. It might have been a bit wobbly, but it was a start. "I'd like that. I also have to tell my mother." Hailey wasn't sure which she dreaded worse—telling the kids or June. "I just hope this doesn't send her right back to the bottle. I'm pretty sure she was hoping for a reconciliation with Aaron."

Mac squeezed her tight, which helped a lot. She wondered why she felt so numb, as if she couldn't yet process anything. "From what you said, your mom has made impressive progress. Think positive. There's a good chance she'll take all this in stride."

"Really?" Detective Logan looked from one to the other. "Would anyone take all this in stride?" Shaking his head, he walked away without waiting for an answer.

"She's a strong woman, Hailey," Mac continued. "We've got to believe she's strong enough to finally conquer her addiction. She may surprise you."

Gut churning, Hailey got out her phone. She didn't know what she'd do if her mother relapsed and knowing June, it was entirely possible. "I might as well get this over with."

"You're calling her now?"

"Why not?" She grimaced. "I have to do it sometime. I'll feel better with one less thing hanging over my head." Or so she hoped. Dimly, she knew she should be feeling something—relief or joy, or maybe that knee-buckling rush of adrenaline now that everything was over—but she didn't. At least this would be a good time to talk to her mother. One of them needed to be calm. It might as well be her. Good old reliable, steady Hailey. No one would know how close she'd come to being pushed off the edge of the tight rope on which she walked.

"Would it be better to tell her in person?" Mac asked, his voice gentle.

To her dismay, her eyes filled with tears. "I can't," she said, hating to admit this. "I just can't." Because one more thing, such as the sight of her mother breaking down, might just do her in.

Hitting redial, using the last number June had called her from, Hailey waited, listening to the other phone ring. After a moment, someone answered.

"May I speak to June Green?" Hailey asked pleasantly, she thought. A moment later, her mother came on the line.

"I was just about to phone you." June sounded frantic. "The police called, saying something about my car being at the scene of a murder. They were asking a lot of questions about Aaron. Do you know what's going on? Is everything okay?"

Hailey sighed, kind of glad for the numbness. "No, Mom. Everything is not okay." Sticking strictly to the facts, she relayed what had happened, ending with the news that Aaron would be charged for the two recent murders and eventually for Brenda's.

June must have been shocked, because she went utterly silent. When she finally spoke again, Hailey could hear the tears in her voice. "I can't... It's hard to process this. I really want a drink."

"I know," Hailey responded gently, though her stomach twisted at her mother's words. "But you've got to find the strength not to."

Silence. Hailey knew June was most likely struggling with the concept of not having a crutch to fall back on when the world went crazy.

"Just promise me you won't start drinking again. Mac says he'll continue to pay for your stay there until you get well."

"Mac?" Again Hailey had clearly shocked her. "He's paying for my rehab?"

"Only what Medicaid won't pay, but, yes, he is. Someday I hope to be able to pay him back."

"Oh, my word. I thought you and Aaron had gotten the cash together somehow." This knowledge seemed to give June strength. "Please, tell Mac I'm fighting hard to stay clean, and I'll continue to do so." June took a deep breath. "I won't let something like this be my excuse to drown myself back in a bottle."

Something like this. If June only knew. But Hailey hadn't told her how close she'd come to becoming Aaron's next victim, or that she was concerned he would have gone after Tara.

"Hailey? Are you there? I give you my word I'll continue on my path to stay sober."

"I'm so relieved." Hailey swallowed hard, aware she'd drifted off. She wished she truly could feel what she knew she should. "I just have to figure out a way to break the news to the kids. I want to do it quickly, before they find out from TV or someone else."

"That's a good idea. You know—" June's voice cracked "—I should have known it was Aaron. All along, there had to be something I missed, a sign. I might have been able to save my Brenda."

Oddly enough, this statement coming from her mother cut through a little of the fog surrounding Hailey. "You can't rewrite the past," Hailey said, as she knew she had to. In addition to being responsible, she'd always been the reasonable one, too. She took a bit of comfort from the fact that she was stepping back in to the role she'd grown familiar with. "At least now, we know the truth. It's awful two more girls lost their lives…" She paused, struggling to hold back her tears. "But Tara is safe, and that's what matters."

"Was Tara ever in danger?" June's voice rose.

Hailey winced. Again, she'd clearly shocked her mother.

"I think so." For some reason, Hailey didn't tell June that Aaron had meant to kill her, too, and if not for Mac's intervention, he'd probably have succeeded.

But June was speaking again. "Thank goodness she had you to keep her safe."

"I've got to go." Keeping her tone gentle, Hailey said goodbye. For the first time she understood what it felt like to be shaking inside but trying to remain calm on the outside. "Are you sure you're all right?"

"Maybe not right now, but I will be. I'm strong, and I want to feel well enough to come back to my family."

After ending the call, Hailey stared at her phone for a few minutes, before realizing there was somewhere else she needed to be. And if she was going to hold on to her increasingly fragile sanity, she needed to do exactly what she was supposed to.

"Tom's basketball game," she told Mac, tugging at

his sleeve. "I almost forgot. If we hurry, we might make it in time to watch some of it before it gets over."

Mac stared at her, his expression concerned. "Are you sure you're up for that right now? Tom will understand once he finds out the reason why."

"Of course I'm up for it." Her perky answer fooled no one. Both Mac and one of the uniformed officers eyed her, neither bothering to hide their concerned disbelief.

"What's going on?" Detective Logan walked back over, looking from Mac to Hailey to his officer, who shook his head and moved away.

"I've got to get to my little brother's basketball game," Hailey said. "I'm already late."

"There are statements to make," Logan said. "Plus you need to be checked out medically."

"Not right now. Please. I have to be there. I promised. Can't we do the rest later?"

The detective glanced at Mac, who shrugged.

"I'm really late," Hailey repeated, aware some of her desperation had leaked through to her voice.

"I can help with that. Would you like a police escort?" Detective Logan asked, smiling. "The FBI is handling transport, and I'm done for the night."

She nodded, before remembering her car was now evidence. "I'll need a ride," she said, eyeing Mac.

After holding her gaze for a long moment, Mac finally smiled back and nodded. "Since that's what you're determined to do," he told Hailey, "we might as well make sure you don't miss anything."

On the way to the game, staying right behind the police cruiser with lights flashing, Mac broke every speed limit. Hailey had no idea how long a basketball game lasted, but no one seemed to think it was already over, which was good.

While she'd started to come back to herself, the shaking and the foggy numbness having begun to dissipate, Hailey knew she'd have to work harder to appear unaffected and normal. If anyone would guess something was wrong, her three siblings would. They knew her better than anyone.

Even Mac. Though he constantly shot worried glances at her, he never questioned her ability to continue on with her normal life after having been tied up and assaulted and almost killed. She only hoped his apparent faith in her was justified.

Right now, she just needed to straighten her spine and get through the next several hours. If she could do that, she could collapse later, in the privacy of her bedroom, where no one would see strong, capable Hailey breaking down.

Oddly enough, this thought buoyed her. And Mac, so sure and strong and kind and loving, made her feel better, too. Watching his capable hands on the wheel as he drove, Hailey realized one truth that she should have known all along. She loved him. Always had and always would. Not that knowing made any difference. She'd never abandon her siblings.

They pulled up to the middle school auditorium, and Mac drove right to the doors. "Go," he said, smiling, though his eyes remained worried. "I'll meet you there once I park."

"Thank you." She leaned over and pressed a quick kiss to his cheek. "See you inside."

Hurrying through the hall toward the crowded gymnasium, she hoped she wasn't too late. Though she had an extremely good excuse—being tied up and held captive by a serial killer—she knew how much this first game meant to her brother. She wouldn't miss it for the world.

The game was still going on. Whew. She slipped inside, glad to see such great attendance. Every time her thoughts skipped back to earlier, she forced herself to focus on the task at hand.

There. Tom. Out on the court, circling around a guy on the opposing team who had the ball. While she watched, Tom made a move, stripping the basketball from his opponent and dribbling it right past several other players.

As he neared the basket, he shot and made it. The entire grandstand erupted, jumping to their feet and cheering. Hailey, too, though when she opened her mouth to yell, all that came out was a croak.

And then, as everyone began to sit back down, the room started spinning. The last thing Hailey saw was the person in front of her, about to unintentionally cushion her fall.

Walking into the gymnasium, Mac located Hailey and headed toward her, just as she jumped to her feet, her attention on the game. On his way, he glanced at the court, just in time to watch Tom confidently steal the ball and score. He cheered and then looked back at Hailey to see her reaction. Like everyone else in the stands, she'd gotten to her feet, clapping. Her blond hair gleamed in the artificial light.

Marveling at her beauty, he kept his eyes trained on her as he hurried toward her. Right as he reached the edge of the grandstand, she appeared to go boneless.

She pitched forward, crumpling and falling onto the person in front of her.

His heart stopped, then adrenaline surged through him. Pushing through the onlookers, he reached her, scooping her up from where she lay, draped over the bleacher like a broken rag doll.

"Don't move her," someone called out. "I'm a doctor."

So Mac laid her down gently on the floor at the edge of the court. The official called a time-out. And Tom rushed over. A second later, Tara and Eli appeared. All three kids clung together. They wore identical looks of shock and worry.

"What happened? Is she all right?"

The man who claimed to be a doctor hurried over. He took Hailey's pulse, examined her eyes and then turned to Mac. "Did she take anything?"

"No." Glancing at the three kids, Mac swallowed. "She's been through a very traumatic event. I think the immensity of it just caught up with her."

"I called 911," another woman volunteered.

"She needs to go to the ER," the doctor said, standing and dusting his hands on his pants. "From what I can tell, while she's in shock, she isn't in any critical danger. They'll need to run tests to learn more."

As relief flooded him, Mac held out his arms. Tom, Tara and Eli crowded in without hesitation. "She's going to be all right," he repeated. "I promise, she'll be fine."

The paramedics arrived just as Hailey regained consciousness. Her eyes fluttered open. "What happened?" she asked, glancing from Mac to her siblings, her brows lowered in a perplexed frown. "I remember getting dizzy, and then…did I fall?"

Tara, Tom and Eli surrounded her, all talking at once. Mac stayed in the background, ready to help in case she needed him. The paramedics helped her up, asking if she could walk, and helped her outside the gymnasium, Eli and Tara on their heels. Tom hesitated, looking from Hailey to his team.

"Go back and play," Mac finally told him, giving him a little push toward the game. "Your sister is going to be fine. I'll come back and pick you up when the game is over."

After a second of hesitation, Tom nodded and dashed back to his team.

Mac hurried outside, just in time to see Hailey being loaded into the ambulance, her expression confused. Eli and Tara huddled together, looking lost. When they saw Mac, they both brightened.

"They're taking her to the hospital as a precaution," Tara declared. "Will you drive us there?"

"Of course."

At the hospital, they saw the ambulance parked under the loading bay at the ER. "Stay with me," Mac ordered, and he and the kids hurried inside. Hailey had been sent to Room 12 to be checked out. When they got there, she was sitting up in bed, shivering despite the blanket wrapped around her. She smiled wanly once she saw Mac and the kids.

"Are you cold?" Tara cried, wrapping her arms around her older sister as if her body heat would be enough to warm her.

"She's in shock." A stranger's voice came from the doorway. A woman in a white coat walked into the room. "Apparently, she had quite a traumatic day. We're going to give her some IV fluids and some medicine to help her calm down. After we keep an eye on her for a few hours, she should be able to go home, pending the test results, that is."

They all nodded and the doctor left the room.

"What happened?" Tara asked, moving in close and taking Hailey's arm. "Why did you have a traumatic day?"

"Where's Tom?" Hailey asked instead of answering. Her voice wobbled because her teeth were chattering.

"I sent him back to the game," Mac told her. "I hope you don't mind. It seemed like the right thing to do."

"It was." Hailey attempted a smile, her gaze sliding past him to her brother and sister. "Kids, I'm afraid I have some bad news to tell you."

When she'd finished speaking, both Eli and Tara stared at her. She'd given them a cleaned-up version of the day's events, but the end result remained unchanged— their birth father most likely was a serial killer. And he'd killed the other sister none of them remembered.

Wide-eyed, the two kids stared at her when she'd finished speaking.

"But you're okay?" Eli squeaked. "He didn't hurt you?"

"No," Hailey answered. "Thanks to Mac, I'm okay."

"That's all that matters." The fierceness in Tara's voice matched her expression.

"I am." Some of the color had come back to Hailey's face. "Please, let me talk to Tom before you say anything. Will you both promise me that?" The kids all nodded. "Thank you." After taking a deep breath, Hailey swallowed. She dragged her fingers through her hair. "This has been a day."

"It has," Mac agreed. He turned to look at Eli and

Tara. "Would you both go wait in the waiting room for a minute? I want to talk to your sister alone."

Immediately and without question, they turned to go. "Here," Mac said, stopping them before they reached the door and handing each of them a five. "I know you haven't eaten yet. Get yourself something out of the vending machine while you wait."

They exchanged glances. "Hailey already gave us money," Tara said. "We'll find something to eat." They left the room.

"That was nice of you," Hailey began.

"Shh," he cut her off, cupping her face with his hand and kissing her, slow and deep. When he finally came up for air, breathing hard, he took in her dazed expression and kissed her again.

"I almost lost you today," he said, his mouth inches from hers. "Do you have any idea what that did to me?"

"I…" With a tremulous smile, she shook her head and sighed.

"I love you, you know." One more kiss, more insistent than the last. "I want to be with you for the rest of my life."

"I love you, too." Gaze troubled, she turned her head away, so his lips grazed her cheek. "But, Mac, I can't give you what you want. I won't leave my brothers and sister."

"Who said you had to?"

Her incredulous expression made him laugh.

"Seriously?" She frowned. "You have to take care of Gus. I have to take care of them. What kind of life would we be able to have?"

"We'll figure it out. Though it breaks my heart, my situation with Gus is only temporary. And when June is better, she'll come back home. I'm thinking she'll want to take more of an active role in raising her children."

"Maybe." Hailey still sounded doubtful.

"You don't have to decide anything today."

At his words, she relaxed, her relief palpable. "I don't want to lose you, Mac."

One more kiss, this one sending heat blazing through both their veins. "You won't," he promised. "We'll take this one day at a time and see what the future holds. As long as we're together, everything will be all right."

"Together," she agreed, her eyes drifting closed.

"Together," he repeated, his words a fierce promise, even though she'd already fallen asleep.

Epilogue

Gus had been thrilled to learn the actual killer had confessed and was in custody. Though Hailey had wanted to be there when Mac told him, she hadn't been able to, so she'd listened in on the phone while Mac gave him the news. He'd whooped out loud, the Texas A&M battle cry, and then, according to Mac, he'd wept.

Gus had insisted on a celebration, and once Hailey felt well enough, she and Tom, Tara and Eli went over with homemade cupcakes and bottles of sparkling water and a gallon of homemade sweet tea. Dolores brought brightly colored balloons and a pot of baked beans made, she said, from an old family recipe. Mac's contribution was the one the kids were most excited about—foot-long hot dogs cooked on the grill.

The day had dawned with the promise of a perfect spring day. The cloudless bright blue sky, the blooming flowers and the temperatures in the high sixties made it a beautiful time for a celebration.

With everyone together, it felt like a family get-together. The only one missing was June, but she'd been absent so long, Hailey doubted any of the kids actually noticed her absence. She knew once June had been deemed well enough to return home, she'd have to spend some time rebuilding her relationship with her children.

Meanwhile, Hailey had resolved to focus on each day as it came. Right now, she'd savor this moment, with these people. Being around Gus had taught her to take nothing for granted. His brief recovery hadn't lasted, but he hadn't declined further either. He was maintaining, she supposed, though the pounds continued to melt from him. He claimed not to be in any pain, so Dolores had withdrawn the morphine. She'd made him promise he'd let her know if he hurt, so she could take care of it.

He loved having the kids running around, and his joy made Mac happy. Mac's delight shone from his eyes, which made Hailey's heart sing with pleasure.

Even though Gus couldn't eat much, he took a single bite out of one of Hailey's cupcakes, pronounced it delicious and smiled. He'd gotten weaker, but Hailey thought he seemed happier, more at peace.

The kids had been subdued around him until Mac set them up a volleyball net in the backyard, and once they got outside, their natural exuberance returned. She was glad to see this. For the first few days after Hailey's release from the hospital, they'd stuck to her like glue, afraid to let her out of their sight.

But life went on. She'd made them go to school, and she'd returned to work at Mac's caring for Gus. Now

Saturday had swung around again, and they were cel-
ebrating the clearing of the Morrison name. Detective
Logan and the FBI had promised to try to rush through
an official exoneration, but no one knew if it would arrive in time.

Mac and Dolores had managed to wheel Gus's hospital bed and IV outside, so he could enjoy the warmth
of the sun on his skin. He grinned, winking at Hailey
when Mac wasn't looking. She hurried over, eager to
get him anything he might need.

Instead, he held out his bony hand for her to take.
Once she had, he motioned her to come closer.

"What is it, Gus?"

"Are you going to make an honest man of him?" he
asked gruffly. "The one worry I have about leaving is
being sure my son is happy. He's been alone for way
too long."

A warm glow flowed through her veins, making her
blush. "We're taking it one day at a time," she began.

The sound of Mac tapping a knife on a glass interrupted her. The afternoon sun lit up his dark hair with
spikes of gold, shadowing his craggy face and making
her chest ache. She'd always found his raw masculinity so damn beautiful.

"Attention, everyone," he said, eyeing Eli until the
boy dropped the volleyball and watched him. "I have
something I want to say." Holding out one large hand, he
locked gazes with Hailey. "Will you come and join me?"

Everyone stared as Hailey slid her fingers into his.

Still holding her hand, he dropped to one knee in
front of her.

"Hailey Green," he began.

"Wait." She knelt down with him, her eyes filling with tears. "I thought we were going to go slowly."

"Hailey?" Tara's clear voice cut across the silence. "Remember what I said? It's time to grab some of that happiness for yourself."

Just like that, Hailey's eyes filled. While Tara was right, she was too young to understand how complicated things were.

"Miss Hailey?" Now Gus spoke up. "I'd sure like to see you and my son married before I go on to my next adventure to the life after this one."

"I'd like that, too," Dolores chimed in, seconded by Eli, jumping up and down with excitement.

More than anything in the world, Hailey longed to say yes. "There's nothing more I want than to be your wife," she said quietly, looking only at Mac. "But where will we live?"

"We'll figure that out," Mac said, holding out the ring. "With love, anything is possible. Now, are you going to answer me?"

He was right. Loving him so much, she managed to smile back through her tears. "You haven't actually asked me yet."

With a hoot of laughter, he did. "Hailey, my darlin', will you marry me?"

Holding his gaze for one more moment, she looked past him to all the expectant faces. His father, at the end of his life. Her brothers and sister, at the beginning of theirs. Dolores, so caring and kind. "Yes," she said. "Yes, I will."

He whooped and kissed her then, right in front of everyone. Sliding the ring on her finger, he whispered in her ear. "It'll all work out in the end. You'll see. One day at a time."

They were married a few weeks later, in the same spot in the backyard where Mac had proposed. In attendance was Gus, whom they'd once again wheeled outside in his hospital bed, as well as Dolores, Tom, Tara and Eli and, as a surprise, June, who'd gotten a day pass from the rehab facility to come.

The kids were overjoyed to see their mother, lavishing her with attention, which gave Hailey hope that things would finally work out with June and her children.

Today, though, she'd focus on Mac. Her Mac. Waiting eagerly for her to come to him and finally, finally, join her life with his.

They said their pledges to each other as the sun set, hearts full of love and joy. There were no longer any shadows across their love. They used the traditional vows, with one slight change. They'd had a single word written in for each of them near the end, right before the preacher told them to kiss.

"Together," Mac said.

"Together," Hailey echoed.

After that, they both spoke at once. "Forever."

And then the groom kissed the bride.

* * * * *

COMING NEXT MONTH FROM

H HARLEQUIN®

ROMANTIC suspense

Available May 9, 2017

#1943 CAVANAUGH ON CALL
Cavanaugh Justice • by Marie Ferrarella
When detective Alexandra Scott is transferred from Homicide to
Robbery, her new partner is *quite* the surprise: Bryce Cavanaugh
is just as headstrong and determined to get his way as she
is. When they go head-to-head while solving a string of home
invasions, fireworks are sure to ignite!

#1944 PREGNANT BY THE COLTON COWBOY
The Coltons of Shadow Creek • by Lara Lacombe
Thorne Colton knows his life is way too crazy for a relationship,
which is why he pulls away after an amazing night in
Maggie Lowell's arms. But when a pregnant Maggie is
endangered by a bomb planted in her car, Thorne is drawn back
into her life, determined to protect her and their unborn child.

#1945 A STRANGER SHE CAN TRUST
Escape Club Heroes • by Regan Black
Just before closing time at The Escape Club, a woman stumbles
out of a taxi and into the arms of off-duty paramedic Carson Lane.
Melissa Baxter doesn't know who she is, but she knows she
can trust Carson to keep her safe. Now the two of them must
bring a killer to justice before he can silence them forever!

#1946 REUNITED WITH THE P.I.
Honor Bound • by Anna J. Stewart
Her star witness is missing and assistant district attorney
Simone Armstrong has only one person to turn to:
Vince Sutton, P.I. Only problem is, he's her ex-husband—and
she put his younger brother in prison. Once they team up, it
becomes harder and harder not to remember how good they
had it, but a killer from Simone's past is determined to put a
stop to their second chance at happily-ever-after—for good!

**YOU CAN FIND MORE INFORMATION ON UPCOMING HARLEQUIN® TITLES,
FREE EXCERPTS AND MORE AT WWW.HARLEQUIN.COM.**

HRSCNM0417

SPECIAL EXCERPT FROM

◆ HARLEQUIN®
TM

ROMANTIC suspense

*When a pregnant Maggie Lowell is endangered
by a bomb planted in her car, Thorne Colton is
drawn back into her life, determined to protect her
and their unborn child.*

Read on for a sneak preview of
PREGNANT BY THE COLTON COWBOY,
the next book in the
THE COLTONS OF SHADOW CREEK
series by Lara Lacombe.

"Is that..." Thorne's voice was husky and Maggie realized he was now standing next to the bed. She'd been so focused on the screen she hadn't even noticed his approach. "Is that the nose?"

Maggie's gaze traveled back to the head, which was shown in profile. She ran her eyes along the line of the baby's face, from forehead to chin. How could something so small already look so perfect?

"Yes. And here are the lips." Dr. Walsh moved an arrow along the image, pointing out features in a running commentary. "Here is the heart, and this is the stomach and kidneys." She moved the wand lower on Maggie's belly. "Here you can see the long bones of the legs forming. And this is the placenta."

Maggie hung on her every word, hardly daring to breathe for fear of missing anything she might say. She glanced over and found Thorne leaning forward, his expression rapt as he took everything in. He must have felt her gaze because he turned to look at her, and in that moment, all Maggie's hurt feelings and disappointment were buried in an avalanche of joy over the shared experience of seeing their baby for the first time. No matter what might happen between them, they had created this miracle together. They were no longer just Maggie and Thorne; they had new roles to play now. Mother and father.

"Congratulations," he whispered, his brown eyes shining with emotion.

"Congratulations," she whispered back. Her heart was so full she could barely speak, but words weren't needed right now.

Thorne took her hand in his own, his warm, calloused fingers wrapping around hers. In silent agreement, they turned back to the monitor to watch their baby squirm and kick, safe inside her body and blissfully unaware of today's dangerous encounter.

I will keep you safe, Maggie vowed silently.

Always.

Don't miss
PREGNANT BY THE COLTON COWBOY
by Lara Lacombe, available May 2017 wherever
Harlequin® Romantic Suspense books
and ebooks are sold.

www.Harlequin.com

Love Inspired
SUSPENSE
RIVETING INSPIRATIONAL ROMANCE

Meet the FBI special agents of the elite Classified K-9 Unit!
Classified K-9 Unit: These FBI agents solve the toughest cases
with the help of their brave canine partners.

Collect the complete series:

GUARDIAN by Terri Reed

SHERIFF by Laura Scott

SPECIAL AGENT by Valerie Hansen

BOUNTY HUNTER by Lynette Eason

BODYGUARD by Shirlee McCoy

TRACKER by Lenora Worth

CLASSIFIED K-9 UNIT CHRISTMAS
by Terri Reed and Lenora Worth

Available wherever books and ebooks are sold.

 www.Facebook.com/LoveInspiredBooks

 www.Twitter.com/LoveInspiredBks

www.LoveInspired.com

Turn your love of reading into rewards you'll love with
Harlequin My Rewards

**Join for FREE today at
www.HarlequinMyRewards.com**

Earn **FREE BOOKS** of your choice.

Experience **EXCLUSIVE OFFERS** and contests.

Enjoy **BOOK RECOMMENDATIONS**
selected just for you.

PLUS! Sign up now
and get **500** points
right away!

Earn
FREE
REWARDS
HarlequinMyRewards.com
Join
Today!

MYR16R

THE WORLD IS BETTER WITH

Romance

Harlequin has everything from contemporary, passionate and heartwarming to suspenseful and inspirational stories.

Whatever your mood, we have a romance just for you!

Connect with us to find your next great read, special offers and more.

 /HarlequinBooks

 @HarlequinBooks

www.HarlequinBlog.com

www.Harlequin.com/Newsletters

HARLEQUIN

A *Romance* FOR EVERY MOOD™

www.Harlequin.com

SERIESHALOAD2015